GUARDING BELLA
CRIMSON POINT SECURITY SERIES

NEW YORK TIMES AND USA TODAY BESTSELLING AUTHOR

KAYLEA CROSS

GUARDING BELLA
Copyright © 2024 Kaylea Cross

∼

Cover Art: Sweet 'N Spicy Designs
Developmental edits: Pamela White
Line Edits: Pamela White
Digital Formatting: LK Campbell

∼

This book is a work of fiction. The names, characters, places, and incidents are products of the writer's imagination or have been used fictitiously and are not to be construed as real. Any resemblance to persons, living or dead, actual events, locales or organizations is entirely coincidental.

All rights reserved. With the exception of quotes used in reviews, this book may not be reproduced or used in whole or in part by any means existing without written permission from the author.

ISBN: 9798873633678

Her past should have stayed buried.

Bella thought she could escape her past. For a while, she did. She even found happiness and the chance for a future she never thought possible. Until one day when it was all taken away in an instant, forcing her to leave behind the man she loved just to survive. Now her nightmare is finally over and she needs to reclaim everything she lost. Except she doesn't know whether he'll take her back. And she's about to discover that the past won't let her go so easily.

Now it's coming after them both.

Professional bodyguard Creed's whole world caved in the day Bella left without explanation. Now, over a year later she's back without warning, and what she tells him leaves him reeling. She's been through a hell far worse than he'd ever imagined, but one thing is certain. He will love her until he draws his last breath—and won't let anything or anyone take her away from him ever again. But when deadly forces from her past life come for her, they find themselves in a fight for survival unlike anything they've faced before. And the only way out is to make an impossible choice that could tear them apart forever.

AUTHOR'S NOTE

Get ready for Creed and Bella's intense second-chance love story! It's one of my favorite tropes, and I loved bringing these two back to each other after all they'd been through. I hope you enjoy it.

Kaylea

PROLOGUE

Fourteen months ago

Multicolored Christmas lights glowed in front yards and along the eaves and windows of the houses Creed passed as he drove into his neighborhood. He was jetlagged and beat from the punishing schedule during this latest overseas contract and the long two days of travel to get home, but when he turned up his street, all that vanished under a rush of anticipation and excitement.

It had been twelve weeks since he'd last seen Bella. They'd talked every day he had the chance, but it hadn't been nearly enough for either of them. Missing her had been a physical ache in his chest, and finally, in just another few minutes, she would be in his arms again.

His heart kicked hard when their house came into view ahead. A little post-war bungalow at the end of the street up on a low hill, where they could see the mountains to the west. Her car was parked in its usual spot on the left side of the driveway, signaling she was home. The living room light was on and he could see the Christmas tree standing front and center in front of the window.

It was bare because she'd wanted to wait until he got home so they could decorate it together. He was looking forward to it as much as she was, and to spending the holidays together for the first time.

He picked up the bouquet of flowers he'd snagged at the airport before grabbing his gear from the back and heading for the front door. A wreath covered the small window at the top, decorated with brightly-colored baubles and a little sign in the center that read *Welcome To Our Home*.

He unlocked the door and set his gear inside, excitement rushing through him as he took off his boots and picked up the roses. It was so quiet. "Bell?"

She didn't answer.

He carried the bouquet into the kitchen. The light over the range was on, a pot of something sitting on the element. "Bella?" he called louder, turning around. The house was small. She would definitely have heard him come in. Unless she was on the phone or in the shower.

Or maybe she was waiting naked in their bed for him.

He started for the hallway, a grin on his face. Then something sparkly caught his attention on the island.

He stopped. Stared in confusion at her diamond engagement ring sitting there on the granite surface, along with a folded note with his name on the front.

The grin faded. He picked up the note, read the two lines.

I love you, but I can't do this. I'm so sorry. Please don't try to find me.

Bella.

His stomach dropped like a boulder, his guts clenching. What the fuck? Was this some kind of weird prank? But that wasn't like her, and it wasn't fucking funny.

Unease coiled up his spine, the silence and empty feel of the house closing in on him.

He shook it off. *There's no way she'd just up and left.*

He dropped the note and bouquet on the island top and rushed for their bedroom at the end of the hall, his heart pounding sickeningly against his ribs. He flipped on the light. Their big bed was neatly made, as usual. A paperback romance was sitting on her bedside table. But that empty sensation was even stronger here.

He spun around and went to the closet. Wrenched the folding doors open.

The blood drained from his face.

Her side was completely bare. All the hangers and shelves were empty. And her suitcases were gone.

"What the fuck," he breathed, feeling queasy and as though he'd walked into some alternate universe instead of their home.

His mind whirled frantically. What the hell was going on? Had something gone sideways without him having any clue? Something to hurt her so much that she would up and leave like this? He wracked his brain. They hadn't had a fight. Everything had seemed normal when he'd talked to her yesterday. She'd been so excited about the wedding plans she was making. And at the end of the conversation she'd told him she loved him and couldn't wait to see him when he got home tonight.

Fuck. He whipped out his phone and called her.

An automated voice answered. *The number you have dialed is no longer in service, or temporarily disconnected. This is a recording.*

No. No, this couldn't be happening. His mind raced, heart thudding in his ears. Bella had no family and no really close friends. But she must have reached out to someone about this.

In desperation he dialed her boss. "Kim, it's Creed. Have you seen Bella today?"

"Yes, of course, we were both in the office today. Why, is something wrong?"

Yes. Everything was fucking wrong, and now he was scared. "I just got home, and she's gone. All her stuff is gone. She left a note saying goodbye."

"What?" Kim exclaimed in shock. "That makes no sense. She was beyond excited about seeing you tonight. She even left work early to go get groceries to make you your favorite dinner, and—are you sure she's really gone?"

Tears burned the backs of his eyes. What the hell had happened? Had Bella been faking it all this time? Lying to him and her coworkers about being happy? He just couldn't believe that. "Yes, I'm sure."

The only explanation was that something seriously wrong had to have happened. Something or someone had made her do this.

His stomach clamped even tighter.

"Have you called her?" Kim demanded.

"Her phone's already been disconnected."

"Oh my God, I... Creed, I'm so sorry, I don't know what to say. I don't understand any of this, I—"

"Thanks," he choked out, his throat so tight he could barely breathe. "I gotta go."

He ended the call. Dialed her two closest friends, praying they would have answers or at least some insight.

Neither of them had seen her today, but they both had the same reaction as Kim. Disbelief. Confusion. They told him how excited Bella had been about him coming home.

Creed ended the last call and lowered the phone to his side. Something really fucking bad had happened, and he didn't know what it was. Didn't know where she was, or how to reach her.

Reeling from the shock, wanting to scream at the anguish

building in his chest, he made his way back out to the kitchen. First he went to the stove. The pot she'd been cooking with was cold, part of the dinner she'd planned for them still sitting in it.

He crossed to the island to stare at the note, trying to pick it apart. Make sense of it or find another clue. The writing was messy, contrasting sharply with her normally neat script. As if she'd scrawled it in a hurry.

The evidence in the kitchen told him she'd been in a rush, yet she'd still had time to clear out her entire closet before leaving.

None of it made any sense, and he couldn't figure out what had happened. Had she been forced by someone? Coerced? Threatened in some way that would make her leave?

That seemed harder to believe than her leaving. Because who in the hell would ever threaten Bella?

He called the police because his instincts were all telling him she must be in danger. Only to be told there was nothing they could do for him right now. She hadn't been gone more than a few hours yet, not even close to the twenty-four hours needed to file a missing person's report.

He hung up, feeling frantic and sick and desperate. There were no signs of forced entry in the house, no signs of a struggle or other violence to suggest that someone had broken in and threatened her at gunpoint or something. And the empty closet, ring, and note were pretty damning. The cops would take one look at that and conclude she'd left him of her own free will.

He couldn't accept that. Wouldn't.

So why? Why had she done this, and where had she gone?

Swallowing against a sudden wave of nausea, he picked up the ring, held it between his fingers. The diamond sparkled in the overhead lights. The symbol of his love for her. It had never left her finger from the moment he'd put it on. Until now.

The emptiness of the house surrounded him. Closing in on him until it felt like he would suffocate.

He sank to the floor, knees buckling. He sat there with his back against the island and buried his head in his hands, struggling to breathe through the agony tearing at him. "Bella, where the hell are you?" he choked out as a rush of scalding tears blinded him.

His whole world had just crashed around him without warning or explanation. Bella was gone.

He had to find her to at least make sure she was okay. Because he couldn't accept this. Couldn't shake the awful certainty that something horrible had happened.

And if he was wrong, if she truly wanted to leave him after he found her…

Then she was going to have to tell him straight to his face.

ONE

The mixture of anxiety and hope that had been building in Bella for the past three days was currently at an all-time high, a constant buzzing inside her that she couldn't shut off. From her seat in a corner booth at the back of the small diner outside of Portland, Oregon, she stared out the front windows into the darkness, her food practically untouched before her.

The past fourteen months had been the darkest of her life, and even though there was now a glimmer of hope at the end of the long tunnel she'd been trapped in, the last three days on the road had taken their own toll.

Since leaving St. Paul, she'd only slept a handful of hours each night, crawling into bed at whatever roadside motel she came upon when she was too tired to continue. She did a slow blink and focused on her dinner, her eyelids like sandpaper. She needed to eat but had no appetite.

She was still numb inside from everything that had happened. Still reeling from the shock of it and this final twist in the roller coaster that was her life.

She was free now. Finally safe from the dangers that had stalked her from childhood.

It still didn't seem real. Didn't seem possible after all she'd been through.

But her freedom had come at a terrible price. Because she was completely alone and had lost the man she loved.

The three other patrons in the diner were quietly eating their meals at other tables, all of them seeming without a care in the world. The stark difference between them and her was jarring. She'd never known and *would* never know what that kind of normalcy felt like. Even now she felt exposed sitting here alone in this diner, couldn't help casting furtive glances outside, watching for any sign of danger.

There had been a time, a lovely too short time in her life, when she'd naively believed she was safe. A time when she'd felt able to be who she wanted to be, been able to open herself up to truly live for the first time. A home of her own. Friends of her own.

And a man who had loved her as much as she loved him.

She tore her gaze away from the front windows and forked up another bite of chicken and mashed potatoes. It stuck in her throat when she swallowed, but she kept going until she'd eaten a third of it. She needed the fuel. She'd been running on empty for far too long, and it showed in the shadows beneath her eyes and the baggy fit of her clothes.

Another wave of nerves hit, and her hand tightened around her fork. She was less than three hours from her destination. The one she'd driven halfway across the country to reach. And she was starting to have second thoughts. Was she really going to do this? *Should* she do it?

It wasn't too late to back out. It wasn't like he knew she was coming. And for all she knew, he might slam the door in her face.

He had every right to hate her. And while she was a little afraid of how he would react, the need to see him outweighed everything else, so intense it had compelled her to pack up her trunkful of belongings and her cat and drive all the way here. Calling him wasn't anywhere close to good enough. The things she needed to say to him had to be said in person. She owed him that much.

Thinking of him, the hope that she might see him again one day, had kept her going all this time. Had kept her alive.

A sudden wave of tears threatened. She'd fought so hard to make things right in her life, only to have it all snatched away from her in an instant. Now she finally had another chance. If this didn't work…

She pushed her plate away, dropped some cash on the table, and hurried outside, the pain tearing at her. The chilly February night air surrounded her, damp but less cold than it had been in Minnesota.

A heavy cloud of fatigue made it feel like she was sleepwalking as she made her way to her little secondhand car parked across the darkened narrow lot, a numbing fog creeping over her. She slid her hand into her pocket. Her fingers had just found the keychain when she heard rapid footsteps coming behind her.

She whipped around. Sucked in a breath when she saw the shadowy figure of a man bearing down on her.

She barely had time to throw her arms up to block the hands coming at her. She threw a right cross at his face, putting all her weight behind it. He wrenched his head back, but she managed to clip the edge of his jaw just as his hands closed around her upper arms with bruising force.

Her scream cut off as they hit the ground with a thud. She wrenched to the side to escape him, but his fingers locked around her left wrist, his grip digging the band of her watch into her skin as he tried to rip it off her.

The sudden shift in momentum yanked her backward. He

grabbed her again, one arm snaking around her chest this time. In desperation, she threw an elbow at him, slamming it into his face.

He swore and released her momentarily, allowing her the second she needed to lunge away and scramble to her feet.

"Hey! Let her go!" someone yelled.

The man was on his feet again. Bella yanked her keys out of her pocket and held one sticking out between her clenched fingers like a weapon, ready to drive it into her attacker's face. But he spun around and took off, vanishing into the darkness of the vacant lot beside the diner as two people came running over to her.

"You okay, honey?" the elderly man said, taking hold of her shoulders in concern.

Bella stood there sucking in short bursts of air while her heart hammered in her ears, her gaze riveted on the spot where the man had melted into the shadows. Her wrist throbbed and stung where he'd tried to rip the watch off.

"Mark, call the cops," the man said to his companion.

"N-no," she managed, taking a step back and lowering her arm. No cops. No more. She was okay, just scared. All she wanted was to get the hell away from here and back on the road.

"Are you hurt?" the younger man asked.

She faced him, noticed through her amped-up state that the two men looked a bit alike. Father and son, maybe. "No." Shit, she was shaking. A fine, rapid tremor spreading throughout her whole body. "I'm okay," she forced out. He'd tried to steal her watch. "Just a mugger."

Was he? her subconscious whispered. Or had it been targeted and she'd just narrowly avoided being kidnapped or worse?

She shuddered, then shook her head. That nightmare was

over. No one was after her. *Don't be stupid. Max is gone. He can't hurt you anymore.*

Never again, she thought as her throat tightened. Though God knew she already bore enough emotional scars from the damage he'd done to last her several lifetimes.

Neither of her rescuers seemed convinced.

"Come back inside," the older man urged, gently taking her by the elbow. "Mark and I'll sit with you for a bit. We'll get you a cup of coffee and let you get your legs back under you."

She started to shake her head, didn't want to stay here a moment longer, but with the way she was trembling, she was in no shape to get behind the wheel right now. "Okay," she whispered, and allowed them to take her back inside.

The waitress hurried over, fussed over her, and poured her a hot cup of coffee. "Here, eat a few bites of this, sweetie, get your blood sugar up. It'll help." She slid a slice of cherry pie in front of her.

Bella murmured a thank you and forced herself to take a few bites. She felt queasy now, but steadier. And she appreciated how these strangers had jumped in to help her. A much needed reminder that there were good people in the world.

"Are you sure you don't want to call the cops?" the younger one asked. "This area's usually pretty safe, but with all the drug smuggling activity around here recently, there've been attempted robberies like this reported over the past few weeks."

She shook her head, adamant. "No. He didn't steal anything. I just want to get back on the road." And get to the address on her GPS.

Father and son exchanged a look, but neither of them argued. "Is there someone we can call for you?" the older man asked.

She shook her head again. There was only one person she

could reach out to, and she wasn't going to make that call until she was alone in her car.

"You look a bit steadier now," he said.

She nodded and set down her fork, unable to eat another bite of the pie. Now more than ever she just wanted to get to Creed. Even if he turned his back on her and shut her out. Even if he screamed at her and sent her away, she just needed to see him. Had to try to explain. It was all that was keeping her going. "Yes. Thank you."

"Not at all. Can we do anything else?"

"No, but I appreciate the offer."

The father grunted. "We'll at least see you to your car and follow you to the highway. That be all right?"

She nodded and slid out of the booth. This time she was hyper vigilant on the way to her car. She made it there without incident, both men hovering over her and looking around the nearly empty lot. Her cat meowed from his carrier in the passenger seat when she got in and locked the door.

"I'm okay. We're both okay," she told him, reaching her fingers through the wire cage in the front to scratch under his chin. Then she pulled out her phone and dialed the emergency number she'd saved on it.

"We're sorry, the number you have dialed is no longer in service. Please try—"

Frowning, she ended the call and rechecked the number. It was correct. She dialed again. Got the same recorded voice. Understanding dawned, and with it, cold swept up her spine because the message could not be clearer.

She was on her own now. There was no one left for her to turn to except for the man whose heart she'd broken when she'd suddenly disappeared from his life without explanation more than a year ago.

She shot off a quick email to the address she had for her

contact, explaining what had happened and unsure whether he would receive it. Then she started driving.

Her good Samaritans followed behind her to the turnoff for the highway and flashed their lights. She raised a hand in thanks and farewell and kept going, keeping a close eye on what was happening behind her.

The road remained empty for the next five miles. There was zero sign of anyone following her, confirming that the attack had been random. And when she reached the junction to turn west and head for the coast, not a single pair of headlights was behind her.

She sighed in relief and let the tension drain out of her muscles. A wave of exhaustion rolled over her. She barely remembered the next few hours, aware of nothing except the road in front of her, half-shrouded by mist.

A nervous buzz started up in the pit of her stomach when she took the exit for Crimson Point. She followed the GPS directions to the little silver-gray house perched high on a hill at the end of a dead-end street and parked a little way down from it. She'd dreamed of this moment so many times. Of this chance, not believing it would actually happen, yet not able to stop hoping for it either.

Now that it was happening, she was suddenly scared to death. Being rejected by Creed after everything she'd gone through might kill her.

"Rrrroww."

She glanced over at the cat carrier. Nick's little black paw stuck out between the wire grate on the front. She stroked it gently with a fingertip. "I know it's been a long day, big guy. But now we're here."

She looked at the house, a small two-story with cedar shingle siding that looked like it must have been built just after WWII. The driveway was empty. According to the intel she had, Creed had only moved here to Crimson Point recently. Had he bought this place? Or was he just renting?

She remembered so vividly the first time they'd met, when he'd walked into the animal shelter where she'd been volunteering in Tucson to pick out a cat with his elderly aunt. She'd never believed in love at first sight, but that's pretty much what had happened. At least for her. One look at him, and everything inside her had stilled, some ancient, intrinsic part of her knowing right then and there that she'd just met the man who would change her world.

It didn't look like he was home now, but the porch light was on. It was after business hours, so hopefully he would be back soon. Until then, she'd wait.

She took a steadying breath and climbed out, taking Nick's carrier to the front door. She tried the bell just in case. When no one answered, she took Nick over to the porch swing and sat, watching the quiet street out front. She would wait here for as long as it took, sleep in her car if necessary.

She yawned, curled up tighter on the swing. It was so quiet out here. Peaceful, if chilly, the dampness in the air tinged with the slight tang of the sea from down below at the bottom of the hill.

Her eyelids began to droop. She shifted into a more comfortable position and soon began to drift off, only to be brought upright at the sound of an approaching vehicle.

She watched, pulse accelerating as an SUV pulled into the driveway and the engine turned off. A moment later the driver stepped out, a tall silhouette backlit by the streetlamp.

Her eyes closed for a moment as Creed's deep voice reached her, rolling over her with a thousand bittersweet memories that made her throat tighten.

He was talking on the phone to someone. Didn't see her as

he rounded the hood of the vehicle and started for the front steps.

Her moment of reckoning was here.

Swallowing, she stood.

He froze, his attention riveted on her.

She forced herself to step toward the stairs, into the glare of the porch lantern that suddenly felt like a spotlight in an interrogation room.

The sight of him almost made her knees buckle. Tall, strong, his dark hair cut short, angular jaw clean shaven, and those incredible, piercing gray eyes locked on her.

Somehow she remained standing, didn't move as he muttered "I gotta go" to whomever he was speaking to and lowered the phone, staring at her the whole time.

"Bella," he croaked out.

Drawing a breath, somehow resisting the urge to run to him and fling her arms around him, she found her voice. This was so hard. The hope. The fear. The chasm of space and time that had divided them. "Hi."

He didn't move. "What are you doing here?"

She deserved the cautious tone, the wary expression, even though she'd been secretly praying for a joyous reunion. But it still hurt. "I know I shouldn't have just shown up like this, but…" Her voice caught. Dammit, she could barely force the rest out. "I didn't know where else to go," she blurted in a shaky whisper.

Creed stared at her for another few agonizing seconds, then dropped the backpack slung over his broad shoulder and rushed toward her. An instant later she was being pulled to his chest, those strong, achingly familiar arms closing around her. Holding her tight. So tight, as if he was afraid she might vanish if he let her go.

Bella grabbed the back of his jacket with both fists and held on, a tidal wave of relief crashing over her. She didn't deserve this response or kindness from him, but she'd ached for it with every cell of her being. Her knees wobbled, the strength of his grip the only thing keeping her from crumpling to the ground at his feet.

She choked back a sob and pressed her face into his chest, the familiar smell of his cologne triggering a thousand bittersweet memories as he held her.

His face was buried in her hair, his grip almost bruising. "Bella," he rasped out, his voice unsteady. "Oh, Christ, where have you been?"

TWO

Reeling from shock, Creed crushed her to him, part of him afraid she would disappear into thin air if he let go. Was this actually happening? This couldn't be real. He was dreaming. Had to be. Because how else could he be holding Bella in his arms right now?

She made a soft, choked sound that twisted his insides and held on tight, her hands fisting the back of his jacket.

His eyes stung, and his throat closed up. He'd imagined this moment so many times. Had prayed for it from the day she'd left, even as he'd told himself it would never happen.

She looked so different. Felt different. Fragile almost, and too damned thin. It only confirmed that whatever had happened to make her leave him, it must have been bad.

He swallowed hard, struggled to find his voice. Why was she here? What had brought her back to him? "Are you okay? I mean, are you in trouble?"

She shook her head and kept clinging to him, making his heart swell and breaking it all over again.

"Come inside," he urged. It was freezing out here, and she'd clearly been through hell.

Bella didn't move for a long moment, just kept holding on. She seemed to gather herself before pulling in a shaky breath and releasing her death grip on his jacket. When she stepped back and turned away to wipe at her cheeks, he had to stop himself from reaching for her again. God, what the hell had happened to her?

She went to the porch swing, then bent to grab something. A pet carrier. "I have my cat with me. Is that okay?" she asked him.

The significance of her finally adopting a pet wasn't lost on him. She'd told him she'd always wanted to and never felt settled enough to bring one home. They'd been planning to adopt one together after the Christmas holidays, but she'd up and left before they could make it happen. "Yeah, it's fine."

She could bring a fucking tiger inside if it meant she stayed here with him.

He entered the code into the lock on the door, stepped in and turned off the alarm. She came inside after him and stood there on the rug in the entry, and his guts clenched when he got a good look at her up close in the light.

She looked haggard and pale, her deep blue eyes dull with fatigue. Shadows dark as bruises beneath them. And her clothes were hanging on her. "Do you have a place to stay?" he asked, concerned.

She shook her head, her appearance and demeanor alarming him. "I didn't plan anything beyond coming here."

"Do you want to stay here?" he heard himself ask before he could think better of it. But what was he gonna do, turn her out when she'd suddenly reappeared out of nowhere and looked like she was on the verge of collapsing?

A sheen of tears flooded her eyes. She sniffed, blinked fast. "I don't deserve that, but thank you."

It took everything he had not to drag her to him again,

scoop her up and just hold her. Demand that she tell him what had happened to make her leave, make her tell him what was wrong so he could fix it. "Guest room's upstairs on the left. You got any luggage with you?"

"Yes, there's some cat stuff in the backseat and a couple bags in the trunk."

"Why don't you go get the cat settled upstairs, and I'll grab the rest."

"Okay, thanks. My car's parked just down and across the road. Black Toyota with Minnesota plates."

Minnesota? Is that where she'd been all this time?

"It's unlocked." The tremulous, apologetic smile she gave him hurt his heart.

He went outside, still grappling with this sudden shift in his reality. He had a thousand questions, but one look at her told him she was in no condition to answer any of them. At least not yet.

Minnesota. That was a hell of a long-ass drive.

In the backseat he found a clean litter box, a bag of litter, and food. He brought it all inside before going back for her luggage. Just two medium-sized suitcases in the trunk. Nothing else. Was this just a brief stopover then? His heart sank. How was he supposed to let her walk away again?

He carried the cat supplies upstairs. Bella was on her knees trying to coax the cat out of the crate. "Should I put the litter box in the bathroom?"

"Sure, thanks. I'll leave him in there for a while until he settles down."

He glanced into the carrier on the way by and caught a glimpse of a single yellow eye peering at him from the shadows. He set the litter box down, left Bella to organize everything, and went downstairs for her bags. When he returned, she was pouring food and water into little dishes she had set on the en suite floor.

She took the door off the carrier, tried to coax the cat out, but it wouldn't budge. "He's a rescue, so he's really shy. He'll probably hide in here all night or under the bed, molting."

He could see the cat was black. It looked like it only had one eye. "What's his name?"

"Nick Furry."

It took him a second to make the link to the Avengers character who wore an eye patch, then he let out a startled laugh. "Nick Furry. That's awesome."

The smile she flashed him made the haunted, exhausted look in her eyes disappear for a moment and set off a painful ache in his chest. Christ, he'd missed her. It was killing him not to know what had happened and why she'd suddenly reappeared out of thin air tonight. "I thought it suited him. He's been through the wars, this guy."

"How long have you had him?"

"Seven months. He was a stray rescued by the animal sanctuary I was working at."

"In Minnesota?"

She nodded and didn't elaborate while she went back to trying to coax the furry avenger out of the crate.

Creed eyed her while her attention was diverted, concern and an acute protectiveness welling up. Her jeans were hanging on her hips and thighs, her once rounded curves whittled away to nothing. "When's the last time you ate something?"

"I stopped at a diner outside of Portland a couple hours ago," she said, pouring litter into the box.

"Did you eat?" Didn't look like she'd eaten much at all for the past few weeks at least, maybe longer.

"A little bit."

"Come down when you're done here. I'll make you something."

"You don't need t—"

He was already out the door and heading downstairs for the kitchen. She needed food, and he needed time and space to get his shit together and think. His mind whirled with a thousand different thoughts and questions as he made her a toasted tomato sandwich with mayo, salt and pepper. Used to be one of her favorites.

He shook the thought away and focused on the task at hand as he moved around the kitchen. Getting stuck in the past right now wasn't going to fix anything. She'd come back for a reason, and her condition was evidence enough that she'd gone through a rough time. She would tell him when she was ready. Until then, he needed to use every bit of patience he had left and give her space to rest.

He was just slicing the sandwich on the diagonal to slide it onto a plate when she emerged into the kitchen, the shadows under her eyes like bruises. "He darted under the bed as soon as you left, so I closed the bedroom door to keep him in."

"Sure. Here, start with this." He slid the sandwich across the center island toward her. "I don't have any juice or wine, but I've got some beers in the fridge."

"Just water would be great, thanks." She tucked a lock of dark brown hair behind her ear and sat on a stool on the opposite side of the island. She'd cut it so that it swung just past her shoulders, no longer spilling down to the middle of her back. Lifting half of the sandwich, she looked up at him. "You look well."

This was killing him. Seeing her again without warning. Her being in his space after all this time. Staying in his house. Not understanding what had gone wrong. The two of them acting like polite strangers when he'd once been closer to her than anyone else on earth.

Every breath hurt, his chest squeezing until it was hard to

get any air. "I'm doing okay." As best he could after having his heart ripped out the day she'd left. "What's going on, Bell? Are you in trouble?" Because there was no other reason he could think of why she would suddenly just show up here.

She tensed and swallowed a bite of sandwich. Seemed to force herself to meet his gaze, and when she did the pain in her eyes sliced him inside. "I'm so sorry I hurt you," she whispered unsteadily, her eyes filling again.

Her tears were like acid in the gaping wound where his heart had been. Because he could see that they and the apology were sincere. He could also count on one hand how many times he'd ever seen her cry and still have fingers left over.

But he didn't know what the fuck to say to her right now. Or do. He couldn't just shrug off what had happened. Couldn't pretend it didn't affect him every second of every day or that he didn't give a shit about her anymore.

He still loved her. Always would. And though he'd sworn to himself he would leave this alone for now, he couldn't hold back a moment longer.

"What happened?" His hands curled into fists under his tucked arms. He'd planned to feed her, let her sleep before they did this. But he needed answers, an end to this torture, or he was going to explode. "I looked for you. For months. Called in every favor and used every connection I had to find you." And came up empty at every turn. "I never found a single clue. Not one." He'd been convinced that she'd died, except there was no record of that anywhere either.

"No, you wouldn't have."

What the hell did that cryptic comment mean? He couldn't let it go. "Did you change your name?"

She lowered her gaze to her plate, released a long breath. "It's complicated."

"So that I wouldn't find you?" he pressed.

Another pause. Then, finally, she answered. "I was in WITSEC."

He stared at her, shock hitting him like a punch to the face. "*What?*" He'd known something terrible had happened to her. But this? This was next level, beyond anything he'd imagined.

Those beautiful, haunted deep blue eyes lifted to meet his. "I was in the program long before we met."

"Why?" he asked, completely stunned. "What the hell happened?"

"I testified against my father."

She was telling the truth. He could see it in her eyes. So he stilled. Calmed himself and waited a beat, a sense of foreboding building. "Who's your father?"

"Max de Vries."

"Oh, holy shit," he breathed, and dragged a hand over his face. Max de Vries, the second-in-command of one of the most powerful and lethal drug lords in the US. Jesus. And he was her *father*?

"Yes." She looked back down at her plate, ran a fingertip through some crumbs. "My birth name was Lara de Vries. But I left her and everything from my old life behind when I entered the program and helped put him behind bars. Then I became Bella."

He was too dumbfounded to say anything else, still trying to take it all in. This was insane. He'd had no clue. Never even suspected that she wasn't exactly who she seemed from day one. And yet she'd lied to him. Hidden the truth the entire time they were together, even after they got engaged.

She looked up at him again, guilt etched into her features. "I wanted to tell you. So many times. But I couldn't. I assume you know the price of being in the program, and how strict the rules are."

He nodded slowly, still sorting through all of this. Struggling to accept that the kind, sweet, and caring woman he'd fallen for had a secret and incredibly dangerous past he'd never known about. Never would have come up with in his wildest dreams.

"When I first entered the program, I was terrified," she went on. "It took me years to be able to build a new life for myself, to not feel the need to look over my shoulder at every turn, thinking one of my father's people would come after me in revenge. And then I met you, and..." She swallowed hard, put her fingers to her eyes, her face pinching. "And I allowed myself to believe it was real, because I was finally happy," she said in a choked whisper. "I was so damn happy. Until he took it all away again like I was always afraid he would."

Blood rushed in Creed's ears, his heart swelling until he thought it might burst at any moment.

Bella fought to regain her composure. Cleared her throat and dropped her hand. "I thought that chapter of my life was all done, behind me and dead forever. That I was actually free. Then that night you were due home in December, I got a call saying my father had escaped from prison and that I had to be moved immediately. The Marshals showed up less than five minutes later and wouldn't listen to my arguments." She paused a moment to collect herself. "They wouldn't let me call you. I had less than ten minutes to grab my stuff and get out. That note was all I could give you, and I'm so sorry—" She put a hand to her mouth, eyes squeezing shut, her pain tearing at him.

"Christ, Bella," he whispered, aching for her. For both of them. "Why the hell didn't you say anything to me before?"

"I couldn't," she said, her expression laced with pain and frustration. "I had to follow all the rules exactly if I wanted to stay in the program. You must know I had no choice. That I would never have left, would never have hurt you like that if there had been any other way. I hated all of it. I hate *him* for doing it to us, but if I had stayed, you and I would both have been targets for the rest of our lives, and I just... I couldn't do that to you. I would rather break your heart than be the reason you got hurt or killed, or were forced to live a half-life because of me."

Hell, what was he supposed to say to that? Part of him understood her reasoning. But the other part refused to accept it. She knew his background. Knew his training and the security clearance level he'd had while in active military service. Knew how much he'd loved her and that she could depend on him, trust him. If anyone could have protected her from a threat like that, and if anyone outside WITSEC could have been entrusted with that information, it was him.

In light of everything he'd just learned, her up and leaving without a word felt like she simply hadn't had faith in him.

She held his gaze, desperation in her eyes. "If I had disobeyed them or broken any of the rules, they would have dumped me from the program. And if that happened, it was only a matter of time before someone came after both of us. I couldn't let that happen. Refused to. Don't you see that?"

Sort of. But dammit, she still should have trusted him more. They could have avoided all this pain. He would have found a way to keep her safe. "So what's changed? Why come back and tell me all this now?"

"I'm not in the program anymore."

He frowned. "Why not?"

Her eyes went flat. "He's dead."

The news was yet another bomb. "I didn't hear anything about that."

"They're keeping it quiet because of ongoing investigations with the Department of Justice. The Marshals Service notified me two days ago that he and a few others died after being severely wounded in a prison break attempt during a riot, and died in the subsequent fire."

"Their forensics confirmed one of the bodies was him?"

"Yes. So I packed up my stuff and drove here."

He took that in. To get here this soon meant she must have driven almost straight through with barely any sleep. No wonder she looked ready to drop. "Why come here?" He needed to know. "You could have sent a letter or email or even just called to tell me all this. Why did you drive all the way here?"

Her shoulders hitched as she pulled in an unsteady breath. "Because I wanted—needed to see you. Needed to explain, and —" She lowered her gaze, shook her head. "God, because I've missed you," she finished in an aching whisper that sent a wave of anguish through him. "You have *no* idea how much I've missed you. Every single day since I left. At first I didn't want to be alive anymore. Could barely function for months."

Yeah, that made two of them. "Where did they take you?"

"St. Paul. New name, new life. Eventually, I got a job working for an animal rescue center. That's done now too, but I'm still Bella." Her eyes lifted to his. "And I'm not even asking for your forgiveness. Just your understanding and maybe a little validation."

He let out a deep sigh, suddenly weary to his bones. This was all too much. "I know it wasn't your fault," he finally said. "But I wish you'd trusted me enough to tell me about your past. I would've done whatever it took to keep you safe."

To her credit, she didn't look away. "I *did* trust you, Creed. I still do. That's why I'm here." She abruptly pushed the plate with the mostly uneaten sandwich away from her and stood. "I'm so tired I'm about to drop. Can we talk more later? I need to go get some sleep."

He could see how exhausted she was, and they both needed

time and space now to process everything. He did, at least. "Yeah, of course. Do you need anything else?"

The sadness in her eyes hit him like an arrow to the heart. She looked defeated and ready to keel over. It hurt to see her like this. "No, but thanks for hearing me out and letting me crash here."

Stop her. Don't let her go.

The overwhelming urge to come around the island to grab her, hold on tight, and never let go had his muscles tied up in knots. Everything he'd ever felt for her rushed back to the surface, the deep, aching loss mixing with the shock and joy of seeing her again, and Bella looking so lost and alone fired up that deep, primal protectiveness toward her he couldn't shut off.

"Sure," he said instead, staying where he was. "Good night."

"Good night."

She left him standing alone in his kitchen with nothing but the quiet hum of the refrigerator filling the heavy silence. He closed his eyes, shoved out a long breath and pressed his fingers to his eyelids.

Fuck, what a mess. Where the hell was he supposed to go from here? Bella had been through a hell he couldn't even fathom. At the very least she needed to rest. To feel safe. To eat good food and be taken care of until she recovered.

Immediate problem was, he only had tomorrow off and then he had to work out of town all weekend. He didn't want to go now. The thought of leaving her felt wrong on every level.

But maybe leaving for a couple days was the best thing for now, hard as it would be to be separated from her again so soon. He needed more time to think all this through, then find out what Bella wanted going forward so he could decide what *he* wanted and was willing to do from here.

Right at this moment he only knew two things. He didn't

want her to leave. But the thought of her staying was just as painful.

THREE

Bella paused in the hallway at the raised voices coming from the other end. One was cold. Hard.

Her father's. *"I'll take care of it myself."*

A shiver of foreboding rippled through her as his voice and that of the person he was speaking to faded out of earshot. She followed them, careful to keep her distance and not be seen. She knew better than to come anywhere near her father when he was working, and that tone she'd just heard made it clear he wasn't happy about something.

She stopped by a darkened window off the kitchen and watched the two men leave the house. They crossed the courtyard and disappeared through the edge of the garden into the shadows beyond. She knew where they were going. She just didn't know why.

She wanted to. Needed answers to the questions she had been asking herself for far too long but was too afraid to voice.

When enough time had passed, she took the same route, moving slowly to make sure they were already gone. She rarely came out here. And never to this part of the property. She had been forbidden from crossing the fence line since she was a little girl. But she had to know the truth, even though it frightened her.

Her pulse throbbed in her ears, trepidation building with each step. The warm Florida air was balmy against her skin, a slight breeze rustling the palm fronds around her. It was dark out, the lamps on the exterior of the sprawling mansion behind her lighting the way across the cobbled courtyard and down the path leading through the garden.

She stopped at the spot where all tropical trees and thickly planted borders obscured the rest of the property from view. This was the fence line.

She kept going, found the gate hidden behind more foliage and walked through it. On the other side a low concrete building stood before her in the moonlight. It had no windows. No lights on the exterior. She knew her father and the other man were inside.

Her bare feet were silent on the concrete as she moved forward. She stopped in front of the door, the ominous feeling growing stronger with each passing second. Over the sigh of the breeze in the surrounding vegetation, she heard something else.

Something coming from inside. A muffled cry that sent a shiver corkscrewing up her spine.

She swallowed, heart thudding. Whatever was happening on the other side of that door was evil. She knew it deep down.

She didn't want to see it. The voice in her head warned her not to look. That she wouldn't like what she found, because it might just confirm what she feared the most. That she had been living a lie and turning a blind eye to the reality because it was easier that way.

No, she didn't want to look. And yet some irresistible, invisible force she was powerless to resist compelled her to keep moving forward and enter.

The door magically opened under her hand. More cries reached her. Guttural, agonized cries that echoed off the concrete walls and made the hairs on her arms stand on end.

A bar of light was visible beneath the bottom of the door at the end of the hall. She moved toward it, mouth dry. Someone was being beaten in that room.

Her hand closed around the door handle. It was ice cold beneath her fingers. She opened it and stopped dead at the sight before her, her feet refusing to obey her silent scream to run. She was paralyzed with horror. Numb with shock.

A man was strung up in chains from the ceiling, hanging head down. He was naked. His entire body was covered in bloody slices, his cries and sobs tearing at her heart.

And the man wielding the blade was her father.

As though he sensed her there, her father whirled toward her suddenly, blood dripping from the wicked knife in his fist. His expression froze, a nauseating, sadistic smile stuck on his face. As if he enjoyed inflicting the pain and suffering.

Her skin crawled, and her stomach lurched, bile rising in her throat.

His eerie smile faded. "Lara." His mouth thinned, his brows lowering in a foreboding frown. But he seemed more disappointed than angry. Resigned. And that almost scared her more. "I told you never to come in here."

She shook her head, unable to look away from the macabre scene before her. He was a monster. A sick, twisted monster who had hidden beneath a mask all these years.

Then his face began to ripple, as if the flesh was moving over the bones of his skull. She stood there, flooded with horror as his face melted away to reveal the true identity that lurked beneath the rich, sophisticated veneer.

Evil. Pure, twisted evil.

She backed up a step. Then another.

His gaze locked on her. He started toward her, one measured step at a time, that fixed expression on his face sending ice sluicing through her veins.

It snapped her out of her paralysis. She spun around, lurched for the door, her heart shooting into her throat. The echo of his footsteps followed her. Relentless.

She reached the door. Grabbed the latch and twisted it, shoving hard.

It didn't budge.

The ragged sobs of the man hanging broken and bleeding onto the concrete floor raked over her, her father's unhurried footsteps coming ever closer sending a wave of panic through her.

"No!" she cried, putting her shoulder against the door and straining with all her might.

She had to escape. Wanted as far away from him and this nightmare as she could get.

"I warned you what would happen," her father said in an ominous tone. "It's too late to run now."

She whirled, cowered against the door as he reached for her. Knowing that once he caught her, she would never be safe from him again…

Something touched her shoulder.

She jerked awake in a rush, a strangled cry locking in her chest. She scrambled up and shrank away from the hand, struggling to see in the dimness as Nick Furry hissed and shot off the bed with a warning growl. A scream built in her throat when her eyes adjusted enough to see a large silhouette hovering beside her bed.

"Shhh, hey, it's just me."

It took a moment for the words and voice to penetrate the fog in her brain. For her to remember she was at Creed's house and believe that he was literally right next to her. And that she was safe.

She sucked in a ragged breath and exhaled slowly, closing her eyes as a quiver ripped through her. Shit, she hadn't had one this bad in a while. At least the fear was fading now, but the sudden drop in adrenaline left her feeling weak.

The mattress dipped slightly as Creed sat on the edge of it close to her. He reached for her, and she didn't resist when he gathered her into his arms. "You're safe."

She laid her cheek against the curve of his shoulder, the soft cotton of his T-shirt overlying hard muscle beneath. Another shudder rolled through her. *God.* Those horrific images were still so clear in her mind.

"You're okay," he murmured against the top of her head. "It was just a dream."

Except it wasn't. It was much, much worse than that, even though her subconscious had changed certain elements and events in the dream from reality.

She gulped in a couple choppy breaths, willed her heart to slow down. As it did, tiredness came rushing back, the sleeping pill she'd taken earlier taking hold once more.

"You're safe now." Creed's low, quiet voice grounded her. "He's gone and can never threaten you again. Everything's going to be okay."

Was it? She nodded slightly anyway and forced the vestiges of the nightmare aside, forced her mind to empty until she could focus on the here and now as she'd been taught by a therapist. *Focus on your senses and immediate surroundings. Nothing else.*

Creed was warm and solid against her, his heartbeat a steady, soothing rhythm under her ear. His arms were strong around her, keeping her safe. He smelled of clean, masculine spice.

He'd been her safe place once. Still was.

The fear and horror receded. Her mind settled, and her breathing slowed. Suddenly she was exhausted again. So damn tired right down to her soul, the medication dragging her back toward oblivion.

"Go back to sleep," Creed whispered, easing her down on her side and pulling the covers over her.

Bella sighed and curled up facing him. Part of her wanted to beg him not to leave, but she still had some pride left, and a heavy wave of sleep was already dragging her under. Max was gone, but she still wasn't okay. None of it was. She would never forgive him for what he'd done. For taking her away from Creed. For forcing her to have to pick up the shattered pieces of her life once again after.

Just as she slid under, she thought she felt Creed's hand stroking over her hair. Her heart ached for them both.

She might be safe now physically, but she wasn't okay. Because being ripped away from him had broken something inside her that would never heal.

∽

CREED GLANCED at the digital clock on the stove as he set a pan to heat on the front right element. It was almost 1900 the next evening. Bella still hadn't emerged from her room. The couple times he'd cracked the door to check on her throughout the day, she'd been sound asleep.

He'd left her to rest all day, then decided to make her something for dinner and take it up to her. A minute ago he'd finally heard her footsteps on the floorboards overhead, so he knew she was at least up and moving.

With the exception of that brief few minutes after the nightmare, she'd slept for the better part of twenty hours. He'd gotten up at five to start his day and had been careful not to disturb her while he worked because she was so damn exhausted. More than that, her nightmare last night showed him just how much mental and emotional strain she was under.

He'd never seen her like that. Never seen her so lost and frightened and it still twisted him up inside. That wasn't just simple fear he'd witnessed last night. It was straight-up terror caused by deep trauma.

She hadn't told him the details about her life before WITSEC, but given what intel he did have, he could imagine her position well enough. Max de Vries had a notorious reputation as a brutal, sadistic bastard. He killed anyone who crossed him or got in his way, anyone who posed a threat. Or even a perceived threat.

To think of Bella growing up with that monster was sickening.

He didn't know what her plans were from here or what kind of support she had—if any—but he still cared about her and wanted to help no matter what had happened between them, or how things worked out. He believed that she had never wanted to hurt him, and he was gutted by all she'd been through without him having any idea.

He'd racked his brains trying to think of any little clue or sign that would hint at what she'd endured that he might have missed when they'd been together. But there was nothing, not a single time that he remembered where she'd slipped up or made him suspicious of anything.

He added a pat of butter to the hot pan to melt. His French toast recipe was her favorite meal, so that's what he was making. If she didn't come down soon or was too embarrassed to face him now, he would take it up to her and stay put until she finished every bite. She needed to eat proper, regular meals every day to get her strength back.

Overhead, her footsteps moved toward the bathroom as he dipped the slices of French bread into the custard mixture flavored with brown sugar, vanilla, and cinnamon, coating them thoroughly but not letting them get soaked through.

Squishy, soggy French toast was a sin. And while he might not be the best cook in the world, he'd mastered this dish.

When the butter was sizzling, he added the dredged slices to the pan, using the familiar task to gather himself before he faced Bella again. He still didn't know what the hell to think about all this, had been up most of the night wrestling with it. Wondering what he could have done differently that would have convinced her to confide in him, leave WITSEC, and stay with him.

After she'd left, it had taken a long time before he'd finally accepted that she wasn't coming back. He'd struggled so hard to move on with his life, to try and put the devastation behind him. Now that she'd suddenly reappeared on his doorstep, she'd ripped the scab off that half-healed wound, making him bleed again.

Even though he was trying to stay objective and protect himself, all his feelings had come flooding back the moment he'd seen her last night. Now he couldn't shut them off no matter how hard he tried, and he didn't know what the hell to do with them.

The melted butter popped and sizzled as it foamed around the pieces of bread in the pan. When the bottoms were golden brown, he flipped them over, left them to finish cooking while he gathered everything else he needed and set it all on the island. More butter. Real maple syrup. Strawberries.

He plated all three pieces for her and started another batch in the pan for himself, then slathered hers with more butter, sliced berries on the top, and drizzled on some syrup. He was just fishing cutlery out of the drawer when he heard her quiet treads on the stairs to the right.

He looked up, unprepared for the gut punch he experienced when he saw her.

Bella paused at the bottom, still dressed in pajamas, hair tousled and her eyes puffy from sleep. She tucked a lock of rumpled hair behind her ear and gave him a hesitant smile that tugged at his heartstrings.

He hated this awkwardness between them, all the uncertainty and the need to keep his guard up.

"Hi," she said. "I'd say good morning, but I guess that was over almost eight hours ago."

"You were exhausted and needed the sleep."

She nodded. "I took a sleeping pill before I went to bed, and I guess it must've knocked me right out."

She didn't mention the nightmare. Maybe she didn't remember it, or him holding her after, and he wasn't bringing it up.

He set the fork and knife onto her plate. "Hungry?" If she wasn't, he would insist she eat anyway.

"Starving." Her gaze moved to the plate on the island, her expression brightening, and he was glad to see it. "Is that French toast?"

He could feel her nervousness. It grated against his senses like steel wool. "It is. Come sit down and eat."

He slid the plate across to rest in front of one of the stools opposite him, determined to keep it light and make things feel as normal as possible. He was just going to go with this as if her being in his kitchen was totally normal, and not bring anything else up. Not about them, her past, and definitely not about the nightmare. Not right now.

She slid onto the stool but didn't pick up her cutlery. "Thank you for this."

"No problem." He flipped his toast over in the pan. "Go ahead and dig in. Don't wait for me."

"No, I'll wait."

A brittle tension settled between them as he stood with his back to her, waiting for the toast to finish cooking. He didn't know what the hell to say to put her at ease. Small talk was beyond him right now.

More unanswered questions kept piling up in his mind. They were driving him crazy.

He didn't know whether she'd come here for more than to merely apologize and give him an explanation. Didn't know whether she still might love him or even if he could wrap his head around giving them a second chance.

All he knew was that the stakes were too high for him to open himself up to her on that level again.

"How's Nick doing up there?" he finally asked when he couldn't take the silence anymore. Her cat seemed a safe bet in terms of topic to put her more at ease and get her talking.

"Pretty good, all things considered. He's not used to traveling, and he's skittish at the best of times, but he slept next to me most of the night, I think. This house is beautiful, by the way. Has lots of charm. Is it yours?"

"Could be if I want it." He wasn't sure whether he did or not. Didn't spend much time here except to sleep. "I'm just renting for now."

"Do you like it?"

"Yeah, I do." Though he liked it a lot more with her here. "A local company renovated it last year. They specialize in period houses, update them without taking all the character out of them."

"And what about Crimson Point? Do you like the town?"

"Yeah. The whole area is beautiful, and I've met some

really great people here." It was the first place that had started to feel like any kind of home since she'd left.

He slid his French toast onto a plate and turned around to set it on the island across from her. It was still too damned hard to look at her so he kept his attention on his food. "Dig in."

She cut a bite. "You didn't stay home today because of me, did you?"

"No, I had the day off. But I've got a contract all weekend up in Seattle starting first thing tomorrow morning." He was really torn about it. On the one hand, he wanted to protect his professional reputation and welcomed a solid reason to be away from her. On the other, he wanted to get out of the contract so he could stay here and take care of her in case she needed something.

But he wouldn't bail now. This sudden monkey wrench in his life wasn't technically an emergency, just a personal crisis. He couldn't let his partner Decker down on this contract and didn't want their boss Ryder to know something was going on with him personally.

Though after all the thinking he'd done since last night, he'd come to the realization that he couldn't hold all this inside much longer and needed to talk to someone. He could call Decker later to tell him what was going on over the phone, but it would be easier to tell him in person on the drive up the I-5 tomorrow.

Since Decker was one of the most emotionally closed-off people Creed had ever known, that was gonna be super fun. Deck was gonna love it too.

"You're working for a security firm now?" Bella asked him.

He nodded. "Crimson Point Security, here in town."

"Doing what?"

"Different things. Risk assessment, event security, personal protection. Whatever they need me to do, and it changes depending on the contract." He frowned. "How did you know that?"

"One of the Marshals told me. Once they broke the news about my f— About Max, I asked them to find you. They told me you'd moved out here and taken a job, and gave me your address. I probably could've found you myself in time, but I knew they'd be faster and wanted to get here as soon as I could."

It helped to know that she'd been in such a giant hurry to come straight to him and explain. Still, damn. What was he supposed to do with all this? What was she expecting?

He put a bite of French toast into his mouth, forced it down his suddenly tight throat. Shit, he wasn't going to bring up their past again, demand more answers or make her feel guilty, but all the emotions hitting him were building like a tidal wave.

"I, um, didn't really stop to think things through when I decided to come here," she continued. "Just threw my stuff in the car once I got your location and left. I didn't want to call first because I didn't know how you'd react or if you'd even take the call. I wanted to talk to you about everything in person, but I realize that was really unfair of me. For all I knew, you could be living with someone or…" She trailed off, left the sentence hanging there while the tension ratcheted up inside him until he wanted to scream.

No matter what had happened in their past, he didn't see any reason to lie to her about this. "I'm single." And he didn't want to talk about that with her, either. "So listen, I'm gonna be up and gone early tomorrow morning, and I won't be back until late Sunday night, but you're welcome to stay here if you want."

"Thank you."

"Will you be okay on your own?" She seemed so damned

fragile, and he didn't want her to feel abandoned and alone while she tried to get her feet back under her.

"Yes, I'll be fine."

He looked up at her, unconvinced. Those shadows in her beautiful deep blue eyes told him she was still dealing with a lot of unspoken shit. "Is there someone you can call? Maybe someone to come stay here while I'm gone?"

"No, there's no one." Her tone was matter of fact, not a trace of self-pity.

But it made him ache inside to think of her being so alone in the world. "Why did you choose the name Bella?"

A soft, almost relieved smile curved her lips. "My mom used to call me that when I was little. She was part Italian." She released a breath. "Then she died, and after that nothing was the same. When everything else was eventually taken from me as well, and I had to start over on my own, I thought the name was a good piece of my past to honor her. So I kept that."

He absorbed that in silence, still floored by everything that had happened in the past twenty-four hours. Every new layer she revealed gave him a newfound respect—awe, really—for the person she'd become before he'd met her. To overcome her past and start a brand-new life all alone in a strange place must have been hard. But she'd done it. And she'd thrived—until she'd been ripped away from their life that night. "I'm glad you did. It suits you."

Her lips quirked, then the smile faded and her expression grew somber again. "There's something else about my past I want to tell you, if you're willing to hear it."

His stomach tightened. "Yeah, of course." He set down his fork, gave her his full attention. He had a lot of questions but hadn't wanted to push her too hard when she seemed so vulnerable and he was trying to keep a lid on his own emotions.

She pushed a slice of strawberry around on her plate with

her fork, avoiding his gaze. "When I was in my early teens, I was hospitalized for almost five months for mental health reasons. Severe depression and anxiety that got so bad, I almost…"

She didn't need to say the rest. The pause at the end made the unspoken part clear enough. Jesus, it hurt to think of her suffering that kind of pain, especially when she was so young.

He kept watching her, not knowing what to say. From the moment he'd met her, she'd seemed so well-adjusted and even-keeled, an optimist determined to make the world around her a better place. She had obviously worked incredibly hard to overcome the past and become that way. Her resilience amazed him. "You hid it well. I never guessed you'd been through anything like that."

Her smile held an ironic edge. "Yep. Fake it till you make it, right? That's how I started. But, eventually, it didn't feel like faking anymore. That felt good." She pushed the berry into a puddle of syrup. "I was ashamed about that part of my life for a long time. That's why I never told you."

What else didn't he know? "You always seemed so happy."

She met his gaze. "I was. With you."

The knot in his stomach pulled into a tight, burning ball. He shoved down all the remaining questions he had. "Do you have any support at all right now?"

"Just Nick Furry. But you letting me stay here for now really means a lot. I feel safe for the first time in a long time, and I can't tell you how amazing that is, so thank you."

He gripped the edge of the island to stop himself from going to her, the sudden longing to touch and hold her burning like wildfire in his chest. "I'm glad."

This was torture. What the fuck was he supposed to do?

"Anyway." She reached out to pluck another berry from the

bowl he'd set between them, and when her sleeve pulled up he saw the marks on her left wrist.

Without thinking, he shot a hand out to grab hers, a cold, hard rage filling him as he pushed the cuff up to reveal more blue and purple marks marking her forearm. Finger marks. There were abrasions on the underside of her arm too. And she still wore the watch he'd given her for her birthday last year.

"What happened?" he said in a low, taut voice.

She glanced at her arm. "Oh, there was an incident at the place where I stopped for dinner last night outside Portland."

His jaw tightened. "What kind of incident?"

"Someone came after me in the parking lot and tried to rip my watch off. I fought him off initially. Then two people inside came running out and scared him off. I'm okay though, just a little bruised." She pulled her hand free.

He let her go, reluctantly, still looking at the watch. He'd had the back of it engraved with a special message. Knowing she'd kept it all this time… "Did you report it?"

"No, he didn't get anything, and when he took off, I just wanted to get here."

He met her gaze, a thread of unease twining in his gut. "You're sure it was just a robbery attempt?"

"Yes."

He glanced back down at the marks on her arm. Maybe he was being overly paranoid, but he didn't like the feel of it or the timing. Not after everything she'd told him. "Did you inform the Marshals Service?"

"I called the number I had for my contact, but it was already disconnected. So I sent him an email. Haven't heard back yet though."

"You should report it to the police, so there's a record of it at least. They can check the security cameras if there are any and report it to the Marshals."

"I'd rather just let it g—"

"Someone assaulted you, Bella. If those people hadn't run out to help you, it could have been a lot worse." And given who her father had been…

It wasn't impossible that someone in the organization might have followed her.

Her lashes lowered. "I know. But I just want to put it behind me and move on now."

"Any chance someone followed you here?"

"No," she said without hesitation, shaking her head. "I know what to watch for, and I was extra careful. There's no way."

He relaxed a bit, thinking back to soon after they'd started dating. She'd asked him to teach her how to shoot not long after. Had asked him to show her self-defense moves too. Now he understood the real reason she'd needed to learn all of it. Damn.

"Will you at least talk to the local sheriff about everything that's happened? He's a good guy, grew up here. At least that way his office can liaise with the Marshals if necessary."

She hedged, clearly uncomfortable with divulging her past to a stranger. "Do I need to if the Marshals already know about the incident?"

"I think you should."

She held his gaze for a long moment, thinking, and the attraction between them flared to life, zinging through his gut. "Okay, then."

More tension bled away. "I'll call him and set something up, maybe even for later tonight if that works, because it's fresh in your mind. You up to it?"

"Sure, that's fine." She tucked another lock of hair behind her ear, took a bite of her French toast and made a humming sound that sent an unwanted torrent of heat flooding through him. "This is so great. Thank you. Just what I needed."

"Good." He went back to eating his own food, but all his attention stayed on her, his mind in chaos.

He wished he could make all this go away for her somehow. To take away the fear and erase the past. Make her feel loved and secure and start up where they'd left things. But he no longer had that right and wasn't ready to open himself up to her like that again. Not unless she'd come here to—

No, he told himself firmly. He wouldn't even allow himself to think it.

Losing her once almost destroyed him. Going through that a second time would be the death of him.

FOUR

Bella remained quiet as Creed turned into the Crimson Point Sheriff's Office parking lot several hours later. She still didn't want to do this, but she saw the logic in Creed's argument, and after a good long rest last night and most of today, she felt much better than when she'd arrived at his door.

"It was nice of the sheriff to meet with me so late," she finally said as Creed turned off the ignition.

"He's good at what he does. You'll like him. His wife owns and runs a popular place on the waterfront called Whale's Tale. It's a combination café and bookshop, always busy."

"I'll have to check it out while I'm here." She got out and walked with him to the front door, the palpable emotional distance between them grating on her nerves and tearing at her heart.

She'd hurt him so badly. He didn't seem angry with her per se, and he'd been good to her, even seemed glad to see her initially. But there was a definite wall between them, and it hurt like hell. They were little more than polite strangers now.

She still didn't regret coming here. If nothing else, at least she'd apologized and Creed now knew the truth. So if he wasn't willing to give her—them—another chance, then maybe her explanation would at least help him make peace with their past and move forward easier.

But she was still hoping against hope that he would want to move on *with* her.

Creed held the door for her. She murmured a thank you and walked into the brightly lit reception area. Before they'd even reached the front desk, a man in his thirties with short brown hair and blue eyes strode out of a hallway dressed in jeans and a long-sleeved shirt.

"Creed, hi. And you must be Bella." He gave her a warm smile and held out a hand. "I'm Sheriff Buchanan."

"Hi." She shook with him. "Thanks so much for meeting with me, especially since it's after hours."

"It's no problem. Come on back to my office." He led the way down a hall to an office overlooking the small park next door. Two framed pictures sat on his desk, a black and white of him with his arms around a pretty blonde woman in a stunning wedding dress, and another of her holding a toddler with brown curls.

She smiled. "You have a beautiful family."

"Thank you. Although that's mostly my wife Poppy's doing." He dropped into the chair behind the desk while she and Creed sat in chairs across from him.

"Heard a rumor that you might be stepping aside soon," Creed said.

Sheriff Buchanan's blue eyes filled with amusement. "Really? Who'd you hear that from?"

"Oh, you know how it is in small towns."

Noah grinned, and she knew she was missing out on an inside joke of some sort. "Ah, yes, the Crimson Point gossip mill."

"I dunno, wouldn't exactly call it gossip. My source is pretty reliable."

"Yeah? Well, that's good to hear." The sheriff looked at her. "It's true. I'm leaving as soon as my term is up and going to work for the same people as him," he said, nodding his chin at Creed. "But that's not important right now." He clasped his hands together on top of the desk. "Creed tells me you needed to discuss something sensitive."

She hesitated, then berated herself. Why did talking about this feel so damn shameful and awkward? She hadn't done anything wrong. "It's a bit of a long story."

"My wife owns a bookstore. I happen to like long stories."

She found herself smiling, disarmed. Then she glanced at Creed for direction, wondering what exactly to disclose and how far back to go. He nodded, his solid, reassuring presence easing the hard knot of tension in the pit of her stomach. She turned back to the sheriff. "I just came into town last night. I went to Creed's house," she clarified. "But up until a few days ago, I was in WITSEC."

The sheriff's eyebrows rose slightly, but he leaned back in his seat, his full attention on her. "Okay, go on."

She took a breath and explained about Max, how she'd cut ties with him and joined the program in exchange for testifying against him. How everything had stabilized after that. How she'd met Creed, moved in with him, and gotten engaged.

"Then a year ago this past December, I got a call out of the blue saying Max had escaped from prison. The Marshals came and whisked me away. I did what I had to do to survive, and then the other day was informed that he'd died. I made the decision to leave the program. Then I got in my car and drove straight here. Except there was an incident on the way."

"What kind of incident?"

She explained what had happened at the diner. "I didn't

report it to local police. I didn't see the point and just wanted to get to Crimson Point." To Creed.

"Show him your arm," Creed said.

She pulled up her sleeve, held it out for the sheriff to see, feeling silly. "It's nothing, honestly. I've had a lot worse. But my contact with the Marshals is over. I tried to call anyway, then sent an email, but I haven't heard back." She shrugged. "Since I'm now staying in your jurisdiction, at least for a little while, Creed thought I should let you know what happened in light of the previous security situation. To err on the side of caution."

"I appreciate you telling me," the sheriff said. "I'll reach out to the Marshals Service myself and check in with them, and see if I can get additional information on whether or not they're still monitoring the situation. If that doesn't work, I can talk to an FBI contact." He frowned in concern. "It sounds like you've been through a lot, Bella. I'm glad you're okay now."

She forced a smile. Physically she was okay. The rest she was determined to regain—if possible. Because some things still remained well outside of her control. "Me too."

"Can you give me a description of the man who attacked you? Anything at all that might help ID him?"

"No. I wish there was, but…no. It was dark, and everything happened too fast."

"All right. If you think of anything else, you can let me know. In the meantime, is there something I can help with?"

"Not that I can think of. But thank you for offering."

"Of course. I'll make a call first thing in the morning, schedule permitting. If I get any information, I'll let you know, but I'm sure someone at the Marshals Service will contact you soon to reply to the email."

"Yes, I'm sure they will." There was no way they would just

drop her because she'd left the program. Not in a situation like this.

"Well, if there's nothing else, I'd better head home." He rose to his feet. "Hudson's refusing to go to sleep because it's my turn to read him a story."

"Oh, that's so sweet." A swift pang hit her. What would it have been like to have a father who had tucked her in and read her bedtime stories? If she ever had kids, that's the kind of parent she wanted to be. She'd thought she would have children with Creed, but now…

Nothing was certain anymore, and she was too afraid to ask him about rekindling their relationship at this stage.

She and Creed thanked him again and left. Creed put her in the front passenger seat then drove them back to his place.

"That part about the small town gossip wasn't far off," he said as he turned onto a main road. The streetlamps reflected off the damp pavement, their light shimmering in golden halos, while below at the bottom of the hill, the ocean spread out from shore like an endless, black blanket. "It's only a matter of time before people find out you're in town and start asking questions. Not in a bad way," he added quickly. "But I've thought about it, and I feel I should tell my bosses what's going on. That okay with you?"

"Do you trust them?" she asked.

"Yes. And Decker, the guy I'm partnered with."

"Okay then, go ahead." She didn't love it, but she understood and trusted that Creed would only give them what they needed, nothing more. "You were right about the sheriff. I liked him."

"Most people around here do. When he joins CPS, he's going to be working on investigations with another new member of the company—Decker's fiancée, Teagan. She's great too, and so is Decker's sister and her guy. Warwick. He's a Brit, but he's all right," he said in a teasing tone. "I'll introduce them to you if you want. I mean, if you're going to stay here for a while."

"I'd like that." She missed having friends. Feeling like part of a community.

Except she wasn't sure what was going to happen now or how long she would stay. That all depended on how things went with Creed.

But as long as there was any hope at all of reconciling with him, then she would stay as long as it took.

∽

RYDER WALKED into his house and let out a sigh of relief. It had been a long couple of weeks at the office getting everything in place for the big contract in Seattle this weekend, and he was looking forward to chilling with his fam tonight. Danae was working her magic in the kitchen, because whatever savory, spicy scent hung in the air, it was making his stomach growl.

But no sooner had he shut the door behind him than his phone rang.

He mentally cursed and thought about ignoring it for the time being, but it could be work related. Taking it from his pocket, he saw Creed's name on the display. "Hey," he answered. "You checking in about the details for tomorrow?"

"No, I'm up to speed on everything. I'm meeting Deck at oh-seven-hundred and heading out. That's not why I'm calling."

He paused there in the entryway at Creed's uncharacteristically grave tone. "Everything okay?"

"Sort of. It's complicated. And personal. Do you have a few minutes?"

"Yeah, of course." Creed was about as low maintenance,

solid, and trustworthy an employee as Ryder could ever find. So if he'd called to talk about personal stuff, it had to be serious. "And whatever you say will stay between you and me."

"You can tell Callum. I'm going to talk to Decker about it tomorrow too."

"Sure. What's going on?" He was starting to get concerned.

"My…former fiancée showed up unannounced last night after fourteen months without a word from her. Long story, but it turns out she was actually in WITSEC the entire time we were together and just left the program a few days ago."

"Okay, whoa." He hadn't expected that. Hadn't even known Creed had been engaged before. Didn't really know anything about his personal life other than he was single. "Why was she in WITSEC?"

The story Creed told him was incredible. It left Ryder standing there in stunned silence as he finished.

"And that's pretty much all I know at this point," Creed said. "We just spoke to the sheriff about everything to let him know what's going on in case anything comes of the assault. He's going to contact the Marshals Service and liaise with them personally. I just wanted to make sure we didn't leave anything to chance, that's all."

"Yeah, I get it." He ran a hand over his closely shorn hair. "Okay, so…she's staying with you?" Creed hadn't come right out and said he still had feelings for Bella, but his actions and this call made that clear enough.

"For now. I'm not sure what's going to happen when I get back, to be honest. She hasn't said what her plans are."

"Fair enough. Do you need anything from us?" Meaning him and the team at CPS, which was still a small enough crew that it felt like a big family. He and Callum had a strict policy of only hiring good people. If anything in their background and rigorously checked references even *smelled* like it might not be a good fit, they didn't get an offer.

"No. I'll check in with you from Seattle when we get there tomorrow. We'll be at the venue before noon. But I'm planning to ask someone to check on Bella while I'm away. Maybe Teagan."

"Good idea. All our agents are currently booked on other jobs, but I can go by your place later too if you let Bella know. And if it's all the same to you, I'm gonna hold off on telling Callum about this right now. His wife is overdue. They might induce in the next few days, so he's got a lot on his mind at the moment."

Callum was in overprotective mode, on high alert as he waited for Nadia to go into labor. It was funny to see the battle-hardened former Delta operator so rattled. He and Nadia already had a daughter they'd adopted, but knowing his wife was about to deliver their baby had Callum on edge.

"Yeah, of course."

"I appreciate the heads up about everything though. Talk to you tomorrow. And if you need anything, a few days off or whatever after you get back from this job, just let me know. We can rework the schedule if need be." He knew Creed would never abuse the offer.

"I will. Thanks. Bye."

He put his phone away, still surprised by what Creed had just told him. But Ryder wasn't worried about him losing focus on the job. Creed was former SF and as disciplined as they came. In spite of their contrasting personalities—or maybe because of them—he and Decker made a good team and had become pretty tight since the harrowing incident with Teagan a few weeks ago.

Ryder walked to the kitchen, ready to ask what that amazing smell was, but paused when he saw his wife standing at the kitchen counter. Her back was to him, the line of her spine and shoulders tense. She didn't glance his way or acknowledge his presence, and when he moved closer he saw the tearstains on her cheeks.

He knew instantly what it meant.

"Hey," he said, coming up behind her to curl his arms around her waist. She remained poker stiff as she stirred a bowl of whatever was in front of her. "You look upset. Does this mean what I think it does?"

She stopped stirring. Sucked in a jerky breath and wiped her cheek with the shoulder of her sweater. "Yes."

Thought so. He caught the hand holding the spatula, pulled it from the handle and turned her around to face him. She stared straight at the middle of his shirt, the little hitch in her breathing squeezing his heart. He hated to see her sad, and her tears bothered him even more.

"Come here," he murmured, pulling her into a hug.

She remained stiff and unyielding for another moment, then gave in, sliding her arms around his waist and burying her face in his chest. "I'm n-not r-ready," she choked out, her voice muffled in his shirt.

"Moms rarely are." Let alone such a loving mom who was so close to her son. And Finn was her only child. After her first husband died, it had been just the two of them until Ryder came along. She and Finn had a special and rare bond that he respected deeply.

"He g-grew up t-too fast," she protested.

Ryder made a sympathetic sound and kept holding her, letting her get this out while they were alone in the kitchen. She wouldn't want Finn to know how upset she was. That was just the kind of person Danae was.

"I don't…w-want him to g-go," she said.

"I know." He rubbed a hand up and down her back. She

would have felt the same if Finn had left for college out of state, but this was on another level. There wasn't much he could do or say to soothe her or make this any easier. Except for one thing. "This is what he wants, babe, and he's wanted it for a long time."

She sagged in his arms. "I know," she said miserably. "I know."

She leaned into him for a minute or two, then pulled herself together and hastily wiped at her cheeks as she looked up at him, her lashes wet and spiky. "He's gonna be okay, right?" Fear lurked in her eyes.

He wiped a tear away from the side of her face. "He'll be fine. But I won't lie, it's definitely going to change him. He'll be a different person after this. And he's going to come back with a new confidence and purpose and maturity. That's for sure."

"He wants to make his father proud. And you."

He knew that, and knew that his own service had partly influenced Finn since Ryder had been in his life. But it wasn't just that, and it shouldn't be. "Sweetheart, this is part of his dream."

Danae nodded, sniffed, and squared her shoulders. "Don't tell him I cried," she ordered sternly.

"I won't." He released her, and she immediately spun around and went back to prepping dinner, the way she stirred the contents of the bowl almost savage. "Need a hand in here?"

"No, I'm good." She was beating the hell out of whatever was in the bowl, clearly needed to keep going and burn off some of the feelings still bubbling inside her.

"Is he in his room?"

"Yes."

"I'm gonna go talk to him real quick."

"Tell him dinner's in twenty."

"Will do." Ryder saw Finn's decision as a good thing, although he'd never say that in front of Danae. She was his mom. It was her right to worry about him.

He tapped his knuckles on Finn's closed door. "Can I come in?"

"Yeah."

He opened the door to find Finn sitting at his desk in front of the fancy computer monitor and whatever video game he had going on. Finn pushed his headphones back on his head and looked at Ryder expectantly.

"So you've decided?" Ryder asked.

"Oh. Yeah. I've got an appointment at the recruiter's office tomorrow. You wanna come with me?"

"Damn right I'm coming with you." He reached out a hand. Finn grinned and clasped it. Ryder squeezed tight, holding his stepson's gaze. "I'm really proud of you, buddy."

Finn's face flushed slightly, but there was pride there too. "Thanks. Mom's not too thrilled—"

"She'll come around. It's just hard for mamas to see their boys grow up and join the Marine Corps."

Another little grin. "Yeah. But I hated college. I was bored to death. It's not for me."

"I'm aware." He'd heard Finn complain about it enough over the year he'd taken classes. "You told your buddies yet?"

"Yeah."

"What about Shae?"

Finn's smile fell, and guilt crept into his expression. "No, not yet. But I will. Don't say anything to Walker yet, okay? I wanna tell her myself in person."

"Good call." Ryder didn't envy the kid the task of telling her. To his knowledge they weren't dating per se, but all indications were that they'd been moving in that direction, and Ryder had a feeling they would already be dating if Finn had decided not to enlist.

At any rate, Shae was going to be as thrilled as Danae about this. "Your mom says dinner's in twenty. Don't keep her waiting with your gaming, okay? Not tonight."

Finn nodded, expression still serious. "I won't."

Ryder shut the door behind him and returned to the kitchen.

Danae looked over her shoulder at him, concern shadowing her eyes. "How is he?"

"Good. Gaming with his buddies."

She grunted and bent to slide something into the oven, giving him a perfect view of her rounded ass. Not that he wasn't sensitive to his wife's distress, but one obvious benefit of Finn heading off to boot camp was all the privacy they were going to have around here. He planned to make the most of it.

"He's a good kid," he said. "This'll be the making of him. Wait and see. Hell, one day maybe he'll even take over my company."

She snorted and handed him some glasses to put on the table. "Please, like you'd ever give up the reins to anyone. Control freak."

He smacked her playfully on the butt, earning a squeak and narrowed eyes. "Takes one to know one, sweetheart. And you love that part of me…especially in bed."

She shot him a sharp look, but her lips twitched, and he could tell she was fighting a smile. That was better. He hated seeing her upset, and having Finn go off to serve his country was going to test her. "*Only* in bed," she warned.

Oh, he was well aware of that.

FIVE

Being dead might be the best thing that had ever happened to him.

Seated at a table on the patio beside the pool of his private Bahamas estate, the man who had been Max de Vries added more names to the list he was writing on a piece of paper. Writing it out by hand was cathartic in a way and helped him focus.

"Your breakfast, sir," the maid said in a timid voice, placing a plate of tropical fruit in front of him. "I hope you enjoy it."

"Thank you," he said without looking up from the list. It wasn't complete by any means, but it contained the most important names. All he had to do now was rearrange them in order of priority that he wanted to see each one eliminated, then determine the means.

And the one at the top remained unchanged.

There had been no sign of his errant daughter since a well-paid hacker he used to keep tabs on his enemies got a hit on a security camera in downtown St. Paul last week. The facial recognition software said it was an eighty-six percent match with Lara. The image had been grainy, and she looked so different now that Max couldn't be sure it was her, but at least it was a starting point.

Their long-overdue reunion was his top priority, and he intended to bring her to heel as soon as possible.

He added one last name to the list, a prison guard who had been rude to him, then set it aside and cut a bite of fresh mango and savored the complex, juicy-sweet tang. It had been grown here on the property and tasted better than any mango he'd had before.

This was the first time he'd been here. He'd purchased this former sugar plantation months ago, having one of his people buy it under a complex series of shell corporations his well-paid accountants had set up for him while he'd still been in prison.

As was his custom, he ate alone. The birds sang in the trees, and the sea breeze rustled the palm fronds overhead, carrying the perfume of the lush jasmine vines that scrambled along the brick privacy wall enclosing the patio area. The staff all remained out of sight as expected, except for his bodyguard/assistant, who hovered behind him in the shadows of the veranda that wrapped around the back of the updated nineteenth-century mansion.

Freedom made every moment of it all the sweeter.

He finished his breakfast, folded the list in his hand, and then paused, closing his eyes to drink in the hard-won peace surrounding him. Being locked up in prison for so many years had taken a toll on him. It had taken far too long to come up with a plausible plan to get him out, and then longer still to execute it.

The final cost was worth every penny. The air here even smelled like freedom, and exacting revenge on the people who had locked him away like an animal was his fuel.

He'd gone to a lot of trouble and expense to ensure the world thought he was dead. But he was very much alive, with many personal scores to settle. Beginning with getting his daughter back.

A throat cleared behind him. He opened his eyes and waved Stanton forward. "Yes?"

His bodyguard/right-hand man bent and murmured quietly to ensure that his voice wouldn't carry to any curious ears that might be nearby. Max trusted Stanton as much as he was capable of trusting anyone. And Stanton was well paid for his loyalty and discretion. "I just heard back from Dave."

He stiffened. "And?" He had sent the man to retrieve Lara for him.

"There was another possible sighting of her in Portland two days ago. This time the software said it's more than a ninety-percent match."

His hand clenched around the list. He'd been trying to find her for years without any success. Hadn't been able to find out anything about her or the new identity she'd taken. No amount of money or threats had gotten him what he wanted. Then, right after his *death*, he'd finally found the first plausible lead in St. Paul.

"Let me see." He snatched Stanton's phone. The picture was taken from an angle and at night. Only three quarters of the woman's face was visible, her chin tipped downward.

He studied the image carefully, analyzing every minute detail. Her hair was the right color, the face shape right. It could be Lara, and the software was cutting-edge tech. If so, she'd changed more than he'd imagined. The woman on screen was thin, looked pale and drawn.

She barely resembled the robust, defiant girl who'd turned on him in the most unforgiveable and heinous act a father could experience. "It could be her. Was she followed?"

"Of course. Dave followed her until she stopped at a diner outside of town. He was unable to take her there, as there were too many people around. But he got a tracker on her, so he has her location. Currently she's in Crimson Point, a little town on the central coast of Oregon."

Max thrust the phone back at him, his breakfast suddenly churning hot and acidic in his stomach. "Tell him to bring her to me." Why the Oregon Coast? Had she relocated there? Visiting someone? "And I want to know every fucking last thing about her and her life. Where she's living. Where she works. Who she's fucking."

"Of course." Stanton hurried away into the house.

Max expelled a deep breath and fished in his pocket for the damn blood pressure meds he had to take. He wanted her back. It was high time Lara paid the price for her betrayal. That she finally learned her place and fulfilled her obligations to him.

He would bring her to heel if it was the last thing he did.

∽

DECKER WAS WAITING for him when Creed pulled up in front of the condo building the next morning. He climbed into the SUV wearing dress pants and a dress shirt.

"Look at you, being all fancy," Creed said.

Decker grunted, shut his door, and put his seatbelt on, sipping a cup of coffee he'd brought.

"Good call on the seatbelt. Safety first. Especially since I still owe you for that little stunt you pulled on me at the training in Montana." Creed had been covered with bruises after thumping around on the floor between the front and back seats while Decker evaded an armed pursuer during a close-protection exercise in a course at Rifle Creek Tactical.

At that, Decker grinned fondly. "Ah, yeah, I'd forgotten about that," he said in his slight Kentucky accent.

"Sure you did." He navigated his way onto the main street

that would take them up toward the highway. "You want to go over anything about the conference?" They'd been briefed on everything several days ago, each team given a different assignment, and worked out a plan amongst themselves for coverage and specific duties.

"Not really. You?"

"Nah, I'm good." They were leaving early enough that traffic was still light. A fine mist made everything look gray, the wipers swishing sullenly to remove the water droplets gathering on the windshield as he drove. Several minutes of silence passed before he reached the on-ramp to the highway and took it, heading north.

"All right, what's up with you?" Decker asked.

"Nothing. Why?"

"Something's up. You never pass up a chance to keep the banter going. You had the perfect opening to draw it out with the Montana thing, and you just let it go. So, what's up?"

When he'd woken up this morning, he'd decided not to bring up the situation with Bella today. But gruff as Decker was on the surface, they'd bonded over the past few weeks. They trusted each other and had been through a lot together during Teagan's rescue. And Decker *had* offered to listen if he ever wanted to talk.

So he just came out and said it. "Bella showed up unannounced at my place the other night."

Decker's head snapped around. Creed could feel his stare drilling into him. "Bella, as in your ex-fiancée?"

That description made him flinch inside. "Yep. Was there waiting for me when I got home. I was on the phone with you when I saw her on my front porch. That's why I ended the call so fast."

"Holy shit. What did she say?"

"A lot."

Decker was silent a moment, and when Creed didn't volunteer anything else, he made an irritated sound. "Whatever. You can't just drop a fucking bomb like that on me and then not explain."

He changed lanes, weaving around a couple of semis. "It's bad. Every bit as bad as I was afraid it was."

"You gonna make me drag it out of you bit by bit, or what?"

He sighed, feeling emotionally drained. "She was in WITSEC for putting her dad away. Guy by the name of Max de Vries."

"You're *shittin'* me."

"Wish I was." Now that he'd broken the dam the rest of it just tumbled out. He kept going, hitting all the pertinent details before he stopped.

The sound of the wipers filled the vehicle for several seconds. "And she came to see you because…she wanted to explain?" Decker asked.

"Partly. But I don't know, she hasn't said if there's more. It's…shit, I dunno *what* to think at this point."

"And she's staying at your place until you get back?"

"Well, I wasn't gonna just throw her out on the street, was I?"

More silence. A heavy, grating silence while the pressure in Creed's chest built higher and higher.

"Do you believe her?" Decker asked.

"Yes," he answered without hesitation. He one-hundred percent believed what she'd told him. He just didn't know how to handle it or where to go from here.

Decker nodded slowly. Took a sip of his coffee. "And do you… Never mind."

"No, what?"

"Nah, it's none of my business."

"Just say it." They respected and trusted each other enough to be straight with one another.

"Do you still… You know."

"No, I don't know. What?"

Decker grimaced slightly, looking uncomfortable. "Love her."

Creed swallowed, his hands tightening on the wheel. "Yeah." Fuck him, but yeah.

Surprise showed on Decker's face. "So what are you gonna do?"

"I don't know." That was the hell of it. "Even though I believe her and I hate what she went through, I can't just jump right back in and pick up where we left off." Even though he wanted to. "I'm not ready yet."

He wasn't sure if he just needed more time or what. Part of him sure as hell wanted to jump right back in, though. The part that kept reminding him that they'd lost so much time together already.

Decker expelled a breath and shifted in his seat. "I'm sorry, man. That's rough."

"Yeah, I didn't see this coming."

"No shit. You sure you're up to working this weekend? If you need time off to sort everything out with her, you could talk to Ryder and explain—"

"I already did. I'm not sitting this one out." He sped up slightly, his subconscious telling him that the sooner they got to their destination and finished this job, the sooner he could get back to Bella. "But I'm worried about Bella."

"You think she's still under threat?"

"No. I hope not. But it's not that. I've never seen her like this. So…fragile. And I feel guilty as hell for leaving her."

"Why? You didn't cause any of this."

"No, but she's stretched too thin right now. I'd be lying if I said I didn't feel like I should still be there with her. She came to me specifically, and now she's alone again." Every mile he drove farther away from her, the more torn he felt. "She's got no one now. No family, no friends, no one to help her. I hate knowing she's lonely." She'd always been friendly and social, liked having a small but close circle of people around her. "Hell, even the Marshals Service have gone radio silent on her, even after she informed them of what happened at the diner."

"I'm sure they'll still be monitoring anyone significant in de Vries's orbit. Anyone who might want to target her."

"You'd think." He stared at the traffic ahead, his mind in turmoil. "I need to figure out some things this weekend, then get home as soon as I can. But in the meantime I'd feel better if she had someone there with her in my place, especially at night. Just to make sure she's okay. Someone I trust who I know would be good to her, so she knows she's not alone and doesn't have to worry. Ryder said he'd stop by later, but I think Bella would be more comfortable with a woman."

"Teagan doesn't start work until next week," Decker said, saying what Creed had been thinking.

"I know. You cool if I ask her? Or Marley? Or both? I thought maybe they might go over and meet Bella, hang out with her for a while to start. She could really use a friend right now. Think they'd do that?"

"Yeah, I think they'd both do anything for you," Decker said. "Want me to call 'em?"

"No. I'll do it." This needed to come from him. Bella needed all the support she could get at the moment. At least he could do this for her.

SIX

Bella was on the couch reading one of the paperbacks she'd found in Creed's bookshelf to pass the time when her phone rang. She rushed over to the kitchen table to grab it, a burst of happiness popping inside her when she saw Creed's name on the display. It was a little after twelve. He'd left more than five hours ago, and the house had felt so empty without him since.

She felt empty. "Hi. You in Seattle now?"

"Got here a little while ago. Everything okay there?"

Just hearing his voice set off butterflies in her stomach. "Yeah, it's fine." It was sweet that he'd taken the time to check in with her, and her demons were far easier to shake in the daylight.

"You need anything?"

"No. I was thinking I might even go into town for a bit later. Check out that place you told me about. Whale's Tale?"

"That's the one. Listen…" He paused a moment. "I don't like ditching you and leaving you there alone right now. And I know this is a bit heavy-handed, but I called a couple of friends and asked them to come by and meet you."

A wave of embarrassment washed over her. She didn't want to be a charity or pity case, least of all to him. "No, really, I'm fi—"

"Just meet them. You'll like them, I swear."

She hedged. "Who are they?"

"Decker's girlfriend, Teagan, and his sister, Marley. They live in town too. They're both great, and they've both been through a lot, so they can relate to your story."

Now her curiosity was piqued. "Why? What happened to them?"

"You can ask them yourself after you meet them if you want. They said they'd be over within the next hour. And, by the way, they're both former military. So if you need more sleep, with them there, you can just crash and not worry about anything."

She smiled a little. Between the attempted robbery and her nightmare, he was in protective mode. It was just like him to have someone come stand guard while he was gone, and she would love some company. The chance to make friends and build connections with other people again felt surreal.

She hadn't been up to it in Minnesota. Hadn't felt like interacting with anyone or doing much of anything. Her depression and grief had been way too deep. "They both sound interesting."

"They are. I'll check in with you later tonight to see how it went if it's not too late when I finish up."

"It doesn't matter how late it is, you can call. And hey, Creed?"

"Yeah?"

She opened her mouth. *I still love you. I never stopped.* "Thanks," she said instead. There would be time to tell him the rest when he got back. She wasn't going to blindside him with that over the phone when he was already going through so much.

"Yeah, of course. Talk to you later."

"Bye." She set the phone down with a sigh, then brightened when she saw a little black face and one golden-yellow eye peering at her around the corner of the newel post at the base of the stairs. "Hey, buddy. Look at you being so brave and coming out to explore." She leaned forward and held out a hand, rubbing her fingers together in a coaxing motion. "Come on. Come over and hang out with me."

Nick snuck around the edge of the wall and paused to scan the kitchen and living room, his body coiled and his tail twitching, ready to flee at the merest hint of anything scary.

"It's just us. Nobody else here."

He started toward her one cautious step at a time, pausing twice, the tip of his tail flicking in agitation. He'd broken the end of it at some point, leaving the last three inches sticking out at an angle from the rest.

He made it to the couch, paused again with his ears back as he listened intently, then hopped up beside her and curled against her hip. Smiling in satisfaction, she scratched his head gently and stroked a hand down his spine, his rumbling purr and half-closed eyes the best compliments she'd ever received. Earning a frightened animal's trust and loyalty was the best feeling ever.

She picked the book back up and resumed reading. Halfway through the next chapter, the doorbell pealed. Nick leapt up like he'd been stuck with a pin, eyes wide and ears flat as he took off with a hiss out of the room and disappeared up the staircase.

Bella hurried to the door and checked through the peephole. Two women stood on the doorstep holding shopping bags. A pretty, tall redhead and a stunning Asian woman.

She opened it with a welcoming smile. "Hi, you must be—"

"I'm Marley," the redhead said with a southern sort of accent, holding out a hand.

"And I'm Teagan," the other one said with a smile, shaking hands with her next. "Nice to meet you, Bella."

"You too. Ah, come in." She stepped back, noting that in addition to bearing bags, both women wore holsters on their hips. Creed hadn't been joking about her not having to worry about letting her guard down while they were here.

"So, Creed sprung us on you, huh?" Teagan asked as she walked past her and into the kitchen. Bella's first impression was that she was incredibly confident, a take-charge kind of woman.

She followed her. "He did, just a little while ago."

"Well, we're not so bad. Are we, Mar?"

"Not bad at all." Marley set a bag on the island and pulled out two bottles of wine. "I didn't know whether you prefer red or white, so I brought both."

"That was nice of you, thanks," Bella said, already charmed. "Creed said you're both former military?"

"Yep. I was in the Navy," Teagan said. "Marley was a Marine."

"Was?" Marley said with a lift of an auburn eyebrow. "Once a Marine, always a Marine, thanks very much." She shot a smile and a wink at Bella, then swept her gaze over her. "Well, you don't look nervous or like you're about to run for the hills. You good with us staying a while?"

Had Creed made her out to be shy or skittish or something? "Yes, absolutely. Want to sit in the living room and talk a bit?"

"Love to." Marley carried in a fruit and cheese tray and set it on the coffee table, then sat on the couch with Teagan while Bella took the armchair to the side. "So, how did you meet Creed?"

The slight tension in Bella's middle eased immediately.

She'd been bracing for them to dive into her situation and WITSEC and pepper her with questions she wasn't ready to talk about with people she'd just met, no matter how nice they seemed. This was a welcome relief. "At an animal shelter I was volunteering at in Tucson, actually."

"Aww. Is Creed an animal lover?" Marley asked. "I didn't know that."

"I wouldn't say an animal *lover*. He likes them, but not as much as me. We were actually about to adopt a cat together when…" She cleared her throat and dropped her gaze.

"When you had to leave suddenly," Marley finished. "It's okay. You don't have to talk about any of that if you don't want to."

"Nope," Teagan agreed. "You just met us. We're here for moral support and company, not to interrogate you or make you uncomfortable."

Bella looked up at them, grateful. Both these women had taken the time out of their day to drop everything and come over here to meet her and keep her company. She was good at reading people—she'd had to hone that skill early on in life—and instinctively knew they were good. "Maybe you could tell me about yourselves first."

"I manage a seniors care home in town," Marley said, "and I'm engaged to a guy named Warwick. He's from Newcastle, in northern England."

"And I'm about to start with Crimson Point Security, helping them with investigations," Teagan said. "My better half is Decker. Well, not better. My *other* half. He comes off as grumpy and aloof when you first meet him, but that's just until you get to know him. He's actually quite squishy inside."

Marley shook her head at her. "He'd hate you describing him like that."

Teagan chuckled. "It's the truth, and he knows it."

"And you're both new to town?" Bella asked.

"Fairly. Marley's been here longer than me. I got here in late October," Teagan said.

"And right after that, everything went to hell around here," Marley added with a wry smile.

Teagan snorted. "I guess I do have a tendency for trouble."

"You guess?"

The easy camaraderie between the two women was obvious and put Bella even more at ease. "Creed mentioned that you'd both been through a lot," she said, looking back and forth between them.

They nodded.

"We have," Teagan answered. "Creed helped save my life, you know."

Bella blinked, not expecting that. "He did?"

"Yes. Without him and Decker, I wouldn't be here." She reached out, plucked a handful of different cheese cubes, and sat back against the sofa cushion. "You want the short version or the long version?"

"Long." Bella curled her feet up under her and gave Teagan her full attention. She wanted to know everything possible about Creed's life here.

"It all started with my cousin's murder," Teagan said.

Bella's eyes widened, and Teagan went on from there. She told Bella about the drug smuggling operation that had targeted her cousin and almost wound up killing her as well when she'd stolen onboard a boat one night. Then an incredible recounting of how she and Decker had survived an assassination attempt at a marina, followed by Teagan barely surviving a kidnapping that had resulted in a desperate rescue at sea.

When she fell silent, Bella was gaping at her. "The guy took you from the *sheriff's* office?" Holy shit. She and Creed had just been there last night, and it had seemed completely secure.

The kidnapper must have been either out of his damn mind or desperate or both to target Teagan there.

"Yep, he was strung out and high as fuck when he did it. Anyway, he's dead, the other guy is rotting in jail, and I'm not only alive, I got Decker out of the deal. I'm calling that a triple win."

"And you also got me out of the deal," Marley added, poking her shoulder.

"Yes, a quadruple win," Teagan agreed with a smile. "Marley's pretty rad, not gonna lie."

Bella smiled at them, but Teagan's story left a hollow feeling in the pit of her stomach. Because the drug smuggling operation she'd just described had infiltrated the Coast Guard and could definitely be connected to the organization Max had helped run before his death.

"Anyway, that's me. Now you go," Teagan said to Marley, helping herself to more nibbles.

"You ready for more?" Marley asked Bella.

This was really helping her feel comfortable and less like a freak because of her crazy backstory. "If you're ready to tell me, yes."

Marley's tale was just as incredible. Warwick had disappeared and let her believe he was dead in order to protect her. And when he couldn't stay away any longer, he'd tracked her down, and everything had gone to hell. Enemies from his past had wanted to silence him forever, and Marley had been caught up in the net.

That hit home too. Enough that Bella curled up tighter to ward off a shiver. The only reason she'd remained in WITSEC and gone with the Marshals that day when they'd come to get her in Tucson was because she'd been afraid of exactly what Marley had just described. She'd wanted to protect Creed. Enough that she was willing to give him up to ensure his safety.

"So you shot the guy?" Bella said to Marley, impressed. These two ladies were incredible, and she was honored that they both felt comfortable telling her all of this.

"I did. Thank God I didn't miss."

Bella shook her head. "You two are so badass compared to me." When danger had come to her door, she'd run. Mostly to protect Creed by keeping him out of her nightmare, but still.

"Are you *kidding*?" Teagan asked in astonishment. "Do you know how much guts it took to do what you did? To break free of your past and do the right thing, even when you knew it would cost you everything you'd ever known?"

She didn't consider that brave. It had been about survival. "I didn't really see any other choice at the time." It had been the hardest thing she'd ever done—up to that point. "And I didn't know it would eventually cost me the new life I'd built after that."

Including Creed. That loss was by far the hardest she'd ever gone through.

An immediate silence fell. Marley opened her mouth to say something, then the doorbell rang.

Bella frowned, but Teagan shot Marley a look. "That's not… You didn't," Teagan said.

"Well, what was I supposed to say when she found out why we were coming over here. *No*?" Marley snorted as she rose. "You know how she is."

"How *who* is?" Bella asked as Marley strode for the door. Whom had she invited here?

"You think *we're* badass, wait until you get a load of this one," Teagan said with a snicker. "We've been trying to get the goods out of her for weeks now. Maybe you can get her to tell us."

What? How? They'd never even met before. But Bella

didn't have time to ask anything because Marley was already admitting the stranger inside.

A thirty-something, striking brunette strode in like she owned the place. She looked around as she took off her shoes, almost like she was scanning the house, then her gaze settled on Bella. "Hey. I'm Ivy."

Um, welcome? "Hi."

"We were just telling her about you," Teagan said with a smirk.

Bella was already intrigued. These women were all *fascinating*.

"What were you saying? All lies probably," Ivy told Bella as she walked toward them.

"Nuh-uh, all *legends*," Marley said, coming back to pass the fruit and cheese tray to Bella.

"So, what'd I miss?" Ivy asked, sitting down in a chair on the other side of the sofa. Her eyes were green, and Bella could already tell they didn't miss anything. "Bring me up to speed."

"We were just giving Bella a little background on us," Teagan answered, popping a grape into her mouth. "You wanna go next?"

"Not really." Ivy turned her gaze on Bella with undisguised interest. "I'd rather hear all about you. I know Creed through CPS, by the way. My guy Walker works with him."

"Your *guy*?" Marley rolled her eyes. "They're engaged," she said to Bella. "Ivy's still struggling saying that part out loud, apparently."

"I'm warming up to it. Don't rush me," Ivy said, still looking at Bella. And there was indeed a sparkly diamond ring on her left hand. "So, tell us about you."

The force of all three women's stares on her at once was a little daunting. "Well, I—" She broke off, blinking in shock when a streak of black flew across the living room and disappeared under Ivy's chair. A second later, Nick poked his head out from beneath the bottom of it, peering at them with his single wary eye.

"Oh, who's that?" Marley asked.

"This is Nick Furry."

"Nick Furry, haaaa," Teagan said with a laugh. "Good one."

Ivy grinned and bent forward to look down at him sticking out between her feet. "Hi, Nick. How are ya?"

To Bella's absolute shock, her cat crawled out from beneath the chair, stared at Ivy for a few moments, and then jumped right into her lap. Ivy smiled and scritched his head and back, not realizing how momentous the occurrence was. "What?" she asked when she noticed Bella staring at her.

"He doesn't like strangers." Like, at all. Anyone else would be covered in bloody gouges right now for daring to touch him. "Actually, he doesn't like people in general. He's an old stray, at least part feral and really shy, but… Okay, wow, he really likes you." To the point where it was starting to hurt Bella's feelings a little at how fast he'd warmed up to Ivy. Traitor. It had taken her weeks to win him over, and Ivy only thirty seconds without even doing anything.

Ivy shrugged. "He probably senses I'm a cat person. Don't you?" she cooed at Nick, her whole demeanor transforming. Softening. "You're such a handsome fella. I've got a cat at home too, and he was a stray. Someone literally threw him in the garbage in the alley behind my building before I found him in there."

Bella gasped in outrage. "Seriously? Assholes," she hissed.

Ivy aimed a grin at her. "Let's just say that whoever it was is lucky there was no CCTV camera nearby to catch them doing it. But Mr. Whiskers lives like a king now, so it's all good. He's extremely spoiled. I flew him over from the UK when I moved here." She shot a pointed look at Marley. "After Walker and I got *engaged*."

"That's very good." Marley raised her wineglass in salute. "I'm proud of you."

So, Ivy was a badass who had rescued a stray from the trash. That made her Bella's new favorite person.

Nick opened his eye and turned his head to look right at Bella, totally content to stay where he was. More than her gut instinct, Nick's reaction to Ivy confirmed Bella's feeling about her—she was one of the good guys. Or gals, as it were. "I'd say you've made a new friend," she said to Ivy.

"That's nice to hear, because my circle's pretty exclusive."

Nick curled up in a ball on Ivy's lap and proceeded to go to sleep. Bella grinned. "Oh, my God, I can hear him purring from all the way over here. You're a cat whisperer."

Ivy gave a pleased smile. "Animals always know who they're safe with."

Yes. This woman got it. "They totally do."

"Hey, the sun's finally coming out," Marley looked out the windows behind her into the backyard before facing Bella again. "Creed mentioned you haven't seen the town yet and were thinking about going to Whale's Tale. You wanna go now? We can grab something and walk along the beach after."

Bella exhaled, a smile spreading across her face. She was so glad they had come over to meet her. It had been way too long since she'd had any friends. In St. Paul, she'd been so shut down, preferred to be on her own and not let anyone else in. Just the animals at the shelter. "I'd love that." She would feel safer in general having people with her when she walked around in the open. That was going to take some getting used to again.

Marley's answering smile was bright and genuine. "Great, let's go."

"Sorry, Nick, gotta go get my sugar fix on. Later, furry dude." Ivy gently deposited him on the ground. He stared up at her reproachfully, incredibly offended that his nap had been interrupted after he'd so graciously bestowed her with his presence, then darted out of the room and back up the stairs.

"Shotgun," Ivy said on the way to the door.

"Why do you always get shotgun?" Teagan complained behind her.

"Because I'm the best shot."

"Yeah, okay, you are," Teagan muttered, shrugging at Bella. "It's true. You should see her with a weapon, and I'm just talking firearms. God knows what else she's an expert with, but…a *lot*. If I wasn't her friend, I'd be terrified of her."

"Yep, we're all pea green with envy of Ivy's prowess with a weapon," Marley agreed, tugging on her coat at the door.

"Stop flattering me," Ivy said good-naturedly. "I'm not spilling any more of my secrets. Yet."

"Aww," Teagan said with a disappointed frown. "Just one teensy one to tide us over."

"Nope." Ivy sailed out the front door.

The ride down the hill into town was just as entertaining. Bella laughed at their banter, the good company and the sunlight bursting through the clouds over the ocean lifting her spirits and helping take her mind off her troubles.

For more than a year, she'd felt like she was trapped in a deep, dark pit. Now she was starting to believe she might be able to get her life back. Hopefully with Creed.

There was a lineup at Whale's Tale, an everyday occurrence according to her new posse. They ordered freshly baked pastries and gourmet coffees made by Creed's boss's stepson, Finn, and took them to go for a beach walk. All three women put her at ease and she appreciated their willingness to make an effort to bring a lonely stranger into the fold.

They walked for half an hour before turning back. "For what it's worth," Ivy said to her as they approached the edge of the downtown waterfront, her voice pitched to be heard over the wind but not loud enough that the other two ahead of them could overhear, "I know what it's like to have to leave everything and everyone and start over."

Bella looked at her in surprise. "You do?"

Ivy nodded, her gaze fixed straight ahead. "Done it a few times. All of them necessary, and none of them enjoyable."

"What happened?" Bella asked, unable to stop herself, then immediately winced. They'd literally just met. "Forget I said that, it's—"

"No, it's fine. Let's just say some of it was by choice, and some of it wasn't." There was something in her tone, in her face that told Bella she'd suffered horribly. Then Ivy looked right at her. "But I'm still here, and so are you. And I just want you to know, you *can* find happiness again. I promise."

Bella swallowed, looked away before Ivy could see the sheen of tears that were pricking the backs of her eyes, and hoped the other woman would think it was just from the wind. Yeah, Ivy really did get it. "I want to believe that."

"Good. That's a start."

It *was* a good start.

By the time they walked back to Teagan's vehicle, the sun had been swallowed up by the clouds again and the heavy cast of them promised more rain. They'd only been on the road for a minute when the first drops hit the windshield. The sound of it was soothing, and she was starting to feel drowsy.

"You guys, I really want to thank you for dropping everything and coming to spend time with me today," she said, still overwhelmed by their generosity. "It's been a rough year-plus, and you don't know what today means to me."

"I do," Ivy said, making Bella smile.

"We've got your back, girl," Marley said.

"Yep. We all like you," Teagan added. "So now you're one of us."

"Y'all better not make her cry," Marley warned, and Bella laughed softly. But yeah, she was feeling a little choked up at the moment.

The porch light was on when they arrived at Creed's, the glow cutting through the gathering gloom. "Well, thanks again for everything." Bella unstrapped and opened her door. "I'll think about coming to the book club meeting."

"Please do," Marley said. "Teagan keeps making lame excuses, but if you come, she might."

Ivy got out with her. "I'll stay for a bit. If that's cool with you," she added to Bella as Teagan drove away with Marley and a friendly wave.

Bella cut a sideways glance at her. Was she offering because she thought Bella was too scared to be alone? Bella didn't want that, but also didn't really want to be by herself yet. "You don't have to. I'll be okay."

Ivy met her gaze. "I know you will. But I want to."

"Okay, then." In truth, she'd feel better knowing Ivy was in the house. "Popcorn and a movie?"

Ivy smiled at her. "That sounds awesome." She followed her to the door. "I needed to get out of the house for a while tonight anyhow. My stepdaughter wanted some privacy."

"Shae?"

She nodded. "I think big changes are on the wind in her life, and maybe not the happy kind. So a movie and popcorn would be great right now."

Bella stopped on the entry mat and hugged her impulsively. "Thank you," she said softly. The story about Shae might be true, but Bella knew for a fact that Ivy's reasons for staying went beyond giving her stepdaughter privacy. That Ivy instinctively understood how raw and uneasy she felt right now and was staying to help her feel more secure.

Ivy returned the embrace, and it felt both protective and sisterly. "You're more than welcome. And remember what I said, yeah? About being happy. Just take me for an example. I shouldn't still be alive. Who'd have ever thought I would end up here, let alone with a ring on my finger because I'm engaged to an incredible man? If you knew me better, you'd understand just how unlikely that all is. And next time you talk to Marley, you can tell her I said the word again without flinching."

"I definitely will." Bella released her, then went straight to the living room.

She wasn't giving up hope. But her future happiness hinged entirely on whether Creed was willing to give them a second chance.

SEVEN

Shae went around the living room one last time, straightening the throw pillows on the couch and adjusting things on the shelves that framed the built-in TV. Partly to make everything look tidy and perfect, and partly because she needed to burn off the nervous, excited energy rolling through her.

Both of which were ridiculous, because Finn had been over dozens of times. There was no reason for her to feel nervous.

Except he'd texted to ask if he could come over tonight to talk to her, and he'd specifically requested that they be alone.

He'd never done that before. Never given any solid indication that he wanted to be more than friends, either, and she was too proud and too scared of rejection to make a move. If he wanted her, he was going to have to be the one to say so.

Something was different tonight, she could feel it. And everything in her was hoping that things were finally going to shift for them. Because being just his friend was starting to hurt worse than the constant ache in her chest from the crush she'd been carrying around since she'd met him.

They had the house to themselves, as requested. Her dad was still at work figuring out last-minute logistics for a big conference up in Seattle his company had sent three teams to, and Ivy was out somewhere with Marley and Teagan. So she and Finn would be alone.

Headlights turned into the driveway and swung across the wall. She went to the door, her pulse tripping. When she opened it and saw Finn striding toward her, a warm glow suffused her entire body. "Hi."

He was tall and lanky, but all his recent working out was already showing in the increased muscle along his arms and shoulders. She was a sucker for arm muscles, and Finn's were delicious.

His smile was tight. Uncomfortable. "Hi."

She stepped back, suddenly uncertain. "Come on in." Dammit, she'd set the mood for a possible romantic interlude, dimming the lights and lighting a candle, but the vibe he was giving off was all wrong.

Finn looked around. "Smells good in here."

"Oh, it's just a candle I bought the other day." His stiffness was putting her on edge. "You okay?"

He met her gaze. "Yeah, why?"

He had the most gorgeous eyes. "You just seem…tense."

"No, it's just…" He sighed and gestured to the couch. "Can we sit down?"

Dread twisted in the pit of her stomach. "Sure." She went over and sat on the smaller couch, curling up into the corner as trepidation spread inside her. "Is something wrong?"

He sat across from her on the larger couch and leaned forward with his elbows resting on his knees, watching her with those incredible, piercing blue eyes. "I came to tell you something."

"Okay," she said, concerned about what was going to come out of his mouth next.

"I've thought long and hard about it, talked it over with my mom and Ryder, and made an important decision about my future."

Her stomach contracted into a tight ball. Because suddenly she knew what he was going to say. She'd known it was a possibility, but she hadn't realized how serious he'd been and wasn't ready for it to happen.

He sat up taller and rubbed his hands on his thighs, his hesitation to tell her confirming her fears. "You know I hated college—or at least the courses I was taking. But I don't see a future for me at the end of that path right now. I need something else. Something more."

Shae didn't move, even as grief speared her, sharp as a blade. *He's leaving.*

"I'm enlisting tomorrow."

Shit. Oh, shit, shit, shit...

She pressed her lips together a moment to keep them from trembling. Had to swallow before she could get her voice to work. "Oh, that's... I'm happy for you."

She wasn't. Not at all. She didn't want him to go away, didn't want to lose him, and she was so afraid that's exactly what would happen now.

He would go to California, become a different person over the course of his training, and then serve his country for years afterward. The possibility that he would be sent overseas or deployed to a combat zone was pretty much guaranteed.

Oh, he might come back to Crimson Point on leave or to visit from time to time, but she knew his enlistment was the end of any chance she had with him. The distance between them meant he would outgrow her. Over time, she would become nothing more than a memory of an old friend he used to hang out with back home.

Finn flashed her a relieved smile that made her want to cry. "Thanks."

She cleared her throat, fidgeted with the edge of a throw blanket as she struggled to hold back the waves of emotion threatening to swamp her. The last thing she wanted was to break down in front of him and make this worse. And thank God she hadn't told him her true feelings for him. "When would you leave for boot camp?"

He held her gaze. "Next week, my recruiter said."

"Next *week*?" she blurted before she could hold it back.

Finn nodded, guilt and something else moving in his eyes. "I know, it's a quick turnaround."

Her heart plummeted but somehow, thankfully, she didn't cry. Shock, maybe. Whatever it was, she was grateful. "And how long will you be gone?" she managed to ask.

"Boot camp is thirteen weeks total, so I'll be gone at least a few months. Maybe longer, depending on what happens. But I'll probably come back to visit after I graduate." He reached across the table to nudge her knee with his hand. "Hey, maybe you could come down for my grad ceremony with my mom and Ryder."

She forced a weak smile. "Yeah, I'd like that."

He sat back, watching her. "Anyway, that's what I came over to tell you. I wanted to make sure I told you in person."

Why? she wanted to ask, that heartbroken part of her stubbornly wanting to know if she meant more to him than just his friend. But what was the point? Even if she confessed her feelings, he was still leaving. "I appreciate that."

"Have you eaten yet? I thought we could order something and watch a movie, or we could go out—"

"I can't," she said quickly. "I promised my dad I'd have dinner with him and Ivy." Lie. But there was no way she could sit here tonight and pretend everything was fine when her world and hopes for the future had just been upended.

"Oh. Sure. Maybe another night then, before I leave?"

"Yes, for sure," she said with another smile that made every muscle in her face hurt.

"Well, I'd better head out then," he said, pushing to his feet.

She followed him to the door, invisible cables tightening around her ribs.

Finn stopped on the mat to look at her, his expression uncertain. "I'll talk to you tomorrow?"

She nodded. "I'm in class until five."

"Okay, I'll text you." He opened the door. Stopped. Seemed to hesitate before turning back toward her. "Can I get a hug?"

She tensed and almost retreated a step. She was barely hanging on now, and the thought of hugging him, really hugging him the way she'd wanted to do for so long, was way too painful.

But the thought of not hugging him was way worse.

"Yeah, of course, you can get a hug," she forced out, and reached her arms up to encircle his neck.

Finn wrapped his around her back and pulled her to his chest, his chin resting on the top of her head as he hugged her. But he didn't give her a quick squeeze and release her. He held on. As if he, too, understood that him leaving meant things would never be the same for them.

Shae squeezed her eyes shut against the burn of tears, and the hard truth she'd been trying to bury came flooding in full force.

She loved him. Had for a while. And now she was about to lose him.

Finn gave her one final squeeze and stepped back, flashing her a smile tinged with something that looked a lot like regret. "G'night."

She could only nod and force a horribly brittle smile before letting him out. As the sound of his car faded away into the night, she stumbled back to the couch and collapsed on it, grabbing a pillow and cradling it to her chest as the dam broke. Heartbroken sobs tore from her, wrenching her chest and throat.

She cried so much her eyes felt swollen and her throat raw. Cried the way she'd cried after her mother's funeral. Her mom had been her best friend. She'd lost her too soon. Now it felt like she was about to lose Finn.

"Mmmreow."

She sniffed, wiped her face with her hands as Ivy's cat, Mr. Whiskers, jumped up onto the arm of the couch she was wedged against and butted his head into her chin. Shae scooped him up, kissed the top of his soft, furry head and was rewarded with a long, rhythmic purr.

She was still sitting like that when her dad walked in twenty minutes later. He set his keys down, looked over at her and went dead still. "What's the matter?" he asked sharply, seeming to become even bigger as he stood there. He was protective of her.

"Finn's enlisting tomorrow. He's leaving for boot camp next week." She pressed her lips together again to stem another rush of tears.

Her dad didn't say anything. Just gave her a look full of sympathy and understanding and crossed over to her.

Without a word, he sat down beside her and pulled her into a hug infused with love. But just like after her mom died, his love couldn't put the broken pieces of her heart back together.

∼

WELL, that had sucked. Worse than he'd imagined, actually.

And there had been a moment when he'd almost turned the whole situation into a disaster by kissing her.

Thank God he'd spared them both that at least. Saying goodbye was hard enough without giving away his feelings and leaving her to pine for him while he was gone. That would have been beyond cruel when neither of them knew what the future held.

Finn shook his head at himself and drove past the turnoff to his house, heading up into the hills instead of going home. He didn't feel like going back there yet. Not with the leaden weight sitting in the middle of his chest. And he wanted to avoid his mom right now too. Knowing she was upset and had been crying made him feel like shit. She'd been trying to hide it from him, but her puffy eyes and blotchy face told him the truth.

He ran a hand over his face and took the turn toward the lighthouse, needing somewhere to just sit and think by himself for a while.

Going over there and telling Shae in person had been hard. He'd had to do it, but the look on her face when he had…

Grief. Or at least, that's how he'd interpreted it. He'd seen it often enough in his mom's eyes after his dad died to recognize what it was. And again when he'd announced his intention to her to join the Marines.

He pulled into the parking lot on top of the cliff. He'd done the right thing, told Shae straight out, and made the break as quick and clean as he could. But he hated that he'd hurt her. The instant he'd told her he'd felt things shift between them. It was like she'd pulled back from him in a way, putting up an invisible forcefield between them or something.

And that hug. God, he'd been dying for an excuse to hold her like that for weeks. Wanting to do a whole lot more than just hug her, but holding back because of the possibility he was leaving.

The wind whipped over him the moment he opened the car door. There was nobody else up here, and the weather matched his mood perfectly.

He walked over to one of the benches perched near the edge

of the cliff in front of the lighthouse and sat there, staring out at the beam of light it cast over the churning waves while the wind whistled through his hair. Hair that would be buzzed off "high and tight" when he reported to Camp Pendleton.

He didn't know what the future held for him. Didn't expect Shae to wait for him, and it wouldn't have been fair to ask her to. But he'd be lying if he didn't admit that he wanted more than friendship. He was going to miss her like hell. Already did.

Staring out at the light skimming across the turbulent ocean, he felt that same wild energy churning inside him, as if he was a bird perched on the cliff's edge, about to spread its wings as it stared down at the towering drop below.

But even though that first step into nothing was huge and scary and he was feeling sad right now, he'd never been more certain of anything in his life.

Becoming a Marine was something he'd dreamed of since he was a kid. He had to do this. Follow in his father's and Ryder's footsteps and prove that he had what it took to be one of the few and the proud.

He wasn't a kid anymore. It was time to grow up and become the man he was destined to be, no matter how hard it was to leave Crimson Point, his mom, Ryder and Shae behind.

He trusted his gut. Sometimes he thought it might be his dad's spirit guiding him.

Whatever it was, it verified that he was doing the right thing. And it also told him that if he and Shae were meant to be together, they would find their way back to each other eventually.

EIGHT

"So what's this charity you told me about that your sister runs? What kind of work do you do for her?" Bella stroked a hand over Nick's sleek back as he lay stretched out on her thighs. It had been an extremely lazy, relaxing Sunday, and he'd spent the afternoon and evening dividing his time between her and Ivy.

"This and that, whatever she needs help with," Ivy said evasively, reclining full length on the long couch in front of the low fire going in the gas fireplace.

It was so cozy in here with the rain pattering on the roof and windows. Ivy had been here since three in the afternoon, and Bella had decided there was something very catlike about her. She looked completely chill and relaxed right now, but it was deceptive. Bella sensed that Ivy was ready to pounce at any moment without warning.

"A lot of computer work," Ivy added.

She narrowed her eyes at Ivy's vagueness. "Is it all legal?"

Ivy half-grinned. "Well, mostly. But I have zero problem with working in the gray area when necessary. And it's unfortunately necessary a lot more often than people realize."

Yes, Bella imagined it was, and rather liked the thought of justice being done by people like Ivy and her sister. "But what kind of charity is it?"

"Oh. We manage a big fund that helps ensure vulnerable orphans don't wind up being exploited or trafficked. Especially in high-risk environments like combat or natural disaster areas."

Bella's eyes widened. "Well, wow! I wasn't expecting that."

Ivy shrugged. "Just trying to do our part."

"It's an admirable cause. Why did you guys decide to start doing that kind of work?"

Ivy took a sip of her wine, swirled the ruby red liquid in her glass. "Because we were exploited orphans ourselves."

Whoa. "You…both of you?"

Ivy nodded. "All my sisters and me. Nine of us."

"Oh, my God, that's horrible!" Outrage punched through Bella, the same anger she felt when she found out about an animal being mistreated or neglected. "Children and animals are innocent and vulnerable, and they should *never* be abused— they should all be protected by society. It *enrages* me that there are predators and abusers out there hurting innocent victims." Her own past made her extra sensitive to it.

Ivy's smile held a sharp edge. "Exactly. That's why we do what we do."

"Well, I'm glad," Bella said fiercely, scowling as indignant fury bubbled inside her. "It makes me insane, the sort of evil that goes on in today's world." She knew all about how it felt to be exploited. It was a horrific experience she wouldn't wish on anyone.

Except for the people who subjected others to it.

"Is that why you started volunteering at the shelter in Tucson?" Ivy asked. "Because you love animals so much?"

"Yes. It's something I'd felt strongly about for a long time, but I couldn't do it before because the…timing wasn't right."

She felt oddly comfortable with Ivy. Had the strongest urge to just blurt out everything to her. Every dark, sordid detail of her past that even Creed didn't know about. But she held back because Ivy had been through enough of her own trauma, and Bella wasn't about to add to her emotional burden by dumping her past on top of it. "Animals are so much easier than people. They don't judge, and they love unconditionally."

"And you needed that," Ivy said with an understanding nod.

"So badly."

"I hear that, sister."

Her phone buzzed before she could say anything else. She grabbed it from the coffee table and couldn't help the smile when she found a message from Creed.

"That him?" Ivy asked.

"Yep. He says he won't be back for another few hours yet, probably after midnight."

"That's fine with me," she said, stretching her arms over her head. "I can hang out here until he gets home."

"Ivy." Bella gave her a pointed look. While she appreciated the company and the sense of community Creed had surrounded her with to make her feel less alone, she didn't want anyone to think she was weak or scared or needed to be looked after. She wasn't weak, even if she looked it right now. "I don't need a babysitter. For real. I love hanging out with you, and I really appreciate everything you and the others have done for me, but seriously. I'm okay." She was going to be. "And you've barely had any time with your family this weekend. I bet Shae needs you right now."

Things hadn't gone well with Finn last night, apparently.

"I've already talked to her about it. She's upset right now, but she's sensible. She's got her dad's level head. She'll be okay, and Walker and I will be there for her."

Bella thought of how tough it had been when Creed was

overseas on contract jobs. Back before she'd known what it really felt like to miss someone so much she physically ached. "Were they together long?"

"They weren't romantic. Yet. But I think it would have happened pretty soon if he'd stayed, and Shae was certainly hoping for it. She's been into him a long time. I mean, she didn't tell me or anything, but I saw it."

"That's so hard. Crushes suck."

"Yep, they do."

Bella saw her way in and took it. "How long did you crush on Walker before you guys got together?"

"About a year. Felt longer though."

Ivy wasn't exactly forthcoming about her past or details of her personal life, but even from that small description, Bella knew there was a bigger story there. "I want to hear all about that one day." She opened her mouth to say more, only to pause when her phone rang. The caller was unknown, but only one other person aside from Creed had her number.

"Sorry, gotta take this." She snatched it up to answer. "Hello?"

"Bella, it's Nico."

One of the Marshals assigned to her case. He'd been her favorite, the most human of the agents she'd dealt with in the Marshals Service. She felt like he genuinely cared about her as a person. "Hi."

"Listen, sorry I didn't get back to you sooner. I was on another assignment when you reached out. Everything okay there?"

"Yes, except for a few nights ago—"

"Outside the diner. That's why I'm calling. We've looked into it and determined it was a random incident of opportunity for the guy who attacked you. From where we're sitting, there's no ongoing or credible threat to your safety. The people connected to your case who we've been monitoring are all accounted for, and none of them are in Oregon. There's been no chatter about you at all. The only serious threat to you was Max, and he's gone."

She exhaled, a massive invisible weight lifting from her. "That's great news. Thanks for letting me know."

"You're welcome. Anything else I can do? Anything you need?"

"No, that's great."

"Off the record then, did you find him?"

Creed. "Yes, I'm here now."

"And?"

"And we're…working on it."

"That's fantastic. I hope it all works out for you. Really. You deserve it."

She smiled. "I hope so too. Thanks again. Take care."

"You too."

She ended the call and looked over at Ivy with a soft sigh, the residual tension she'd been carrying melting away. *It's over. I'm safe.*

"Good news?" Ivy asked.

"Great news. The official word is, no credible threats against my safety after the incident the other night."

"Glad to hear it." Ivy set her glass down on the table and sat up. "Are you sure you don't want me to stay until Creed gets back?"

"I'm positive. But thanks for offering. You go home and be with Walker and Shae and Mr. Whiskers."

"Okay, but I like you, and we're definitely hanging out again soon." Ivy winked, got up, and carried her glass to the kitchen.

"Just leave it in the sink. I'll wash it in the morning." She walked Ivy to the door, hugged her. Ivy might still be a mystery to her in a lot of ways, but they connected on so many levels. Bella was certain they'd laid the foundation for a strong friendship this weekend. If things worked out between her and Creed and she stayed, she got the feeling that she and Ivy would become close. "Thanks for hanging with me. This is the best weekend I've had in forever."

Ivy patted her back. "Anytime. Get some sleep. And keep me posted about any…developments I should know about." She stepped back, her eyes twinkling in the porch light.

Bella grinned, an excited buzz starting up in her stomach. She was anxious to see Creed when he got home tonight. Had been thinking about him constantly, and knew that if she wanted another chance with him, she was going to have to be the one to put herself out there this time.

She was going to have to take a leap of faith and trust that he would catch her. "I will."

She locked the door, set the alarm, and did a sweep of the house to ensure all the other doors and windows were shut and locked, then scooped Nick up and started for the stairs. "Bedtime for us, big guy." She planned to take a bath, put on her coziest jammies, then read in bed until Creed got back. And take it from there.

She had a lot of things she needed to say to him, and they couldn't wait until morning. She'd waited long enough already.

Upstairs, she had a bath and got ready for bed. Before she slid under the covers, she took her weapon out of the nightstand drawer to check it as she did every night. While rain tapped on the roof, she tucked herself in with a book, Nick a purring puddle in her lap.

Fatigue hit her hard. As she almost nodded off for the second time, she finally set the book aside and groggily reached out to switch off the lamp. Within a minute of curling up on her side, sleep rushed at her.

But instead of the deep rest her body craved, once again her subconscious threw her straight back into the past she couldn't seem to escape.

~

THE FRONT PORCH light was on when Creed arrived, and Bella's car was parked in the driveway. Seeing it there filled him with a deep sense of relief and gratification, easing that part of his subconscious that had been afraid she would up and disappear on him again before he got back. He hadn't actually thought she would, but the past had left a mark.

He quietly unlocked the door, walked in, and reset the alarm to home mode. Bella was in bed, but she'd left a soft light on in the kitchen for him, just like she always had when they'd been together.

Starving, he stopped in the kitchen to wolf down a piece of fruit and some water, then made his way up the stairs, his heart rate increasing. It was after one, and she had to be fast asleep. Still, he had to see her, even if it was only from the doorway. But as he neared her door he saw a band of light appear beneath it, signaling she'd turned on a lamp.

"Bella?" he said softly, and turned the doorknob. He opened it a few inches and stopped dead.

Bella was hunched over on the edge of the bed with her back to him, breathing fast. She looked over her shoulder at him, a sheen of sweat glistening on her face, and the panic-stricken look in her eyes tore through him like a gunshot.

He rushed forward, but she threw out a hand to ward him off. So he stopped, even though it was the last thing he wanted to do.

"I'm okay. Just…gimme a second," she gasped out.

His muscles knotted with the need to go to her, hold her, but he stayed where he was, feeling helpless. How often did she have these nightmares?

After a minute, her breathing steadied, and she pushed to her feet, running a shaky hand over her face. "God. Sorry about that."

"Nothing to be sorry for. You okay now?"

"I'm good." She headed for the bathroom and shut the door behind her.

He went and sat on the foot of the bed, wondering if she'd been wrestling with the same demons as last time.

Water splashed in the sink for a few minutes, then stopped. Bella reemerged and came back to slide under the covers, smelling like soap and toothpaste. "How was Seattle? Everything go okay?" she asked as if nothing had happened.

He didn't want to talk about Seattle. "Yeah, it was fine. Bella—"

"It's nothing," she said quickly. "Just my subconscious working through some things, I guess. I'm fine."

So much for putting herself out there this time. She wasn't fine. He'd never seen her less fine. He'd come home burning with the need to talk about them, their future, but now the timing felt all wrong. "What was it about?"

"The usual," she said evasively.

Max, he guessed. Or something connected to him. "Do you want to talk about it?"

"Not really." When he didn't respond she heaved out a breath, as though resigned. "I didn't know how dangerous he was. Not for a long time. He went to great lengths to hide it from me."

Yeah, Creed bet he had. He still couldn't believe someone as sweet and kind and caring as her had come from a murderous psychopath like de Vries.

"He never did business in front of me. Or…other things. He

even sent me away to an all-girls boarding school to keep me away from it all." She looked down at her hands, gathered in her lap, and the shame on her face was like a gut punch. "Not for the education's sake, but so that I would be monitored twenty-four seven and stay 'pure' for the boss's son he was going to marry me off to when I turned eighteen."

"What the *fuck*?" he burst out before he could stop himself, his entire body going rigid. That sick motherfucker had been grooming his own daughter with the intention of forcing her into a twisted, archaic arranged marriage with his boss's son like she was a prize mare?

"Yes. That's why I left when I did. Well, that's not the whole reason."

She twisted her hands in her lap, and his heart went out to her. How in the hell had she moved past all of this and had any kind of normal life at all? How had she been able to hide it all from him for so long without giving any sign that anything was wrong?

"I came home after finals in my senior year and went to the storage facility on our property to get something. I'd never been in there before. It was forbidden. But something made me want to see what was in there. I heard sounds of pain from inside it. Awful, haunting cries, and went to investigate."

Creed reached for her hand, curled his fingers around hers and held on, knowing that whatever she was going to say next would be horrific.

"Max was torturing someone," she rushed out in a strained voice. "A friend of his, someone who I'd called uncle for years. I don't know what he'd done. He was strung upside down from the ceiling and bleeding all over. When I pushed the door open, Max slit his throat like he was slaughtering a pig."

Holy fuck. "Bella," he whispered, sickened that she'd had to see that.

"I ran. He came after me, but somehow I got away. I think it was because he hadn't expected me to be there. I wasn't supposed to come home until the next day. Otherwise I have no doubt he would have taken steps to ensure I was nowhere near that building."

She must have been fucking terrified. "What did you do after that?"

"Went to the police in a different county, and they brought in the FBI. I went into WITSEC shortly after that, and the rest is history. And that night is also why I'm a vegetarian, by the way. The thought of an animal being slaughtered to wind up on my plate makes me sick. I think of that night and I…" She shrugged.

He shook his head. Heartbroken for the hell she'd been through. Desperately wishing he could take it all away, wipe it from existence or at least her memory, and he didn't know how to help beyond just being here for her. "Sweetheart, I—"

"No, wait." She gripped his hand, looked directly into his eyes. "I told you that because I feel I owe you an explanation for everything. For why I hid so much from you. I don't want to hide anything from you ever again."

"I don't want you to either." There was so much else he was dying to say. That he would always be there for her. That he didn't want to lose her. That he would do anything for another chance if they could just work through this together. But he dared not.

She drew another breath, raised her eyes to his, and his heart skipped at the resolve in them. "I've thought so much about what I was going to say when you got back. But I'm just going to go with how I feel."

He forced himself to breathe, hoping for the best but bracing for the worst just in case. Because he had no idea what she was about to say.

"I know we've been through a lot," she began. "I know I hurt you badly when I left, and I'm not sure how you feel now. But my feelings for you have never changed. I still love you, and I always will."

He inhaled sharply, her words rocking him to his core. He hadn't expected her to say it. Definitely not this soon. And now that she had, he couldn't stay detached from her for another moment.

He grabbed her, pulled her to him and held on tight, absorbing the feel of her. "I never stopped hoping you'd come back." The rush of endorphins flooding his bloodstream left him dizzy. Even if he couldn't bring himself to say the words back to her yet, his feelings for her hadn't changed. He needed more time. Needed—

Her arms wound around his back. "I'm here."

He nodded, all choked up as his heart raced a thousand miles an hour. This was so much more than he'd dared hope for. It was everything. *She* was everything, yet he was so afraid to trust this was real.

His hands were a little unsteady as he took her face between them. Her beautiful, precious face as he drank in every detail, committing them to memory.

In that instant, all his reasons for maintaining distance between them were wiped from his mind. Staring into her eyes, he was lost.

He lowered his mouth to hers and kissed her with every ounce of pent-up longing that had been building since she'd been torn from his life. Bella shifted to her knees, her hand coming up to hold the back of his head as she flattened herself against him and kissed him back.

Raw hunger exploded in his gut, the need to claim her a searing wildfire inside him.

Bella. His Bella.

A deep, rough groan came from him as his tongue stroked hers. He couldn't get enough. Couldn't touch enough of her. They explored each other with greedy, worshipful hands as they kissed, roaming over curves and angles that had once been so familiar. Rediscovering one another.

What was meant to be a slow and tender reconnection on his part quickly got out of hand. He was lost in a rip current of desire, the feel and taste of her flooding his senses.

Slow down. Slow down, he told himself, struggling to rein in the raging desire. He wanted her more than ever. So much he could hardly breathe.

He forced himself to slow down, soften the kiss before he lost control. Teasing her with flicks of his tongue. Sucking at her lower lip until she made a mewling sound and shifted to straddle his lap, the sweet pressure of her ass nestled against the bulge beneath his fly.

He needed more. They both did. Right now.

Creed eased her backward until he had her lying flat and came down on top of her. Bella moaned and surged beneath him, her legs wrapping around his hips.

The urge to strip her naked right then and there was so overwhelming, he had to close his eyes as he kissed his way down the side of her jaw to her neck, finding all the sensitive little spots that made her gasp and twist. He wanted to drown her with pleasure, wipe away the nightmare and the dark memories it had brought up. Heal the rift between them once and for all.

His fingers found the top button of her pajama top and slipped it free. His lips sought the soft, bare skin he'd revealed, followed it all the way down to her navel. Then he lifted up on his forearms and pulled the undone halves apart, exposing her pretty round breasts and their tight pink centers.

Bella's hand curled around the back of his neck as he bent

and covered a nipple with his mouth. She made a soft, hungry sound and lifted toward him, her eyes falling closed.

He sucked and flicked one pert nipple before moving to the other, his right hand sliding down to push inside the waistband of her pajama bottoms to cup her in his palm. Bella sucked in a breath, a tiny quiver rippling through her before she impatiently reached down and began shoving at her waistband.

He settled back on his knees to help her, drawing the pants off her legs, leaving her bared to him for the first time in more than a year. She was so much thinner than before, but every bit as gorgeous. Even more so now that he knew everything she'd withstood and overcome.

She gazed up at him with hungry blue eyes, her trust in him humbling. The urge to tear his own clothes off and plunge into her was riding him hard, but he refused to do it. He was going to love her slowly tonight, build back the intimacy and trust that had been taken from them.

He slid his fingertips between her legs, parting her to reveal the slick, flushed folds waiting for him. Holding her gaze, he eased one finger inside her. Watched her face when he curled it and rubbed just inside her while stroking his thumb along the edge of her clit. She gave a throaty moan and opened her legs wider, her breasts rising and falling with her erratic breathing.

He teased her more, relearning what she enjoyed most. Focused on binding her to him with pleasure.

She reached for his shoulder. Dug her fingers in and tugged him. "Creed," she whispered.

He licked his lips, focused on the sultry flesh he was stroking, and eased down until his face was directly above it. The bite of her nails through his shirt sent a bolt of lust through him. He dipped his head, gave her a slow, soft stroke that ended in a swirl around her clit.

"Oh, my God, don't stop," she whispered breathlessly.

He had no intention of stopping. Not until she was limp and collapsed against the pillow.

He slid his tongue to the top of her clit, moved a fraction to the right and lingered there while his finger rubbed that sweet spot inside her. Over and over and over, only increasing the pressure of his mouth when her fingers clenched in his hair and she was straining against his tongue.

She was so wet, so sweet as she rode his tongue, her moans rising. He felt her clench around his finger, reached his other hand up to play with her nipple as his tongue zeroed in on its target.

Bella's cries of need raked along his spine, making him draw it out, driven by the need to ensure she craved him with every cell in her body. When she was on the verge of begging, he increased the pressure of his tongue and finger slightly.

In moments, she started coming, her core clenching rhythmically around his finger. Only when she pushed at his shoulder did he stop, press a firm kiss to the spot just under her navel and work his way back up to her mouth.

"I want you naked," she whispered against his lips, impatiently pulling his shirt up his torso.

He helped her draw it off, made short work of the rest of his clothes, and then settled on top of her again, groaning into her mouth at the feel of his cock nestled against her abdomen. She reached between them, wrapped her fingers around his length and squeezed, making him shudder all over.

Sensation ripped up his spine, blotting out the ability to think. He pumped into her hand, craving the friction more than he needed his next breath. He wouldn't enter her. Didn't have a condom and wasn't going to stop and bring up birth control now. But just the feel of her stroking him so perfectly…this was heaven too.

He was hard as hell and swollen to bursting. Couldn't stop, the pleasure swamping him as he thrust his hips. *Bella. Bella...*

His hand fisted in her hair, a raw, animalistic groan wrenching from him, muffled by their kiss as he came across her belly in long, hard spurts that stole his breath and made him see stars. He shuddered, dropped his forehead onto her shoulder and just lay there, wrecked, struggling to catch his breath.

Bella drew a hand up and down his bare back, her touch so achingly familiar it put a lump in his throat. He started to lower his weight back onto her, felt the stickiness between them and drew away. "Be right back," he whispered, dropping another kiss on her lips.

He went to the bathroom, quickly cleaned up, and returned with a warm washcloth. Bella lay there quietly while he gently wiped her clean, running her fingers through his hair. "I've missed you," she said in a rough whisper.

He set the cloth aside, switched off the bedside lamp and lay down beside her, drawing her into his arms. She nestled against his chest with a deep, contented sigh, one leg draped over his and her cheek resting in the crook of his shoulder.

A feeling of complete contentment filled him. Goddamn it, he'd missed her. Didn't know how he'd even functioned while she was gone.

"I missed you too," he murmured into the darkness, holding her to his chest.

Bella didn't answer. It took a few moments for him to register her slow, even breaths and realize she had already dropped off to sleep.

His heart squeezed.

Lying awake in the darkness as he held her, he made a vow. Nothing and no one would ever take her away from him again.

NINE

Creed's eyes snapped open in the darkness when something woke him. He lay still, listening, taking in his surroundings. He and Bella were in the guest room bed. She was still curled against him, her breathing soft and even. She hadn't stirred since she'd first dropped off to sleep, and he was gratified that she felt safe enough in his arms to just let go.

A light flickered on the ceiling. Coming from his phone on the bedside table.

He let go of Bella to roll slightly and reach back to grab it. She inhaled sharply and sat upright in a rush. "It's all right," he told her quietly.

"What's going on?"

"Just an alert on the exterior camera in the backyard." It had happened before, triggered by a family of raccoons nesting in a tree just over the fence. It could be them again, but he was checking it out. "Stay here, I'll be right back."

He kissed her forehead and slid out of bed, quickly tugging on his clothes on the way to the door. The house was dark and still as he made his way to his own room to retrieve his weapon, then headed downstairs.

Nothing seemed wrong on the camera feed showing on his phone as he crept soundlessly toward the kitchen. The quiet hum of the refrigerator was the only sound in the silence. None of the motion-sensor lights in the backyard had been triggered, but a thin swath of moonlight spilled through the sliding glass door leading to the back patio, illuminating a path on the floorboards.

He paused in the shadows near the corner of the wall, checking a live view of the front camera, and caught a large shadow flitting past the edge of his field of vision.

Human-sized.

A surge of adrenaline flashed through him. He raced to the front door to disable the alarm, eased it open, and snuck outside, then crept along the front of the house—just in time to see a man's silhouette detach from the shadows ahead of him.

"Hey!" Creed yelled, rushing down the front steps.

The masked man whirled to face him. Creed stopped and automatically dropped to one knee as everything moved in slow motion. He saw the man's hand come up. Started to raise his own weapon.

A shot went off behind him.

Creed's head whipped around, shock blindsiding him when he saw Bella standing there aiming a pistol at the suspect. He quickly looked back at the man, who was now lying on his back on the grass, groaning, legs writhing.

Creed stood and rushed at him, weapon up and ready to put another bullet in him if he made one wrong move. His route triggered the security light on the side of the house. The bright beams flooded the area, illuminating the suspect. He'd dropped his weapon. It lay on the grass near his hand as Creed stalked toward him.

"Don't move," Creed growled, kicking away the fallen pistol,

The guy made a guttural sound and tried to roll to his side.

"I said don't *move*," Creed snarled.

The man was dressed all in black, his face covered by a balaclava. His gloved hands were clutching at his upper belly where Bella had gut shot him.

The porch light flicked on behind him, helping him see better. Creed tucked his weapon into the back of his waistband as Bella's footsteps approached the end of the porch closest to him.

"Go back inside and call the cops, Bell," he told her, darting a quick look around before focusing back on the wounded suspect. Someone in the neighborhood had probably already called after hearing the shot, but he didn't want to take the chance of her being exposed out here if this guy wasn't alone.

He slipped off his belt, knelt beside the guy, and rolled him onto his side. The man struggled, an agonized cry coming from between his gritted teeth. Creed ignored it, quickly secured the man's hands behind him, then ripped off the balaclava and checked his pockets. There was no ID on him, no phone. He was Caucasian, probably early thirties, and losing a lot of blood.

Creed stripped off his shirt and used it to apply pressure to the wound. It wasn't spurting, so it wasn't an arterial bleed, but he was losing a good amount. The grass around him already glistened with it.

Creed pressed down over the entry wound. The man twisted under him, letting out a strangled bellow. Creed didn't let up, pressing hard as he leaned over him and stared down at his face. "Who the fuck are you and what are you doing here?" he growled, rage and growing alarm hitting him.

This guy was no ordinary thief looking for a place to rob.

No answer. Only a defiant snarl.

Creed's patience was running out. He wanted answers.

Wanted to know if this was about Bella. "If I take my hands off you, you're gonna bleed out in less than five minutes, way before any emergency personnel get here. So start talking, asshole."

The man bared his teeth and glared up at him with a low growl.

Creed looked up and glanced around again. If this guy wasn't acting alone, it looked like his buddy or buddies had left him behind, or they would have made a move by now. And while Creed had threatened to let this asshole bleed out, they wouldn't get any answers if he died.

The chances of this being a simple robbery attempt gone wrong were low. Not in this neighborhood, and not with an armed guy dressed like this who refused to talk even with a bullet hole in his gut.

Creed heard a window slide open behind him.

"The police will be here soon," Bella said.

"Get back inside," he ordered, protectiveness on overdrive.

"I *am* inside. You okay?"

"I'm fine. Shut the window and close the blinds."

The window closed. He stayed where he was, his hands already turning numb from the pressure he was exerting, the smell of blood thick in the air. The man was still conscious, now staring defiantly up at the night sky as he shook from shock and blood loss.

All Creed's instincts said this guy was a pro.

"Who sent you?" Creed snapped. He was running out of time, needed to know if he had to get Bella the hell out of here. Her life had been blown apart too many times already, and he didn't want to move her again unless it was necessary. And he was already pretty sure it was.

It seemed like a long time before he heard the approaching sirens, but he breathed a little easier when the vehicles arrived and flashing lights lit up the front yard. He explained who he was to the cops and what had happened, maintained pressure while they moved in to secure the scene. They left Creed where he was to keep applying pressure to the man's stomach and began questioning him.

The bastard refused to answer, eyes now half-closed and the shaking slowing. Getting close to unconsciousness.

"How long until the EMTs get here?" Creed asked, shivering in the cold night air.

"Another couple minutes," the female cop said.

By then the guy would likely be unconscious. Not that his being awake was giving Creed or the cops anything they needed.

The fire department finally arrived, and the EMTs took over from Creed. He rose and stepped back, shirtless, his hands and the knees of his jeans soaked with blood. The cops took him to the front porch and started questioning him as he cleaned up with a towel someone had given him.

"Is there anyone else home?" the female officer asked, handing Creed a blanket to wrap around his shoulders.

"Yeah, my—" What was Bella now? Not his fiancée. The love of his life. "Bella's inside. She'll verify my statement."

"We'll need to take you both down to the station individually."

Creed nodded, jaw tight. He didn't like it, but it was standard procedure in a situation like this.

The officer went in to talk to Bella. While the male cop talked to his supervisor on the radio, Creed stood on the porch and pulled out his phone to call Decker.

"You okay?" Decker answered in concern, no surprise considering what time it was.

"No. We had a situation here. Bella shot an armed intruder. The cops are gonna take us down to the station to question individually." Much as he hated the thought of being separated from Bella any longer, there was no way to avoid it. "Can you and Teagan meet us there and bring us back to my place after?"

"Yeah, of course. You both okay?"

"Yes." Thank God. But he had a bad feeling he and Bella wouldn't have been if he hadn't seen the alert on his phone.

"We'll be there ten minutes after you text me."

"Thanks, man." He ended the call just as the EMTs were loading the suspect onto a gurney, and turned to look through the window in the top of the door where all the downstairs lights were now on.

He exhaled deeply and pulled the blanket tighter around him. Bella was inside talking to the female cop right now. She was safe. But given the evidence he had, he needed to get her out of here as soon as possible.

~

THE POLICE INTERVIEW seemed to take forever. In the interview room at the Crimson Point Sheriff's Office, Bella kept darting anxious glances between the clock mounted on the wall and the door, impatient to end this so she could see Creed. She hadn't seen him since the female officer had put her in a cruiser and brought her down here. She had already admitted to shooting the suspect and turned over her weapon as evidence.

She didn't feel an ounce of guilt over her actions. The instant she'd seen the weapon in the man's hand, she hadn't hesitated, her sole concern protecting Creed.

But that didn't mean the experience hadn't shaken her. Because she was scared as hell that someone had sent him after her.

"We're almost finished," the male officer said to her in a

soothing tone that was beginning to grate on her nerves. "You're doing great."

Bella focused back on him and answered the remaining questions that were now beyond annoying because she was repeating herself. She understood why he was doing it, but she just wanted this done so she could see Creed and talk to him alone.

"You followed Creed downstairs, saw him go out the front door, and when he yelled 'hey' at the suspect, you went outside. Where were you standing when you first saw the suspect?"

She drew in a breath, fighting for patience, and once again went through the series of events leading up to her taking the shot. Thankfully, they finished up a few minutes after that. She signed the paperwork to verify the statement she'd given and was finally released. "The sheriff will contact the Marshals Service?" she asked to verify.

"I'm going to call him right now and tell him what's happened. He'll be in touch."

Okay, then. She shot off a quick text and email to Nico to tell him what had happened, then exited the room. As soon as she walked into the waiting area, she saw Creed waiting there with Teagan and a big, imposing man who had to be Decker.

Bella rushed straight to Creed. He caught her and pulled her to his chest, hugging her tight. "You okay?"

She nodded, gripping him hard even though the smell of blood coming from him made her stomach twist. It reminded her too much of that awful night she'd seen Max kill that poor, defenseless man. "Any update on the man I shot?"

"He's in surgery. That's all I know." He kissed the top of her head, ran a hand over her back.

Bella eased back to look up into Creed's face, her throat tightening at the love shining in his gray eyes. "Did he say anything to you? The officer wouldn't tell me anything." She was so worried that this had been targeted.

"No, but he's still alive. If he makes it through surgery, they'll question him again after."

"Where did I hit him?" It had been so dark, she'd just aimed for center mass and taken a shot.

"Just below his diaphragm." He searched her eyes. "You sure you're all right?"

She nodded, not wanting to let go, but she did, her gaze straying to Teagan and Decker. Creed must have called them. "I'm so glad to see you."

"Same." Teagan came forward to hug her. "This is Decker, by the way."

The dark-haired man was even bigger than Creed, and she could see the family resemblance with Marley. "Hi," he said, standing there with his arms crossed in an imposing posture.

"Don't mind him, he always looks like that. Used to be an MP in the Corps," Teagan said as if that explained everything. "You ready to get out of here? We'll take you guys home."

Home. She hadn't had one in over a year, but home was wherever Creed was. "Thanks."

"Of course. Come on."

Creed wrapped an arm around her, and they left the building. He sat in the back with her, keeping her tucked close to him, kissing her temple and the top of her head while she leaned against him. Bella was too caught up in her head to talk to any of them. She'd gone over everything so many times in her mind.

It *could* have been a robbery attempt. But it also could have been something far worse. Something that sent a wave of fear crashing through her. But they wouldn't know until the police had finished their initial investigation.

It started raining again on the way back to Creed's place.

Cruisers were still parked out front and a cargo van. People wearing white suits and masks were standing in the front yard when they arrived. A uniformed officer let them under the crime scene tape and into the house.

Teagan steered her toward the couch. "Come sit and relax for a few minutes. I'll make you something to drink, and we can talk while Creed cleans up."

"Thanks, I'll be right back." Creed gave Bella another long look before turning and jogging upstairs, the bottom half of his jeans soaked through with blood.

"Do you want anything? Coffee? Tea?"

"Brandy." She rarely touched the stuff, but if there was ever a time to have some, this was it. "It should be in the pantry on the left-hand side." That's where Creed had always kept it before.

"Coming up." Teagan returned a minute or two later with a tumbler holding an inch of amber liquid. "Here."

"Thanks," she murmured, and took a sip. It burned all the way down but settled into a nice warm glow in the pit of her stomach, helping take away the shaky edge. "Did Creed tell you everything?"

"Pretty much," Decker said. "He didn't know you'd followed him, though."

"I got my weapon and followed him down, just in case."

Teagan nodded in approval. "Good."

"I stayed back so I wouldn't be in the way or distract him, but he went outside almost immediately and didn't know I was behind him. I saw the guy at the edge of the yard. I saw his hand come up, saw the gun, and just reacted. One shot. He went down hard."

God, what if he'd come here for her?

"You did the right thing," Decker said.

She nodded, still wrestling with it. Max was dead. There

was only one other person she could think of who might still want to target her. "I mean, I know how good Creed is," she went on, unable to stop herself from babbling. "I know he didn't need my help and would have handled it on his own without me, but I…"

Teagan reached out to put a hand over hers. "It's okay. You were just trying to protect him."

She let out a shaky laugh, because that was only partly true. She'd also been trying to protect herself. "I know it's ridiculous. Me trying to protect a former Green Beret."

"You neutralized the threat," Decker said. "That's all that matters. You didn't do anything wrong."

"No, I know," she murmured, and took another sip of brandy. She was tempted to knock it all back at once but was afraid it might come back up if she did.

The hierarchy within the organization would have shifted the instant Max died. The only other person left who might target her was Andreas, her intended fiancé. Her stomach roiled at the thought. It still made her sick to think that her own father had planned to force her to marry a man like that.

Teagan got up and moved to sit beside her, draped an arm across her shoulders. "You did good, girl. Did you get a good look at him?"

"No, and he was wearing a mask." She hadn't seen him up close or even heard him say anything except for the cries of pain. "He was wearing all black, including his gloves. But I just keep thinking that this happened too close to the incident at the diner the other night." She rolled the near-empty glass back and forth between her hands, unable to stem the wild energy coursing through her. "That it might be connected."

Until the police ruled that out officially, she was going to remain worried.

Teagan and Decker shared a look, then Teagan squeezed her

tighter. "Hopefully he'll start talking once he comes out of recovery."

Creed came back downstairs a few minutes later, freshly showered and wearing jeans and a T-shirt that hugged his muscular chest, his dark hair slicked back. His gaze cut straight to her, and he crossed the room to sit on her other side, wrapped an arm around her and pulled her into him. "How you doing?"

"Okay." But not really. She was scared. Scared that she was still in danger. And that she had likely endangered him too.

"Did you get anything on the perp?" Decker asked him.

"Nada. No ID on him and no phone either. Hopefully they'll be able to find his prints in the system. If not, then we need something to make him start talking."

The knot in Bella's stomach tightened, Creed's response tipping her toward the conclusion she'd instinctively feared from the moment he'd received the alert.

The man she'd shot was a pro, probably sent from someone within the organization, and he'd come here for her. To either bring her back by force or kill her.

She set her glass down and wrapped her arms around herself to stave off a shiver.

Creed ran a hand up and down her arm and said what she'd been thinking. "Bella and I can't stay here."

"You can come to our place," Teagan said without hesitation. "We've got an extra bedroom."

Bella looked up at him, unsure. Was going to their place smart? If she was being targeted, then someone else might already be in the area watching her. She might bring the danger to Decker and Teagan's place. But a hotel wasn't secure enough under the circumstances, and they wouldn't be able to get a rental in the middle of the night.

"Okay," she finally said. "Thanks."

"No need to thank us for that." Teagan stood. "You need any help packing up?"

"No, I—wait, what about my cat?" She looked at Creed. She could leave Nick here alone for a day or so with his food, water, and litter box, but not longer than that.

"Can you leave him here just for tonight until we figure things out? Maybe Ivy can come drop by to check on him. You said he likes her."

That eased her mind a bit. "Okay. I'll call her in the morning."

He nodded. "Let's go grab what we need for a few days."

In the guest room, she began packing her smaller suitcase. Nick made a chirping sound and jumped up on the bed to watch her. She picked him up, ignored the way he pushed his front paws against her to make her let him go, and kissed the top of his head.

"I'm sorry, buddy, but you won't be alone for long. Promise. I just need to leave until we're sure it's safe to come back." She let him go, and he immediately leaped onto the floor, tail twitching as he gave her an indignant look.

She picked up a sweater to fold it and stopped suddenly, her mind still churning. And an instant later, her inner turmoil skyrocketed.

This was wrong.

Under the circumstances, staying with Creed any longer was wrong. Her gut kept insisting that the armed intruder tonight had been targeting her. That if she stayed, she would make Creed and anyone else who tried to help her a target as well.

She couldn't let that happen. Wouldn't. She needed to leave right now. Get in her car and put Crimson Point behind her, disappear again before anyone else got hurt.

Although—shit, she'd just shot someone. She couldn't

leave the area until the DA or whoever cleared her. She wasn't thinking clearly. WITSEC might be her only option to make this stop and protect Creed. She would contact Nico once she was on the road.

She bent, scooped up Nick and hurried over to put him in his travel carrier. "Change of plans," she told him, locking the screen door in place before rushing to the bathroom to grab her stuff in there, the frantic need to leave before she changed her mind making her skin buzz all over.

Creed stepped into the bedroom just as she came out. He took one look at her, saw Nick in his carrier, and his expression tightened. "What's going on?"

She shook her head, fear driving her. There could be more people coming for her. They might already be in Crimson Point. "I have to go."

He quickly shut the door and stood in front of it. This was what he'd feared. Why he hadn't said the words back to her earlier. He couldn't trust that she wouldn't up and leave him again. "No."

Her mind was made up. She spun and shoved her toiletries into the suitcase. God, she'd been so stupid to think anything had changed with Max's death. Dammit. She'd known coming here still held a certain amount of risk and selfishly done it anyway, endangering Creed. "This is because of me. It's my fault. I should never have come here."

"Whoa, stop," he said firmly.

She kept packing, the need to flee clawing at her insides. "Max is gone but I'm still not safe. They'll never let me go." Max or Andreas, it didn't matter.

"Bella. *Stop*." Creed was in front of her, spinning her around and taking her by the upper arms. "Look at me. You're not running. Not ever again. Not from me."

She went rigid, pulled in an unsteady breath, and slowly

looked up into his face. The understanding and tenderness in his eyes made her want to cry.

"I've got you. I've *got* you," he repeated when she opened her mouth to argue, "and I swear I'll keep you safe. Just don't run. You don't have to run anymore, because I'm here. You know I won't let anyone hurt you. We'll figure out everything together this time."

Her throat clogged up, her heart thudding hard in her ears. "You don't know what they're like. Max is dead, but Andreas isn't. This could be because of him. And if it is, he won't stop sending people for me."

"Let him." Defiance burned in Creed's eyes.

She stared up at him, heart lurching. God, she wanted to be with him more than anything, but not if it put him at further risk. It was her worst nightmare, and a big part of the reason why she'd gone with the Marshals and cut all contact with him last time.

"You're safe here with me, I swear." He wrapped his arms around her and crushed her to him, holding her so tight she could hardly breathe.

But you're not safe with me.

She squeezed her eyes shut, his distress carving her up inside. She could feel his desperation, his fear that she would leave and disappear again, but he didn't know what she knew. Didn't realize the kind of danger they would both be in if that man had been sent for her.

"Bell," Creed whispered when she didn't respond, his arms locking her to him. "I know you're scared, but we'll work this out. Because I'm not letting you go again. I won't. I *can't*—" He broke off, his voice catching as his grip turned desperate.

His pain broke her, shattering all resistance. She leaned into him, wanting to scream at the unfairness of it all. She still loved him as much as ever. Would love him the same way until her dying breath. Yet tonight had proven beyond doubt that she might be a constant source of danger to them both.

She wasn't sure whether she could live with the guilt.

Sensing her surrender, Creed exhaled in relief, the awful tension in his body easing slightly. "Everything's gonna be okay now," he said against her temple.

She inhaled a shaky breath and wound her arms around him, wanting to believe him. Was this completely selfish of her? If she stayed she would be subjecting him to constantly having to look over his shoulder, constantly having to watch over her.

But how could she leave? It would kill her to be torn from him again, to hurt him like that again, especially since they'd just found their way back together.

He squeezed her. "Say the words, Bell. Say you'll never leave me again."

"I— I'll stay," she whispered, terrified that she had just sealed their fates. But if she left him she would essentially die anyway.

He made a rough sound, cupped her head in his hands, and brought his mouth down on hers. There was nothing gentle about this kiss. It was a claiming. A raw, desperate declaration of intent to bind him to her forever.

She pushed up on her toes to give it back to him and more, losing herself in the dizzying tide of need that punched through her.

"You guys about ready?" Decker called upstairs.

Creed broke the kiss, the raw possessiveness in his stare making her ache inside. The look on his face told her that if they'd been alone, they would be naked with him buried inside her seconds from now. "You're mine, Bell." His voice was low and rough, his eyes dark as storm clouds. "No one's taking you away from me ever again."

She nodded because it was true, and they both knew it.

Even if he hadn't told her he still loved her. He cared. Cared enough to stay beside her, be subjected to the danger she'd brought, and protect her.

They belonged together until the end, for better or worse.

She just hoped that her decision wouldn't get them both killed.

TEN

Creed eased from the bed in Decker and Teagan's guest room and pulled on the clothes he'd changed into last night before coming here. It was still early, just after six, but he couldn't sleep anymore, and he'd heard someone moving around in the kitchen as of a few minutes ago.

At the door, he paused to look back at Bella. She was curled up on her side facing him, fast asleep, her dark hair tousled across her pillow. The sight of her like that made him feel like an invisible fist had reached through his ribs to grip his heart.

Last night had been intense for both of them in a lot of ways. Even though he'd wanted her more than he wanted air to breathe, she'd been so exhausted she'd dropped right off when they'd crawled into bed at just before two. He didn't have the heart to wake her up now.

Especially since he would have his face between her legs and wouldn't stop until he was inside her. When that happened, he wanted complete privacy for them without anyone else around to overhear anything.

Last night had changed everything, had turned back time in so many ways. He'd meant what he'd said. She was his, and he was hers. He was sticking by her, no matter what consequences came his way as a result. Any risk was worth it as long as he still had Bella.

He'd never known he could love anyone as much as he loved her. Except for his aunt, the only family he'd had. The overwhelming power of what he felt for Bella rocked him. He would do anything to protect her, and nothing short of death would ever tear her away from him again.

He snuck out of the room, shut the door quietly, and made his way to the kitchen in the center of the condo, the scent of brewed coffee filling the air.

Decker was at the pot, pouring himself a mug. He glanced over his shoulder at Creed. "Hey. You want some?"

"Please, yeah."

Decker reached up into a cupboard and pulled down another mug to fill it. "How's Bella?"

"Still asleep. Where's Teagan?"

"Gym. Any messages from the cops about last night?"

"Not yet." He was going to call Sheriff Buchanan soon. "You going into the office today?"

"In a bit. You coming in?"

"I'm gonna call Ryder and tell him what happened. I'll work remotely today if he's cool with it." He wanted to be here for Bella and to get a plan together. Once the police started digging into the situation, he and Bella could make a decision about what to do from here. Together. Because letting her go wasn't happening.

"I'm sure he will be."

Creed thought so too. Ryder had high expectations of his employees, and rightly so, but he was fair and cared about the people who worked for him. Callum as well. "Thanks again for letting us crash here."

"Yeah, no worries." Decker slid the mug of coffee across

the island top to him, then leaned back against the counter and folded his arms to regard him. "So, everything good with you guys again?"

Creed eyed him in surprise, taken off guard by the question. Decker was one of the least touchy-feely guys he'd ever met. "You really wanna know?"

Decker's shrug was a little defensive. "Just wondering. You don't have to answer if you don't want."

"No, I'm fine with talking about it. I'm just surprised you wanna know."

"You gonna tell me or not?"

Creed huffed out a laugh. "We're working through it. But whatever happens, I'm not letting her go."

Decker nodded in approval. "Nice."

"It is nice," he agreed.

"She sure held her own last night. One shot, center mass in the dark under that kind of stress?" He whistled softly.

"Fuckin' amazing."

"Where'd she learn to shoot?"

"I taught her. She asked me to soon after we got together. Never knew the real reason she wanted to learn until she told me everything when she showed up at my place." He took a sip of coffee. It was sweet and creamy. "What'd you put in this, anyway?"

"Some creamer stuff Teagan likes. French vanilla or something."

"I thought you liked it black."

"Me too, until I tried this."

He grinned, enjoying the easy back and forth. "Look at you, getting all comfy with your sweeter, softer side. Love to see it, brother."

Decker grunted, his eyebrows crashing together in a scowl. "Fuck off."

A sharp ding filled the kitchen. He fished his phone out of his back pocket, scowled harder as he read whatever was on the screen.

"Bad news?" Creed asked.

"It's my brothers." He tucked his phone away without answering. "They're both coming out to interview with CPS."

"That's great, I know how much you and Marley have been hoping for it." Their family had been through a lot and all of them were scattered to the wind during their various military careers. Now they were all out, and Marley and Decker both wanted the twins to come here. Not that anyone would guess it by Decker's expression just now.

Decker grunted again and drained his mug, turned to pour himself another one and added a healthy dose of the flavored creamer.

"You don't look too happy about it." What was up with that?

"I'm happy."

"I mean, yeah, you look fucking ecstatic."

Decker gave him a hard stare and raised his mug, but Creed saw his lips twitch. Decker loved playing the hardass, didn't like anyone knowing it was partly a front or that he had actual *feelings* under that aloof exterior. But Creed knew him now and saw all the way through that.

"You're not gonna answer them?" Creed enjoyed needling him a bit. All in good fun.

"Nope."

"Are they gonna keep messaging you until you do?"

"Yup." He gave a long-suffering sigh. "I'll text them in a bit when I'm not busy. After I've had my coffee."

"Oh, you're busy right now?"

Decker shot him a look. "Like I said, I'm having my coffee."

Creed chuckled and passed his empty mug over for a fill-up. "So, all three Abrams boys in Crimson Point, huh? That sounds like a recipe for trouble."

"With those two?" He snorted. "Practically guaranteed."

∽

"MAN, who knew little Crimson Point was such a hotbed of criminal activity," Tristan said to him.

"I know," Gavin replied as he drove them through the quiet neighborhood. "Now I'm even more excited to get there."

It felt weird to have a Monday off. A few older people were out walking their dogs, and some young moms out pushing their little kids in strollers.

"What do you think the real story is?"

Decker had finally deigned to respond to their message about the interviews by saying he was busy because a situation with his partner Creed had gone down last night. Which, given what had happened in Crimson Point recently, could mean anything from drug running to human trafficking to murder. It was frickin' annoying that Decker wouldn't give them the details. That was just like him, all stony-faced and acting like a human vault. Luckily, they had a way around that in the form of a sister who was more than happy to include them in the loop.

"Dunno, but we'll find out soon enough because I'm gonna call Marley after we're done here."

"Good idea. Autumn know we're coming?" Tristan asked as Gavin turned the truck down her street.

"No."

"She'll be working. You don't think we should at least text her to say we're coming over?"

"Why? It's Autumn. She won't mind. If she's busy working on something important, she'll just say so, and we'll wait."

He'd always just shown up at her place when he felt like it, starting way back when they were kids. She'd always been cool with it. Besides, this news had to be delivered in person. Autumn was his best friend. Well, other than Tristan.

"That's because she's too polite to tell you that you're an inconsiderate shit and throw you out," Tristan said to him as they turned into Autumn's driveway.

"What? I'm not inconsiderate. I'm spontaneous."

"Oh, is *that* what it is?" Tristan hopped out and headed for the side door.

Gavin hurried ahead of him, knocked once before punching in the code on the keypad and pushing the door open. "Hey, it's just us."

They walked in and took their shoes off on the mat inside. She had a little bench set up against the wall with a storage unit tucked under it filled with little shoes in all kinds of colors. Highly organized even with footwear.

Autumn appeared just as they stepped into the kitchen, dressed in snug black yoga pants and a long top that came to mid-thigh. Her sandy-blond hair was pulled up in a messy bun, and her green eyes sparkled when she smiled at them.

Seeing her always brightened his day, but especially lately. For reasons and to an extent he didn't want to analyze too closely.

"Well, hi," she said. "This is a nice surprise to start my week."

Gavin threw his twin a pointed look. "See?"

He walked over to hug her, breathing in the familiar scent of her perfume that smelled like green apples. And tried to ignore how good she felt in his arms. Soft and curvy in all the right places. Something else he'd also not paid attention to until recently. "How are ya?"

"Hanging in there. Hi, Tris." She hugged his brother.

"I told him to message you before we came."

"No, don't be silly. Y'all are family."

Gavin shot him a smug smile and got an eye roll in answer. "Carly at school?"

"Yes. They're starting to plan their grad today, so she's pretty excited."

"Can't believe she's finishing seventh grade in a few months." Or that he wouldn't be able to attend her grad in person. That sucked. He'd known her from the day she was born and hated the thought of disappointing her. Or Autumn. He didn't ever want to let either of them down.

"Believe me, I know. I'm so not ready for her to leave elementary school. Can I get you guys anything?"

"No," Tris said, "it's—"

"What've you got?" Gavin asked, ignoring Tristan's look of exasperation. He was hungry, and Autumn was almost as good a cook as Marley.

Autumn's lips quirked. "Chocolate zucchini muffins."

Oh, yeah. "Awesome. I'll take two."

"You'll take *one*, so your brother can have the other." She walked over to the counter. And, hell, he couldn't stop his gaze from dropping to admire the way those tight yoga pants hugged every inch of her legs right up to where the hem of her top stopped just under her rounded ass.

He'd started doing that sometime over the past few weeks since he'd returned home, and it was becoming a real bad habit. But he couldn't seem to shut off the voice in the back of his head that kept reminding him of things he'd sworn long ago not to think about. The same voice that whispered about that one sultry summer night that was best left in the past.

They'd never talked about it. Not once in all these years. And neither of them had told anyone else about it either. Not even Tristan knew. Now he wished they had.

"So did you guys just drop by for a visit?" she asked.

"Partly," he answered, tearing his gaze from her ass as he and Tris sat on the stools tucked under the island.

She looked over her shoulder at them, in the midst of popping the plated muffins in the microwave. "What's the other part?"

"Tell you after we eat."

She hit a few buttons, and the microwave whirred to life. Fourteen seconds later she pulled them out, one second before the clock had run down completely—why did people always do that?—and set a plate down in front of each of them. "Want coffee with them?"

"That'd be great," Tristan said.

She poured them two cups, put creamer in Tristan's, and left his black. "Okay, dig in." She leaned her forearms on the island top, watching them expectantly.

He let out a little groan of pleasure when he took his first bite. The warmed muffin was just hot enough to make it taste oven-fresh, partially melting the chocolate chips she'd put in them. "You sure these have zucchini in 'em?"

"I'm sure. And nonfat Greek yogurt. They're low fat, high fiber, and high protein. That's a triple win in my books."

"They don't taste healthy."

"That's the whole point," she said, her eyes laughing at them.

The sunlight streaming through the window over the sink lit up those eyes, making them glow in the most gorgeous way. He'd never realized how many different shades of green were in them before.

Beautiful. But then she'd always been beautiful in a fresh, effortless way he loved. Even before the night when—

Nope. They'd both buried that deep and moved on. Or he'd thought he had. Except…

Something about their dynamic had changed for him lately. Shifting things into a new and powerful focus he couldn't shut off or dismiss.

"What?" she asked.

"Nothing." He wrenched his eyes from her and got back to eating his muffin. What was up with him lately? The prospect of moving away permanently seemed to be dredging up all kinds of things from the past.

"This is great," Tristan said beside him. "What are you working on now? Another big project?"

"Pretty big. Just signed a new client for a big marketing campaign that should give me a decent chunk to sock away into Carly's college fund."

"Good for you," Tristan said, the pride in his voice unmistakable. She and Tris had always had a brother-sister thing going on between them.

As for Gavin… His feelings ran deeper and way more territorial than that. And given the way he'd just been ogling her ass, the past clearly wasn't dead and buried for him after all.

"Yeah, proud of you, Autie." It wouldn't surprise him if she'd managed to squirrel away enough for a full undergrad degree already. Autumn was one in a billion. She'd always had her shit together, even as a kid, right through her teens, through college.

Even through being dumped while pregnant and left to raise a child all on her own—and Gavin still sometimes fantasized about finding that deadbeat and breaking his face. The few times he'd seen her frazzled, juggling life's challenges while being a single mom, she'd still managed to hold it together.

She gave him a soft, pleased smile that hit dead center in his heart. "Enough about me. You've eaten. Now tell me your news."

He sat up a little taller, suddenly feeling hesitant. There was a twinge of guilt too. "Tris and I are going to Oregon to interview with Decker's company in a couple weeks."

Her smile slipped a notch. The light in her eyes dimmed, and he winced inside. "Oh. What are you both interviewing for?"

"They have a few openings we're interested in. Risk assessment, undercover work, personal protection. We want to meet them, explore our options, and see if there's a good fit."

"And if there is, will you be moving there permanently?" She looked at him as she asked. Not Tristan.

Another twinge of guilt hit him. Sharper this time. And there was something else too.

Something deep and tinged with regret for what might have been. "Probably. But that's still a ways down the road," he rushed out. "We need to see how it goes first."

She nodded, smile gone now, gorgeous eyes serious. "I hope it goes really well for you both. It would be so great if you guys got to live so close to Decker and Marley."

That was the biggest reason he and Tristan were looking at this. While Autumn and her daughter were his biggest reasons not to go. "Yeah."

But I'd miss you like hell.

"Don't go missing us yet," Tristan said, drawing her gaze to him and giving her a gentle smile. "It's not a done deal by any means, and we'd only take the job if both of us decide it's what we want."

She put on a smile for his twin, but Gavin could tell it was forced. "I understand. But I'm happy for you guys. Really. It would be an amazing opportunity for you and your family."

But she was part of the family too. Especially to him.

"We'll be around for a couple weeks, then we'll come see you when we get back," Gavin said, trying to take the sting out of the announcement.

"Okay. Holding you to that."

The comment threw him. Did she really think he or Tristan would up and move across the country without coming to say goodbye in person?

"Hey, is that bookshelf in Carly's room still busted? Gav and I can take a look now and fix it for you," Tristan said.

"Oh, that'd be great, yeah." She turned and hurried for the hallway.

And, yup, Gavin's eyes went straight back to her ass. Damned pervert.

Tristan nudged him as they rose. "She's taking it pretty hard already."

"I know," Gavin said, aware of a heavy weight stuck in the middle of his chest. A combined weight of regret and loss that refused to go away.

Leaving Autumn behind was going to be way harder than he'd ever imagined.

ELEVEN

Creed kept a hand anchored on Bella's lower back as he escorted her from the elevator and down the upper-floor hall to the conference room. When he'd called Ryder to tell him what happened, his boss had promised that the Crimson Point Security team would do whatever it could to help, then asked them to come in for a meeting at 0900, the soonest they could schedule it with everyone there.

Creed was grateful for the help and anxious to find a solution that would guarantee Bella's safety until the threat against her was identified and neutralized.

Ryder, Callum and Walker were all waiting for them. Ryder ran the company with Callum, his number two, who excelled at risk assessment. Walker came from an intelligence background and brought that expertise along with his skills in logistics. Together, the three of them had turned Crimson Point Security from a small company to the most sought-after and fastest-growing security firm on the West Coast.

They rose from their seats at the long rectangular table, laptops, and file folders open in front of them. "Bella, good to meet you. I'm Ryder," he said as all three men stood to introduce themselves and shake her hand.

"Hi. Nice to meet you all." She aimed a small smile at Walker. "I feel like I already know you a bit, from Ivy."

"She told you all good things about me, I'm sure," he said in his Deep South accent.

"Oh, definitely." She sat in the chair Creed pulled out for her across the table from the others, and he took the one next to her. She seemed calm and composed on the surface, but he knew she was still shaken from what had happened. On edge, thinking that someone from her father's organization might have targeted her.

Ryder leaned back in his seat, his attention focused on her. "We know about some of your background—and the gist of what happened at Creed's place earlier this morning. Can you walk us through it in more detail so we get a clearer picture of what's going on?"

"Sure." She began with her family, talked about the intended and unwanted arrangement with Andreas, and worked her way up to last night. "I shot the suspect, saw him go down, and then Creed told me to go back inside and call 911, so I did." She rubbed her hands on her thighs. "The police got there pretty fast after that. We were taken in separately to give our statements, and then Decker and Teagan came to pick us up and let us stay the night at their place."

"Not the best welcome to Crimson Point," Callum said to her with a somber expression. "Have you heard anything from the sheriff's office yet this morning?"

"No, no leads yet on the suspect's identity, and nothing from the Marshals either, though I've reached out to my contact there to update him," she answered. "Until the police ID the suspect, there's nothing more anyone can do."

Oh, yes, there was. Creed was going to take every measure possible to keep her safe. But he kept that to himself.

"There's a good possibility the Marshals will recommend you rejoin WITSEC for now," Callum said.

"She's not leaving," Creed said sharply. Maybe too sharply, given the way everyone's eyes snapped to him. But he loved her and was desperate to keep her by his side through the rest of this. He didn't care what it took or what it cost, he was ready and willing to do anything to protect her.

Anything except let her go. And if that meant going into WITSEC with her, then so be it.

"No." Bella reached for his hand and curled her fingers around it in reassurance. "I'm staying with Creed."

The hard knot of tension in the pit of his stomach loosened at her words, the public declaration easing the fear that she was still planning to run again, even though she'd promised not to.

Callum nodded. "I figured as much. But there's a chance someone has either cloned or been tracking your phones."

"Yeah," Creed said, and slid both phones across the table to him. "They're both deactivated. Thought it wouldn't hurt to see if the tech department can find anything."

"Sure. So what do you guys want to do from here? Because under the circumstances, and given the reach and wealth of the organization, I recommend you go off grid until the extent of the threat is identified."

"That's exactly what I want to do," Creed said. "I was going to run it past all of you first, get your input before we made any decisions."

"We all agree disappearing for a while is the best thing for Bella's safety at this point," Ryder said. "We'll pull you from your upcoming contract for now. Have you got a place in mind?"

"Not yet." He had a few ideas, but nothing concrete.

Ryder turned his head toward Walker. "What do you think?"

"Nothing out of country. If the organization is behind this, then they might know her alias and Creed's name, and could be monitoring their passports. Where you go doesn't have to be far away, but definitely something out of the area until we know if this was targeted and the Feds and Marshals can do a thorough threat assessment. Give me a few minutes to make a couple calls."

"Sure," Creed answered.

Walker rose and left the room, already dialing someone on his phone.

"I've got an idea in mind that might work," Callum said. "I'll check with a contact." He started texting someone.

Creed shifted his grip on Bella's hand, rubbing his thumb over the back of it. Letting her know without words that he was here for her and that they would handle this together. He wasn't letting her go again.

"I'll start working my connections with the FBI and Marshals Service and see what I can find out," Ryder said, pulling out his own phone.

"Thanks."

"Meantime, let's run through a list of what you guys will need for the next week at least," Callum said. "Ivy's already volunteered to get everything together for you."

"I love her," Bella said, earning a smile from Callum.

"She's pretty great all right," he agreed. "She's at our place right now hanging out with Nadia and Ferhana. And you must have made a really good impression on her, because she insisted she be involved with this." He grabbed a pad of paper and pen. "All right, let's break this down, starting with the basics. Food, water, clothes, equipment."

They were almost through the list a few minutes later when

Walker returned and shut the door behind him. "They'll get back to me when they know more."

Callum's phone chimed. He checked it, then said, "Friend of mine owns a place about a six-hour drive from here on a lake in southeastern Washington State that fills your requirements. He uses it for cross-country skiing in the winter and for a few weeks' holiday in the summer. He doesn't rent it out, but it's yours if you want it for now." He set his phone in front of them on the table to show them a map of the area with a pin marking the location of the property.

Creed and Bella leaned forward to study it. The house was remote, in a secluded area in the mountains. Sparsely populated.

"Here's the satellite view." Callum hit a button, bringing up a full-color overhead image. "The entire area's heavily forested. This development is just four years old, so there are only a half dozen other houses built so far, the closest one about four hundred yards to the south."

It was private and definitely off the beaten path.

"How many access roads?" Creed asked.

"Two. One to the east, and one to the south. The closest town is three miles north up this road." He indicated it on screen. "It's got modern wiring and plumbing and a couple wood-burning stoves for heat. He says there are four cords of firewood stacked under the carport, so you'll have plenty of fuel. There's also a generator as backup. He put in a new security system last year. It's not state of the art or anything, but the doors and windows are all armed, and he's got security cameras in the front and back."

Creed looked at Bella. "What do you think?"

She was studying the image intently, taking it all in. "I think it's off grid enough that it would be hard for anyone to find us." She met his gaze. "What do *you* think?"

"I think it's perfect, and we'll be taking burner phones." He was already impatient to get her there and hunker down until things were settled. And the idea of holing up there, just the two of them, was hugely appealing too. They could use the time to reconnect, get to know each other again without any interruptions.

Relief bled into her expression. "Okay." She looked at Callum. "We'll take it. Thank you."

"Sure. I'll get the details and set it up, then get you a rental vehicle through the company. One of us will pick it up, and you can leave from here once Ivy brings what you need. I'm texting her the list right now." Callum tapped away on his phone. It rang in his hand, and whatever he saw on the screen made him go rigid. He whipped it up to his ear immediately and answered, tension pouring off him. "You okay?"

Whatever the answer was, it must not have been good because he shot out of his chair so fast it flew backward on its wheels and hit the wall. "I'll be there in ten minutes."

"Is it Nadia?" Ryder asked as Callum hurriedly rounded the end of the table, face set. "She in labor?"

"Yeah, I gotta go," he blurted and yanked the door open. "I'll send you the details of the house as soon as I can."

"Good luck, man," Ryder said. "Let us know if you need anything."

"Will do." He disappeared into the hallway, the sound of his rapid footsteps fading.

Ryder gave a rueful smile. "Never a dull moment around here. Now, let's get you two squared away."

∼

CALLUM BROKE at least nine different traffic laws on the way home and pulled into the driveway seven minutes after Nadia's call. He realized that having a baby was natural and women did it every day, but this was *his* wife and baby, and that gave this a whole level of urgency he'd never felt before, not even on the riskiest mission overseas.

The front door opened as he was hopping out of his truck. Nadia appeared on the doorstep, one hand on her swollen belly, her brown hair tied back in a ponytail. She looked up at him, started to smile but then froze, her eyes closing and her face twisting in agony.

Fuck.

He rushed up the pathway and reached out to steady her. She grabbed hold of his upper arms and dug her fingers into him, her face pinched with pain as she sucked in air. And in that moment, he knew they were way past the initial stages of labor.

"How long ago did it start?" He wrapped an arm around her.

Nadia leaned into him, resting her forehead in the crook of his shoulder, a painful moan coming from her before she answered. "Few hours."

Few *hours*? That meant she'd gone into labor while he'd still been home. "Why didn't you tell me before I left for the office? I wouldn't have gone in."

"Exactly. What happened to Creed and Bella was serious, so I thought you should be at the meeting. Besides, I wasn't sure it was labor when it started, and first deliveries are notoriously long. But I'm hoping I'm the exception, to be honest." She winced, shifted her stance, and reached back to rub her lower spine.

He pushed her hand aside and did it for her, applying firm, steady pressure, and was rewarded with a gratified sigh. "Want me to call Ember and Boyd?" They'd volunteered to come over and watch Ferhana when Nadia went into labor, but things were already moving faster than they'd expected. He didn't want to waste time sitting here waiting for them. "We can drop Ferhana off at their place on the way."

"No, I already called—"

"Here." Ivy stepped out carrying Nadia's packed hospital bag, taking him completely by surprise. He'd been so preoccupied with getting to his wife that he must have passed right by Ivy's car without noticing when he'd arrived. "Everything's ready to go, and Ferhana's still asleep. You put Nadia in the truck, I'll take care of this."

Callum bent and scooped Nadia up sideways in his arms, then turned and carried her quickly to the truck. Ivy rushed ahead to open the passenger door for them. Callum set his wife in the seat carefully, feeling fucking helpless as she clung to him and struggled through another contraction.

It had only been two minutes since the last one. "How far apart are they?"

"About four minutes on average," Ivy answered, setting the bag on the backseat. "That one was faster though, and they're definitely getting more intense."

He didn't like the sound of that. "Have you called the hospital?"

"Her doctor. He's going to meet her up there later."

His eyes shot to Ivy. "How much later?"

"He didn't say."

Damn. "Okay." He hugged Nadia to him for a moment, but she pushed him away, wiping at her face.

"Let's just get there," she said, her face pinched, the hint of fear in her eyes turning his stomach into a concrete ball.

He let her go and stepped back to shut the door. "Thanks," he said to Ivy as he hurried around to the other side.

"Don't mention it."

"I'm coordinating with Creed and Bella about a safehouse."

"Got it, and good luck," she called out. "Shae's out buying

everything for Bella and Creed right now while I hang out with Ferhana, but text me if you need anything else."

"You're the best."

"I know."

He fired up the engine and reversed down the driveway. The moment he swung the truck around and put it into drive, Nadia sucked in a sharp breath and grabbed for his right hand. She grimaced, her back arching as she pressed her lips together to muffle a painful moan.

Callum hit the gas and shot them down the road. He hoped to hell they had an anesthetist standing by when they got there. "We'll be there in twenty minutes," he told her, steering with his left hand while she gripped the right.

They made it to the hospital in just over fifteen, after Nadia had snapped at him twice on the way to slow down before he got them in an accident. He pulled up in front of Emergency, ready to run her inside, and a huge wave of relief hit him when Grady came through the automatic doors pushing a wheelchair.

Grady smiled at them both. "Morning. I'll be your L&D nurse today."

Thank Christ. Callum had never been so happy to see anyone in his life. In addition to being an experienced labor and delivery nurse, he was also a PJ with the Air National Guard. "Good to see you." He ran around to help Nadia out.

"How you doing?" Grady asked her as Callum eased her into the chair.

"Been better," she said, shooting a glare at Callum. "Had two near-death experiences on the way here."

Grady grinned good-naturedly. "I guess that means you made good time. How far apart are the contractions?"

Nadia opened her mouth, but Callum answered for her. "Just under three minutes. She's been in labor for about four hours now."

Grady nodded and wheeled her toward the doors. "We'll get you upstairs and see where you're at."

"Is there an anesthetist on shift today?" she asked, wincing as she put a hand on her belly.

"He's on his way."

"Good." Nadia flung out a hand toward him as another contraction hit.

Callum grabbed it, held on as he strode beside the chair on the way to the elevators. Shit, he knew this was natural, but he hated seeing her suffer—and she was in serious pain at this point.

Upstairs on the maternity ward, he and Grady got her into a private room, changed her into a gown and then put her in the bed so Grady could examine her. The contractions kept on coming hard and fast, relentless in their pace and intensity.

Callum quickly shot off a few more messages about the safehouse while Grady did a quick internal exam, then straightened. "Eight centimeters and almost fully effaced," he announced as he stripped off his latex glove.

"How much longer?" Callum asked, trying to hide his anxiety. At the rate things were going, he was afraid there wouldn't be time for an epidural.

"A while," Grady said. "Don't worry, the anesthetist will be here any minute to give you the good stuff." He set a hand on Nadia's shoulder, his calm demeanor a godsend. "I need to get a few things, but I'll be back in a couple minutes. Just keep up with your breathing, and try to relax between contractions." He left the room.

Nadia gasped and tensed, her face screwing up in pain as she threw out a hand for Callum's. He grabbed it, covered a wince and writhed inside while she battled through another long and powerful contraction. The sheer strength and desperation of her grip told him exactly how much she was hurting.

He didn't budge. Didn't flinch as he divided his attention between her face and the digital monitor tracking the strength and length of the contraction. She could break every single bone in his hand, grind them all into dust if that's what she needed to get through this, and he wouldn't make a sound. It was the least he could do for her.

When it was over, Nadia collapsed back against the pillow, breathing hard, her face flushed. "That was a bad one," she panted as he dabbed at her cheeks and forehead with a cool damp cloth Grady had given him. "But I'm okay. I can do this."

She was the one suffering and yet still trying to comfort him. "Don't talk. Just rest." He knew she could do this. But that didn't mean he wasn't dying inside watching her go through it.

Grady came back in a few moments after the next contraction had ended. "Look who I found."

A doctor who must be the anesthetist walked in behind him a second later.

"Oh, thank God," Nadia breathed, and Callum seconded that sentiment, the heavy tension in him easing.

"You're in good hands," Grady assured her as he stepped up to her bedside, gently rolling her onto her side. "Everything's going beautifully, and you're doing amazing."

Callum helped as much as he could, still holding her hand while messaging back and forth with Creed and Ryder with his free one. The instant he was done, he shoved his phone into his back pocket and turned his full attention back to his wife.

She looked up at him, and her expression softened slightly. "Don't worry," she said, giving his bruised hand a gentle squeeze. "I'm ready. I was born for this." Her face was stamped with pure determination.

He'd never loved her more than in that moment. His brave, incredible wife who was enduring so much pain to bring their baby into the world. But it was true. She *had* been born for this, the most naturally maternal woman he'd ever known. She was already an incredible mother to Ferhana.

He raised her hand to his lips to kiss her knuckles, glad she was facing him and unable to see the needle being prepared to go into her spine. "I know. This is going to be the luckiest baby in the world."

TWELVE

Max strode into Stanton's office at the back of the villa and closed the door behind him. His right-hand man looked up from his desk, where he was working on his laptop.

"Well? Have you heard anything yet?" It had been way too many damned hours since his asset had contacted him from Crimson Point, and there hadn't been a single word about the operation to recover Lara since. Stanton had been gathering intel all morning. He must have something by now. "Did he get her or not?"

"No. And it's...not good."

He set his jaw. "Why, what's happened?"

"He's in the hospital recovering from a gunshot wound."

Max frowned. "The police shot him?"

"Don't think so. Looks like it could have been Lara, but it sounds like she might be with a guy. Maybe he took the shot."

"What guy?" A lover? It was possible. And it made sense, could explain why she'd gone directly to Crimson Point of all places after finding out that he had "died." Maybe she'd been going to her lover.

"Not sure of his name yet. The address where Lara was living is owned by a rental company."

"So Dave's done." Useless. Another dead end, and now Lara would know she was a target. So would the Marshals.

Stanton nodded slowly. "As soon as Dave's stable, they'll discharge him and take him into custody."

"Goddamn it!" Max slammed the end of his fist down on the desk with enough force to rattle the framed prints on the walls. "Where is she now?"

"Still in Crimson Point."

But not for long. She was too smart for that, and if she wound up back in WITSEC it could take him years longer to find her. "Find out who she's with. Get me all the intel you can find, and do it *now*." He wasn't worried about Dave talking or giving up anything sensitive about him or the organization. Everyone who worked for him knew the punishment for turning rat. He made a point of making the consequences abundantly clear early on to each person he hired.

"I'm working on it."

"Well, work faster. God knows I fucking pay you enough." He spun to storm out of the office, but his phone vibrated in his back pocket. He pulled it out, bit back a curse when he saw the number on the display. His boss. The head of the entire organization, and the most powerful man he knew. The one man he feared. "Milos, hi."

"Max. I just thought I'd call to see if there's any update on Lara. Do you have her back yet?"

No, he fucking didn't, and Milos probably already knew it because he would have had his own people keeping tabs on everything. "Still working on it. Won't be long now that I know where she is," he said in a tone much lighter than he currently felt.

Milos's sigh was heavy with disappointment. "This…

endeavor has already taken far longer than we agreed on. I don't have to tell you what a disappointment this whole messy situation has been for us. You and I have been friends for a long time, Max, so I'm going to be straight with you."

Friends? They weren't friends. Men like them didn't have friends, only allies and enemies. "All right."

"I'm losing patience, and Andreas is tired of waiting for what was promised to him so many years ago."

Max turned and stalked from the room, his mood plummeting from bleak to black. It wasn't his fucking fault that his daughter had turned on him. He'd given her the best life, had hidden all the criminality from her. If she hadn't walked in on him that night, none of this would ever have happened. "As I said, it won't be long now. We know her location. I have people in the area—"

"What has David reported?"

Dammit, Milos *did* already know. "He was shot last night going after her."

"She shot him?"

"Maybe. I don't know yet." It seemed his daughter had learned certain skills to protect herself since he'd last seen her. Not that it would matter in the end.

"Did he need medical help?"

He ground his back teeth together. "Yes, he was taken to the hospital by ambulance."

"So then he'll be arrested. What are you going to do about that?"

"I'll handle it," Max said, his own patience stretching thin. He would have someone deal with Dave as soon as he was moved from the hospital. A routine cleanup measure.

"I hope so. I would hate for all this ugliness to come between us after all the years of loyal service you've given to me and my family."

A wave of anger punched through him at the thinly veiled threat, quickly followed by an Arctic blast of cold. Milos had never threatened him before. Max had always felt secure in his position.

He had spent the past thirty years working for Milos, busting his ass to win his trust. He had eliminated dozens of threats to both Milos and the organization at great personal risk, sometimes with his own hands when it was necessary. He had neutralized would-be competitors before they could pose a real threat to the organization.

And he'd done it at great cost, losing his own wife and daughter in the process, and serving a miserable fucking prison sentence because he'd refused to cooperate with the Feds against Milos.

But none of that mattered to the old man. If he didn't get Lara back soon and bring her under control, his relationship with Milos and Andreas was as good as dead. And so was he. Once he was shut out of the inner circle, he would be a pariah to everyone else within the organization.

Milos would put a kill order on him. While the old man or Andreas were alive, the organization would never stop hunting him. Even if Max gave up everything and tried to fall off the map, he would have to run for the rest of his life with only whatever cash he could carry with him.

He couldn't let that happen. Refused to. He'd worked too long and too hard to allow anything to jeopardize what he'd built, and he'd only just won his freedom back.

Two could play at this game. He had his own crew. A small, select group outside of the main organization that nobody else knew about and who were loyal to him alone. Enough to take out Milos and his men if it came down to it.

"Max? You listening?"

"I'll handle it," he bit out, and ended the call.

Fuming inside, he stormed through the back of the house, servants scattering in his wake, and burst out through the rear doors leading to the patio. He stood there for a long moment, pushing his anger down and letting his blood pressure settle before taking out a burner phone from his other back pocket and making a call.

"Yeah?" Randy answered, sounding annoyed.

There was a lot of that going on today. "Got an urgent job I need you on, so drop whatever else you're doing and get on a flight to Portland. From there you'll head out to a small town on the coast. Text me when you land, and I'll send you further instructions."

"What's the job?"

"Cleanup and recovery."

He was done waiting. He was getting Lara back at all costs. It was the only way to solidify his position within the organization and lock in his legacy—getting her married off to Andreas and pregnant so that her children would carry on Max's bloodline. His unborn grandchildren were his future. Lara was the means to the end to get them.

There was no way he was losing everything now that he was within sight of securing the position he'd always dreamed of. Part of an empire that he would one day pass on to the next generation that the union between his daughter and Andreas would eventually give him.

THIRTEEN

Bella handed Creed a cup of coffee she'd made him in the reception area and sank down beside him on the plush leather sofa in Callum's office where they were waiting.

"Thanks." He wrapped an arm around her shoulders and kissed the top of her head.

"Welcome." She swallowed a sip of the herbal tea she'd made for herself and leaned her head against his shoulder, savoring the peace and security he made her feel.

Being close to him helped ease the anxiety grinding in the pit of her stomach. Made the fear that she'd sealed both their fates by coming here fade into the background. Even if he hadn't told her he still loved her. Though she hoped that would come in time.

"I hope everything goes well with the birth," she said quietly. Callum had taken off in a giant hurry a few hours ago and they hadn't heard anything yet. As far as distractions went, she was grateful for this one. "Is this their first baby?"

"First biological baby. They adopted a little girl from Afghanistan a couple years ago."

"Aw, they did?" Now she liked Callum even more.

Creed made a low sound of confirmation. "Nadia was doing relief work with orphans in Kabul just before the US withdrawal, and after that, things went sideways. She was trapped there and was targeted by radicals. Callum and Donovan and Walker teamed up with Ivy to get her and the little girl out safely."

"Wow! Just when I thought I couldn't have a bigger girl crush on Ivy." She hadn't said a word about it this past weekend. And what a kind, determined woman Nadia must be to take on that type of risk to help vulnerable children in such a dangerous area. "I'll have to ask her about it next time I see her."

"If she tells you anything, you need to let me know. That woman has more secrets than Area Fifty-One."

"I believe it."

They both looked up at a knock on the door and Ryder opened it. "Hey. The sheriff's here to talk to you guys." He stepped aside to let him in.

"Morning," Sheriff Buchanan pulled an armchair over to sit close to them. "My people have just finished questioning the suspect. He refused to answer anything, but the Feds are taking over now and we have fingerprints and updated photos of him. I wanted to see if you recognized him." He handed his phone over to her.

The moment Bella saw the face on the screen, her blood iced over. "I know him."

"Who is he?" the sheriff asked.

She could feel both men staring at her, waiting for her response. "David. He's one of my fath—one of Max's most trusted guys."

Oh, this was bad. So, so bad. Shit! The organization definitely knew where she was.

"Do you know his surname?"

She shook her head, then stopped. "No, wait." It was something common. Max had referred to him by it instead of the first name. L something. Lee? Larson… "Lynch," she blurted. "David Lynch."

The sheriff took his phone back and started typing into it. "Any idea where he's from?"

"Not originally, but he was living in Miami when I knew him." God, and he'd made it to Creed's house. "Andreas must have sent him."

"Andreas?"

"The son of the founder. I was sort of betrothed to him. An archaic arranged marriage kind of thing."

"You think he's behind this?" Creed tightened his hold on her.

"Has to be. He's cold and cruel and controlling. He wants me as a trophy because his daddy promised me to him when we were both teenagers and his ego demands he collect." Rage burned hot in her veins. "He doesn't give a shit about me, only cares about the status I would bring him and that our children will keep the bloodlines pure amongst the top echelon of the organization. It's beyond disgusting."

"Jesus," Creed muttered.

"You think he sent David here?" the sheriff asked.

She nodded. "David must have come here to bring me back to Miami. With Max dead, only Andreas or his father would have ordered this."

Knowing they were still after her made her feel sick to her soul.

"Would he have acted alone? Or do you think there's someone else?"

"There's definitely someone else. They always have more than one person on a job for insurance purposes, even if the people involved don't know that. God, how did they find me so fast? Max is dead! Why can't they just leave me the hell *alone*?"

Creed wrapped both arms around her and hugged her tight, deflating the bubble of panic rising in her. "They're not going to touch you. I swear."

"We'll find out everything we can on Lynch," the sheriff said. "I just sent his name to my FBI contact. They'll check their databases and cross reference with his prints in case he's using an alias. And I'm sure they'll be in contact with you shortly anyhow. Ryder said you're planning on leaving town for a while."

"As soon as we get supplies," Creed said, and Bella was suddenly itching to leave *now*.

Oh, but poor little Nick… "I need to check if Ivy will look after my cat," she said, pulling out her phone to text her. He'd just started to get settled at Creed's place. Forcing a traumatized stray that had already endured a three-day trek out here into another road trip to a strange place was too much stress. She didn't want to put him through that unless she had no other choice.

Someone else knocked on the door, and Walker poked his head in. "Shae's here with your gear, and Decker's got the rental waiting out back."

"Thanks. I just texted Ivy to see if she'd look after my cat while we're gone." Hopefully not more than a week or so at most, but… Who knew? Everything felt too damned scary and uncertain again.

"She will. She's watching Ferhana right now while Callum and Nadia are at the hospital, but if she can't make it over today, Shae or I will drop by to feed him or whatever."

"Thank you," she said, suddenly feeling emotional. Nick was her baby, and he trusted her. Counted on her. Now he would be lonely and confused, might stop eating like he had when she'd first brought him home.

A wave of rage swept through her. God, she hated that the glimmer of safety she'd felt had been snatched away yet again. Just fucking hated everything about this, that her past wouldn't let her go and was now infecting the lives of everyone around her, especially Creed. "I gave him fresh water and food last night, and his litter box was clean. It's up in the guest room en suite," she finished, fighting to keep her voice steady.

Walker nodded and gave her a little smile. "We'll take care of him, don't worry. When do you want to head out?"

"Sooner the better," Creed answered. "Bella just IDed the suspect from last night. He's one of Max's guys."

Walker's face darkened. "Here." He held out the keys. "You guys are good to go."

Feeling like she was in a kind of daze, Bella was whisked down to the vehicle, wearing a hat to cover her hair and shade the upper part of her face. Minutes later, Creed was driving them through the rain up the hill toward the highway.

She squashed the urge to apologize. One, their current situation wasn't her fault, and she knew Creed would just tell her exactly that. Two, he'd made it clear he intended to weather all of this with her no matter what. She was so damn lucky that he'd let her back in and didn't think she'd have the strength to face this without him.

"It's all right. We're clear," he said on the coastal highway ten minutes later when she checked her mirror for the hundredth time, looking for any hint that someone might be following them.

Hope so, she thought to herself, and tried to relax. Creed was highly trained. He was observant, and he would do everything possible to ensure their safety.

They didn't talk much, and she was glad because there

wasn't much to say at the moment and banal conversation was beyond her at this point. Traffic thickened and slowed as they neared Portland. When they passed through it and turned northeast onto a smaller highway without incident, she began to breathe easier, the tension slowly melting from her spine.

"Feeling better now?" He brought her hand to his lips to kiss it.

"Much." She laid her head back on the headrest and let out a sigh, weariness pulling at her.

"Go ahead and sleep," he told her, correctly guessing her thoughts. "We're okay, promise."

She gave him a smile and paused to study his profile, her heart squeezing tight. Hopefully, the FBI would unravel everything and go after Andreas so they could finally lock him up.

That was the only thing that would truly end this nightmare.

∽

RANDY CHECKED the message one last time before leaving the airport in the rental car. The tone was unmistakable. The boss was pissed, and it was his bad luck that he'd drawn the short straw for this assignment.

The last guy sent after Lara was in the hospital with a bullet wound and facing a life behind bars. Well, not really. Dave had to know as well as Randy that he was as good as dead as soon as he left the hospital. But Randy's first priority was crystal clear.

Get the phone with the tracking app, find Lara, and bring her back no matter what.

The late-afternoon sky was a heavy-leaden gray as he crawled through rush hour traffic out of Portland and turned onto the highway heading for the coast. A few minutes later the clouds opened up with a heavy soaking rain the wipers could barely keep up with.

A little over two hours later, he took the exit to Crimson Point and headed straight to the address the boss had given him. The small bungalow Dave had rented under an alias.

The place was so old there were no security cameras or even an alarm system. Randy drove past it a couple times to ensure it wasn't under surveillance, then parked alongside it and went in through the back. When he didn't find anything in the kitchen or living area, he moved down the hall to the bedroom.

It was standard procedure to never take a phone with sensitive material on it to a job. And sure enough, he found a phone sitting on the bedside table. He carefully used a piece of clear tape to pull the thumbprint from the sensor, applied pressure over it with his own thumb, and the phone booted up.

The tracking app was right there on the home page. He accessed it, his heart beating faster. If this didn't work, he wasn't sure how the hell he was going to find Lara, and then he would be in as much shit as Dave—

The app showed a red dot moving slowly across the screen. He zoomed out, at first unsure what he was looking at. A map of Washington State and Oregon. The dot was moving toward Portland.

He studied it, thinking fast. It was no surprise that Lara had decided to leave the area. But she must not know about the tracker. Apparently the tracker was on her watch and practically invisible to the naked eye.

He texted Max to say he had located her and would follow, then got back in the rental and headed for Portland.

His mission was clear. He had to get her tonight and kill anyone with her so he could bring her back to her terrifying father before his name was added after Dave's to the long list of people Max de Vries had already made disappear forever.

FOURTEEN

Bella woke with a start sometime later when the vehicle made a tight left turn and found them driving around a switchback surrounded by a forest of evergreens. "Where are we?"

"Few miles from the house," Creed said. "Did you get any decent sleep?"

She'd been asleep for that long? "Yes, I feel much better."

And now that they were nearly at their destination, excitement began to stir inside her. No one except the CPS crew knew where they were. They were safe out here. Not only that, she and Creed would be alone at the house with all kinds of time to rebuild their relationship. That was the best silver lining she could have hoped for.

Her mouth was dry so she downed half a bottle of water then reached for his hand. A hot zing shot low through her belly at the sexy smile he gave her, tingles racing up her arm and throughout her body.

But she also felt a pang of regret. Because no matter how adamant Creed was about staying with her through all this, no matter that he'd shown how much he cared about her, she couldn't shake the guilt that he was in danger now too after being dragged into her mess.

"Here we are, our home away from home." He slowed in front of the steep driveway, which was surrounded by trees. From the bottom she could just make out the edge of the house above them.

He turned the vehicle and reversed up the driveway, parking at the top before glancing at her. "Okay?"

"Yes." More than okay. They were far safer out here than back in Crimson Point, and she was looking forward to spending a long stretch of uninterrupted time together. She just hoped the FBI stamped out this threat before it escalated more. "Thank you for being here."

On impulse, she leaned over to cup the back of his head and press a lingering kiss to his lips. Sparks flared to life deep in her belly, quickly becoming a torrent of heat when he slanted his mouth across hers and his tongue delved inside to stroke hers.

When he pulled back, his gorgeous gray eyes glowed with an unfulfilled hunger that made her belly flip. "Hold that thought. I'm gonna check everything out and be right back."

Anticipation built as she waited, her arousal level sharpening. Creed came back two minutes later, his posture and expression relaxed. "All good."

He ushered her straight into the house and insisted on unloading the vehicle by himself. When he was done, he locked the door behind him, got a fire going in the fireplace, and turned to face her with a look that had her whole body buzzing.

He started toward her, the heat in his eyes making her heart thud and her insides melt. And suddenly getting settled was the last thing on her mind. She wanted him naked and inside her.

He stopped in front of her, took her face in his hands. "It's just you and me now, Bell."

Bella pushed up on her toes to kiss him as she wound her arms around his neck, desperate to lose herself in the moment, in this man who owned her heart.

THE DESPERATION IN her kiss set off a dark tide of need he'd been holding back. But no more.

Creed grasped her hips and lifted her, turning to press her flat against the nearest wall, absorbing the quick, tight shudder of her body as he deepened the kiss. Desire shot fast and hot through his bloodstream, ramping the need even higher. Bella moaned and wrapped around him, the way her fingers dug into his back conveying her emotional state as clearly as if she'd told him aloud.

He knew what she needed from him. Could read it in the way she gripped him, the rigid tension in her muscles, and the force of her kiss. An intimate secret he'd learned about her early on in their relationship.

She needed him to take complete control so that she could let go. She liked to be overpowered. For him to overwhelm her. Given her background, it made total sense, because at its foundation this was all about trust.

He gave her what she wanted, keeping her pinned there as he slowed the kiss, soothing the frantic need he sensed in her. Telling her without words that he understood and would take care of her. Soon she was rubbing against him and mewling in her throat, and he was so hard he hurt.

The ugly incident at his place and their ensuing argument about her leaving was still there at the back of his mind, refusing to be silenced. He needed to be inside her. To claim her in the most basic, elemental way there was to drive home the point he'd made. They were in this together now, no matter what, and he would stay by her side through whatever came at them. He would never let her fight her battles alone again.

He slid his right hand under her sweater to cup her breast, rubbed his thumb across the taut nipple where it pressed against the thin material. Bella tore her mouth away and dropped her head back against the wall, arching. Demanding more as she reached down to peel the sweater up and over her head.

Creed made a low sound of approval and tugged the cup of the bra down to expose her tight pink nipple, then bent and took it into his mouth. Her soft cry, the way she rocked against his erection, had him ready to come out of his skin. Having her back in his life only drove his hunger higher.

He turned them, made it as far as the living room and laid her down on the wide, soft leather sofa in front of the fire. They stripped each other in a flurry of movement, then he came down on top of her and seized her wrists, anchoring them above her head. Bella wrapped her thighs around him and gazed up at him with sultry blue eyes so full of trust and hunger, he almost buried himself in her right then and there.

But he backed off, using his intimate knowledge of her body to stroke his fingers along her slick folds, his weight holding her down. He kept her wrists pinned with his other hand and rubbed her clit until she was whimpering and straining under him.

Thank God he had condoms this time. He released Bella's wrists and turned to grab one from his jeans on the floor. Before he could open it, Bella sat up and took it from him.

"Let me." She gripped the base of his cock with one hand, got to her knees and crawled forward to glide her tongue around the engorged head.

He let her play for a minute, until the throb became unbearable. Then he wound his hand in her hair and squeezed it with

GUARDING BELLA

his fist, adding downward pressure in a silent command. She answered by bowing her head and taking him into her mouth.

Creed sucked in a harsh breath and clamped his jaw shut as a tide of pleasure ripped through him. He gripped her hair tight while the heat and pressure of her mouth engulfed him, fighting the urge to thrust over and over until he exploded. No way. Not until he gave her what she needed, until she was clenching around him as she came on his cock. When he lost it, he wanted it to be deep inside her.

But the sight of her like this, naked and kneeling in front of him with his cock between her lips, was almost too much. He savored the sensation for another few moments, allowed her one final pull with that luscious mouth he'd been dreaming about for more than a year.

"Stop," he ground out before his brain shut down completely, then pulled out and flattened her against the buttery leather.

He caught her wrists in one hand again, brought them up high against the arm of the couch and held them there while he settled between her open thighs and eased the head of his cock into place against her opening.

I love you. Always will, until the day I die.

The words were right there, stuck in his throat. His heart pounded hard as they stared into each other's eyes, both of them breathing fast. But he couldn't speak, too focused on the incredible physical intensity they'd always had together. He wanted to drag this out more, make her desperate before he plunged into her heat.

He guided his length up and down her slickness, rubbed the flared head over her clit again and again, adding pressure and friction right where she needed it. Bella closed her eyes, a moan of surrender coming from her lips as her expression tightened with need. A need only he could satisfy.

The dark, possessive edge she brought out in him rushed to the surface. He wouldn't allow her to pull back from him. Not emotionally, and definitely not when they were together like this.

"I want to feel you clench around me when you come." He nudged the head of his cock inside her, steeling himself against the sudden flash of pleasure as her heat closed around him. Waited until her lashes fluttered and she gazed up at him with half-closed eyes before driving deep, demanding that she let herself go completely into his care.

With a choked sound, she cinched her legs harder around his waist, her heels digging into his ass. Pulling him closer even as she arched up, taking him to the hilt.

"Yeah, baby, just like that." Christ, the way she surrendered to him was the hottest, most addictive thing he'd ever experienced. He couldn't get enough. Didn't know how he'd survived so long without her.

Bella was warmth. She was fire, and the beating heart in his chest. His existence had been so damn empty and bleak without her.

Pressing the side of his face to hers, he paused to fight for breath. For the control that was rapidly slipping away from him, the feel of finally being inside her again flooding him with raw, primal triumph and a pleasure so keen it hurt.

He tightened his grip on her wrists, came up on his elbow and slid his free hand between them to find her clit. Applying steady pressure with his thumb, he eased his hips back and surged forward again, watching her face.

"Creed," she cried, eyes closing as she strained beneath him. Clearly getting off on the way he was holding her down.

He loved seeing her this way. Stripped bare in every way, open and vulnerable and needing him. "God, I can't get enough of you," he rasped out.

"Please," she begged breathlessly. "I need—"

He surged deep and took her the way he'd been longing to. The way she needed him to. Hard. A little bit rough, just enough to force her surrender and give her the friction necessary to send her over the edge.

Jaw tight, he drank in her reaction hungrily, cataloguing every shift in her expression, her cries of pleasure as he pushed her toward the edge, ready to soar over it with her. She tightened around him, her breathing rapid and shallow as she neared the peak, the telltale quiver running through her telling him she was right there.

Bending down, he fused his mouth to hers and rubbed his thumb across her clit, driving quick and hard with his hips. Bella convulsed beneath him with a muffled sob, legs clamped hard around him, her whole body bowing with the force of her orgasm.

He held on for a few more seconds before his own release slammed into him. With a guttural groan, he drove deep and stayed buried there as it ripped through him in wave after wave, blotting out his hearing and vision. There was nothing but sensation, the knowledge that he and Bella were finally one again.

Gradually his muscles relaxed. He opened his eyes, released his grip on Bella's wrists and leaned in for a long, slow kiss as she wound her arms around him, cradling him to her. The infinite tenderness she showed him made his heart turn over.

"We'll get through this, Bell," he said into the quiet, and kissed the tip of her nose. "No matter what happens, we'll get through it."

She stroked a hand through the back of his hair. "Yes."

He withdrew from her gently and turned onto his side, bringing her with him and holding her close. The house was quiet, the rain barely making a sound on the roof and windows.

He thought of everything she'd endured to get back to him. Everything they'd gone through to get to this moment.

It didn't matter what threats remained. Didn't matter that they were both targets now.

Whatever happened from here on out, he would be right there to face it with her.

FIFTEEN

"They're here," Stanton said.

Seated in the back of the luxury SUV, Max looked up from the phone with the tracking app on it to peer out the tinted window. A few moments later, the headlights of another vehicle turned through the gates and headed toward where he was parked next to the tarmac at a private airport near Seattle. "Good. Let's go."

He was impatient to get moving. The seven-hour flight from Miami had felt like an eternity and left him restless, but it had also given him enough time to assemble a small team to accompany him on this mission.

He didn't believe in micromanagement and normally let his people carry out jobs without him. As he was supposed to be dead, he wouldn't have risked traveling right now unless it was absolutely necessary, but he'd changed his mind and decided that this mission required his presence and was worth all the risk involved.

An icy, seething rage coiled inside him at the thought of seeing Lara again. A rage that had fueled him through his prison sentence. It was part of him now.

He got out, waited as the other vehicle slowed to a stop in front of him and shut off. Stanton stood beside him. His right-hand man was also a skilled pilot. Not only had he flown Max here in a private jet, he also flew rotary wing aircraft. That came in extremely handy at times like this.

Three men stepped out. Three of his best, consummate professionals handpicked for their loyalty, skill, and ruthlessness. All former military-turned-mercenary, and he paid them handsomely for their service. They would do whatever he wanted, whenever he wanted it done, no questions asked. And the cash payments were high enough to buy their loyalty and keep them from talking.

"What's her location now?" the driver of the second vehicle asked him.

"Same place as she was when we touched down." Lara hadn't moved from the house the entire time he'd been watching. "How long until we can be airborne?" he asked Stanton.

"Depends on whether you want to skip the safety check."

"Skip it." The clock was ticking. He wanted this done and over with *now*. He'd waited far too long to bring his errant daughter back.

"Okay. I'll have us up in five minutes." He strode past Max to where the Bell 407 was waiting on the helipad, its red and gold paint visible in the surrounding lights.

"Everyone else got what they need?" Max asked. Both the other men nodded, so he gestured to one, who shut the back of the SUV and turned with a rifle in his hands. "You wait here with Charlie and keep the area secure. You," he said to the third man, who was also holding a rifle. "Come on."

The rifle was probably overkill considering that Lara and her lover didn't know they were coming, but a show of overwhelming force would make things happen faster. Avoiding bloodshed would give law enforcement little to go on.

They crossed the short distance to the helicopter, its rotors now spinning slowly, and he climbed in the front next to Stanton. "We good?"

"Yep." He flipped some switches, looked at the instrument panel with all its gauges. "Almost there."

Max withdrew his pistol from the holster on his hip for the ride and strapped in as the rotors picked up speed, the vibrations making the aircraft shudder. He put on the noise-canceling headset, and the sound instantly receded.

He hit the mic button. "We take her unharmed," he reminded them. "And we take whoever's with her as well—unless he poses a problem.".

Lara would be far more cooperative if she was concerned about her lover's safety. Whoever he was, the man would prove useful, at least at first. Then it was just a matter of disposing of him earlier than planned and dumping his body in the woods for the predators.

Stanton made a few last-minute checks. "Here we go."

He lifted them off the helipad and eased them forward as they rose into the night sky. A gusty wind buffeted them around almost as soon as they left the ground, and it would only get worse as they flew into the mountains. Max stared grimly ahead at the darkened terrain passing below them, then glanced down at the tracker app, totally focused on the mission.

Lara was coming home tonight. And like her mother before her, she would have to be punished for her betrayal. He had to make an example of her, and he would start by using her lover against her.

This wasn't the way he'd wanted things to go, but even so, he was still looking forward to this reunion. What was about to happen was long overdue.

He was taking his daughter home where she belonged.

CREED OPENED his eyes in the semi-darkness. Bella was curled against him in the master suite bed. They had come upstairs hours ago. The house was quiet, but instantly he knew what had woken him.

Rotors, their rhythmic pulse growing louder as a helicopter approached.

He tensed slightly and lay still, listening intently. The helo flew past them and didn't circle around or come back, its sound fading into the background.

He relaxed. It could be search and rescue. Or a medevac. Maybe the military or a local sheriff's department hunting someone.

But it could also mean danger.

He eased away from Bella without waking her, rolled slowly to grab his phone and check for any alerts. There was nothing from either the exterior cameras on the house or the sensors set up at intervals around the perimeter of the property. When he looked at the feeds, everything appeared as it should, the yard dark and still, just the outline of the forest visible in the background.

The helo hadn't circled back, but he thought he could still hear it faintly, so he remained on alert for another few minutes. When it didn't grow louder, he set his phone down and turned to lie back and study Bella. She was on her side facing him, the moonlight diffused by the thin window shade, making her skin glow and casting deep shadows where her lashes lay against her cheeks.

She looked so damn peaceful. The power of everything he felt came rushing back all at once. He needed to tell her he still loved her. Wanted to make all this go away for her so that she would finally feel safe and get her life back. So that they could start their new life together without anything hanging over them.

Needing to touch her, he carefully draped an arm over the curve of her waist and closed his eyes.

What felt like seconds later, a quiet beep woke him. He bolted upright and lunged for his phone as Bella woke and shoved up next to him.

His insides congealed when he saw the alert on-screen. Something had triggered the perimeter sensors. On both the north and east sides of the property.

He couldn't afford to wait and see what the cameras picked up. He needed to get Bella the hell out of here.

"What's wrong?" Bella asked, fear in her voice.

"Get dressed. Hurry." As Bella scrambled from the bed, he hit the emergency beacon on his phone, instantly transmitting a distress signal to Ryder, Callum, and Walker back in Crimson Point, then grabbed his clothes. "The perimeter sensors picked up something. I heard a helo pass over a few minutes ago, and now there's movement on both sides of the house. We have to move."

"How long do we have?"

"A few minutes." At most. "I transmitted a message to CPS just in case."

He did up his jeans and grabbed his weapon from the nightstand. When he turned around Bella was hurriedly pulling her sweater over her head. "Where's your weapon?"

"In my suitcase," she answered, eyes wide, the fear in her face eating at him. "I left it by the front door."

"I put it here." He knelt and quickly retrieved it, checked to make sure it was loaded, and handed it to her. Then he glanced at the video feeds on his phone, thinking fast. The cameras hadn't picked up anything yet. They still might have a chance to get out of here.

There was nowhere for him to hide her in the house. They had to get downstairs, escape out the back and get to the vehicle before whoever was out there arrived. He didn't like it, but it was their only chance. They couldn't stay here.

"Come on." He grabbed her hand, led her to the bedroom doorway, pressed the keys to the SUV into her palm. "Stay behind me. And if I tell you to run, you go out the back, get in the vehicle, and drive like hell for town."

"No, I'm not leaving you."

They didn't have time for this.

"Yes, you will," he ordered as he led her to the top of the stairs, pausing for a moment to check the cameras again. Still no movement, but the back of his neck was tingling, anxiety crawling up his spine. "We're gonna have to be fast. Get your shoes on and go to the back door while I grab some gear." He had a go bag waiting downstairs. "Got it?"

"Only if you're coming with me."

He didn't answer, too focused on what he needed to do. They hurried down the stairs together. At the bottom he stopped for a second to check again, then ushered her forward to where her shoes sat inside the front entry. "Quick."

She hurried past him. He went the opposite way, going for the gear he'd set near the back door in case they needed to make a quick getaway.

He glanced at his phone. A shadow moved across the screen.

His heart lurched. He whipped around to shout a warning just as something rammed the front door in.

SIXTEEN

Bella screamed as the door burst inward six feet in front of her. She whirled, raised her weapon to fire as Creed shouted a warning to her.

She squeezed the trigger as a man flew through the door. He grunted but didn't go down. Before she could fire again, he'd wrenched the weapon from her grip and locked a forearm around her throat, hauling her back hard against him. She felt the hard shape of his Kevlar vest against her back.

Panic exploded inside her like a bomb. She twisted to attack, teeth bared, then went dead still when she saw Creed standing frozen on the other side of the room, his pistol leveled at them.

"Drop it," the man holding her warned, shoving the barrel of his gun against the side of her head.

Cold slid through her as she stared back at Creed. *Shoot him*, she mouthed silently. *Do it.* He was a deadly shot and well within range. He could make it, and he was her only chance.

The back door burst in with a crash. Creed spun to face the new threat.

But instead of firing, he slowly straightened and separated

his hands as he raised them. She couldn't understand why he was giving up, but then he looked over at her and the pained resignation on his face made her heart plummet.

A moment later another man walked in holding a rifle, and she understood why Creed had surrendered.

They were outgunned, and with her being held hostage, Creed had no hope of taking both men out without endangering her. She regretted not aiming for her assailant's head instead of his chest.

"Drop it or die." The newcomer stalked toward Creed, the muzzle of his rifle aimed at her. "Try anything, and she'll suffer for it."

Creed looked over at her again, jaw tensed, then reluctantly did as he was told, lowering his weapon to the floor. She bit back a cry of protest. The newcomer immediately grabbed Creed's hands, wrenched them behind his back and secured them with flex cuffs.

It tore her heart in two. If it had been only his life in danger, she knew Creed would have fought to the death. But he was surrendering now to protect her in the only way he could. Even if it meant sacrificing himself in the process.

She couldn't let that happen. Refused to let Andreas or his father do this. She planted her feet, drove an elbow into her captor's middle. "No!"

He barely flinched. "Shut up." He increased the pressure of his forearm, cutting off her air as he forced her around to face the door.

This couldn't be it. Couldn't be how their story ended.

She shifted her stance to try again—then froze in shock and growing horror as an all too familiar silhouette appeared in the doorway. Seconds later the man materialized out of the mist and stepped across the threshold.

Her father stopped just inside the entry to stare at her, his blue eyes glittering with a mix of fury and triumph that made all the blood drain from her face. "Hello, Lara."

She couldn't answer. Couldn't force a single sound past the sudden restriction in her throat or tear her eyes away, her heart trying to pound its way through her ribs.

How? How was he still alive?

One side of his mouth lifted in a smirk she wanted to claw off his face. "Surprise."

"Let us go," she rasped out, trying to keep her voice from shaking. She refused to give this monster the satisfaction of seeing her fear.

"I don't think so. Not after all the trouble I've gone through to bring you home."

His words made his intentions all too clear. He didn't want to kill her. He wanted to drag her back into the fold and force her to do his bidding. Fulfill her duties by marrying Andreas and seal whatever sick pact was made when she was still a kid.

"It was never my home. It was a prison," she spat, hating him with every fiber of her being. If she'd still had her pistol she would have shot him where he stood. "And you were dead to me from the day I left."

His expression turned as cold as his eyes, and he shook his head in disappointment before dismissing her and addressing his men. "Let's go."

She wrenched her head around to shoot a desperate glance at Creed a split second before a hood came down over her face, blotting out all light. It disoriented her. She tried to wrestle free of the man holding her, but he subdued her easily enough and bound her hands behind her, rendering her almost helpless.

He muscled her out the door without a word. She swore and kept resisting, stumbled several times, would have hit the ground if he hadn't finally tossed her over his shoulder and kept going. She bucked and fought every step, heard a commotion behind her, then an awful *thunk,* and something hit the ground hard.

"Creed!" she screamed, but there was no answer.

The man holding her carried her uphill for a ways, and then she heard the sound of a helicopter waiting somewhere up ahead. She was hurriedly bundled into it and squeezed between two people. Was Creed still with them? Was he okay?

She was more afraid for him than for herself. As evil as Max was, she doubted he would actually kill her. But without a doubt he would kill Creed.

She frantically tried to think of a way out of this, saw only one option and didn't want to think about it. Creed had alerted the CPS crew. Surely they would figure out she and Creed were in danger and organize a rescue. But if help didn't come and she was forced to do the unthinkable, she would give up her freedom and her future without hesitation to save Creed.

The helicopter took off. It jostled around as it flew them away from the place that was supposed to be her and Creed's safe haven. She sat rigidly between the two men, fear tearing through her the entire time, her terror growing when they began to slow and descend maybe half an hour later.

The helicopter touched down with a wobble, and the pilot turned off the engines. The rotors were still spinning fast when she was dragged out, a hand shoving her head down as she was force-marched across a paved surface in her bare feet. A metal door clanked open, then they were in a stairwell.

Her feet slipped on the treads. She was shoved forward roughly by the grip on her bound wrists. They kept going for ten or fifteen seconds.

She heard footsteps behind her, then another metal door clanged shut, the echo telling her they were in a large, empty space. The man dragging her finally stopped and ripped her hood off. She flinched and squinted against the sudden brightness, another wave of cold hitting her when she saw they were in a concrete room.

Two chains were hanging from a hook in the ceiling, ropes tied to the bottom links. And on a stainless steel table nearby she saw a collection of rods…and a knife.

She sucked in a breath, whirled to confront the man holding her. "You can't—"

Her protest died out as Creed was forced past her. They'd taken off his hood too. He was bleeding, the side of his head and face covered with it. He'd been pistol-whipped.

Her stomach knotted, fear sluicing over her in an icy wave.

The man holding him stalked over to the table and grabbed the knife.

"Don't—" Her captor jerked her hard to silence her. She watched helplessly as the other man sliced through Creed's flex cuffs and wrenched his arms back to cuff his wrists to the ends of the ropes hanging from the chains.

No. Please God, no.

She swallowed a scream. Wanted to throw up, horror paralyzing her.

Think, Bella! She had to figure out a way to stall them. The team back in Crimson Point would be doing everything they could to help them. Rescue would come. She had to make sure Creed stayed alive until then. No matter what it took.

Determination turned her terror into rage. "Let him go!" she snarled, straining against the man holding her, her gaze trained on the one holding the knife. With her arms bound behind her, her movement was limited. But she would go down fighting and do everything in her power to stop this.

"Bella, no!" Creed ordered sharply, his expression set. Prepared to endure whatever was inflicted on him to try and protect her by keeping their attention focused on him.

Like hell. She would rather die than leave him to suffer.

With a cry of fury she turned on her captor, slamming her head into his jaw and slicing out with a foot to kick his feet out from under him. They tumbled to the floor just as Creed drove his knee into the other man's gut, dropping him.

The impact with concrete sent a shock of pain through her hip and side, but she scrambled up and turned toward the man holding the knife, ready to tear him to shreds with her teeth if that's what it took.

Hard hands caught her from behind before she'd taken more than a single step, yanked her off her feet and wrenched her around. Stanton stared down at her, his face inches away from her, expression hard. "Stop before you make this worse for both of you."

"That's good advice."

She whipped her head around to see Max standing just inside the door.

"I'd listen and heed it if I were you." He cocked his head, watching her with a curious, almost proud expression that made her feel sick. "You made things interesting, I'll give you that."

The hair on her arms stood up. "How did you find me?"

He walked toward her. She stiffened, would have backed away, but she was already pressed against the man keeping her in place.

Max reached into a pocket. A soft *snick* sounded as a blade sprang free.

She cringed inside, braced for the burn of the knife, but all he did was slice the tie holding her wrists together. He grabbed her left arm, wrenching it up toward him. "This."

He used the knife to slice through the strap of her watch. Turned it over so the back of the face was visible, angled it so the light caught it.

Only then did she see the tiny dot on the back.

She jerked her gaze up to his, incredulous. "You sent that man at the diner?"

"First found you in St. Paul on a camera downtown. He followed you to Oregon and planted this." Max dropped it on the concrete. Raised his foot and slammed the heel of his boot onto the watch, shattering it.

Then his gaze swung to Creed, and the icy, murderous rage in his face sent a bolt of terror forking through her.

Grief and fear collided, making it hard to breathe. He would never allow Creed to live. And she didn't know how to save him except to buy him time. Enough time for help to arrive. "Let him go. You'll never get what you want this way. I'll kill myself before I let you take anything else from me." She meant every word and let him see that truth in her eyes.

Max's cold gaze snapped back to her, his face hardening with disgust. But her words had the intended effect. She had him off balance, his full attention on her rather than Creed. "You're just like your mother. She said the same thing, defiant to the end. Such a fucking waste."

The end...

Shock hit Bella like a truck as an old memory flashed to the surface. Something she'd buried so deep it had remained fuzzy and fragmented until now.

She had woken up in bed one night when she was no more than six or seven to find her mother frantically shoving things into a suitcase in a jumbled heap at the foot of her bed.

"What are you doing, Mama?" Something was very wrong. Something worse than her parents arguing and shouting at each other.

Her mother jumped and turned around, her face streaked with tears. "We have to go, Bella. Right now."

The fear on her mother's face frightened her. "Go where?"

"It's a secret. Come now." She held out a hand, put on a

brave smile that did nothing to reassure Lara. "Hurry, before he gets back."

"Who?" Someone bad. Someone her mother was afraid of. Father maybe? He was away again.

"Quickly!" The urgency in her mother's tone made Lara scramble out of bed and get dressed.

She rushed down the hall clinging to her mother's hand, hurrying through the quiet, empty house and outside. Her mother's car was waiting under the porte-cochere.

"Going somewhere, my dear?"

They both jumped at the voice behind them. Lara's father stepped out of the shadows hugging the side of the house.

"Don't touch me," her mother spat, edging backward with Lara in front of her like a shield. Her grip on Lara's hand hurt, but Lara was too afraid to say anything. "Don't you dare come near me or our daughter."

Her father didn't move. Never looked away from them. "Stanton."

Stanton appeared behind them and grabbed hold of Lara's mother before she could try to flee. Her mother stood rigidly as Lara's father stalked forward and wrenched Lara's hand from hers.

"You bastard," her mother spat in a shaky voice. "I hope you burn in hell!"

"Take her," he said to Stanton in a dispassionate voice that sent a chill up Lara's spine.

Her mother started to struggle, crying out and swearing as Stanton dragged her away around the opposite side of the house and out of sight.

"Mama!" Lara tried to pull away from her father.

He knelt and captured her chin in his hand. Twisted her face around to look at him.

"Where is Stanton taking her?" she asked worriedly.

Both men seemed so angry. It scared her.

"To talk to her." Then he smiled, though something in his eyes remained cold. "It's late, and you must be tired. I bought you a new teddy bear on my trip. Would you like to see him? We could read him a story once you're tucked back into bed."

She looked over her shoulder. Her mother was gone from view. "Where is Mama going?"

"Away."

His answer confused her. "On vacation?"

"Yes. Now let's go inside." He captured her hand and took her back into the house.

Bella sucked in a breath, returning to the present as it all crystallized in her mind. Oh, my God. That night was the last time she'd seen her mother. She'd later been told her mother died in a car accident in the Bahamas. Lies. "You killed her."

A twisted smile spread across his face. "No. She did it herself. Got hold of a pistol and called my bluff by blowing her brains out."

Fury and grief slammed into Bella, the callous summation of her mother's death making her stomach pitch. A scream of agony echoed in her head. "Why? Because she saw something she shouldn't that night?"

"Betrayal," he answered sharply. "Something you understand all too well. And now you'll pay the price for it." His gaze moved past her to Creed again.

Bella went rigid, a sickening wave of horror swamping her. He intended to punish her by torturing and killing Creed. In front of her.

"She hated you," she spat, venting her hatred on him even as she quaked on the inside.

Max looked back at her, his expression cold. Hard. But something flickered in his eyes.

Keep going. Keep talking. How long until help came? Every

second felt like an hour, and she didn't know how long she could keep distracting Max before he lost patience and vented his fury on Creed. "She hated you and everything you stood for." She remembered the way her mother's posture and face had changed whenever Max walked into the room. And now she knew why. Fear. Fear and secret loathing she'd been too afraid to show.

"Is that so?" Max said silkily.

She clenched her jaw to keep it from trembling. Refusing to give him the satisfaction of seeing how afraid she was. "She knew what you were all along."

He smirked. "Did she tell you that?"

"She didn't have to." She struggled in vain against the man holding her, beyond caring about pride or how pathetic she looked, her terror for Creed overriding everything else. If she didn't do something to stop it, they would kill him right here and now. Slowly. And once they started, she would be helpless to stop it. "She never loved you."

"You think I care, Lara?"

She hated that name. Rejected it on a visceral level. "I know you do. Your ego would never accept that she saw through and hated you."

Max didn't answer, that cold, hard stare drilling into her until her knees began to wobble.

Her heart pounded against her ribs as she held that stare for an endless, terrible moment. Then he looked away from her toward his men. Nodded once.

One of them stepped back and delivered a roundhouse kick to Creed's middle.

"*No!*" she cried as Creed doubled over, fighting for breath as he hung by his wrists from the chains, defenseless and unable to protect himself.

The other man slammed his boot into Creed's lower back. Creed jerked in his bonds, his face contorted in agony.

Scalding, bitter tears welled up, blurring her vision. She reached past them, dug deep for the rage, the determination to save Creed. "Did you enjoy prison, Max?"

His eyes snapped back to her. Narrowed.

She forced a laugh. "I went to bed every night knowing I'd put a monster behind bars. So whatever you do to us now, it was worth it."

He held up a hand. The other man stopped beating Creed.

Please. Please God, get us out of this. Help was coming. It had to be. But how long? How *long*?

Desperation gripped her. Begging would do nothing. Max would never allow Creed to live. But maybe she could stall this by bargaining. If it meant giving up her future with him and subjecting herself to a life of misery with Andreas and enduring whatever other terms her father wanted, then so be it. "Killing him won't make me comply. But if you keep him alive, I will."

Max's face might as well have been carved from stone as he stared back at her. "You made your choice," he said as he turned for the door. Dismissing her and what was about to happen in this room. "This is the price of betrayal."

∼

RYDER BURST through the back entrance into the building as soon as the door unlocked and took the stairs to the top floor rather than wait for the elevator. Time was of the essence, and there wasn't a moment to lose. He'd received an emergency signal from Creed almost twenty minutes ago and there had been no contact since.

Not good. Not good at all.

The others were already in the conference room when he

arrived. Callum, who had just become a father again hours ago, then Walker, Ivy, Decker, and Teagan. "What've we got so far?" He stripped off his jacket, leaning in to look over Ivy's shoulder as she worked on a laptop.

No one should have been able to find them up there. What the hell had happened?

"Signal came from the house." She showed him a map. "Still no response from either of them since."

"Local police are at the house," Callum said. "Both Bella and Creed are gone, and there are signs of forced entry to the front and back."

The place had perimeter sensors and security cameras. They should have been alerted in time to get out. "Do you think they're still alive?"

"No blood at the scene, so that's a positive," Walker answered. "If they'd wanted to kill them, they would've done it upon entry and left. So we're working on the assumption that they've both been taken somewhere."

"Can we track them?"

"I'm on it. But you're not gonna like it," Ivy said. "I had to hack into a government satellite to get the right feed."

They would deal with any repercussions later, although he wasn't worried. Ivy was a pro at covering her tracks. "So where are they?"

"There's been no traffic moving on the roads in the area, but I did pick up a single helo nearby minutes before Creed sent the signal. Here." She typed in more commands, and the satellite image zoomed in and focused on a small helicopter. "Civilian?"

"Yes, best we can tell. We lost sight of it for a few minutes, but we're trying to track the registration now," Callum said. "We think it took off from somewhere near Seattle given the direction of approach. Remaining fuel reserves mean it's going to land somewhere reasonably close by."

"Where is it now?" Ryder leaned in closer, his shoulder brushing Decker's as the other man stood staring intently at the screen.

"Flying almost due south," Ivy answered. "But in another few minutes they're going to be out of range unless I find another satellite to use."

Damn. "Are they going to another airstrip maybe?"

"Maybe." She opened another screen to work on something else.

Teagan was busy working on another laptop farther down the table. "I'm digging into all known addresses or suspected properties of Max de Vries and his boss."

"Wait." Callum's gaze was riveted to Ivy's screen. "It's slowing."

Ivy immediately hit full screen and zoomed in. Sure enough, the helicopter seemed to be slowing. It banked south over an area that seemed to be dotted with farms or ranches and did a circle.

"I don't see an airstrip anywhere nearby," Decker muttered, gripping the back of Ivy's chair as he stood behind her. "They've gotta have a vehicle waiting."

"It's descending," Ivy said.

They all watched as the aircraft slowed more and moved in for a landing…right beside a large building contained within what looked like a fenced compound.

"Where is this?" Ryder asked.

"Southeast Washington State." Ivy zoomed in and enhanced the focus. The picture was so good they could clearly see people stepping out of the front and rear doors. Two men holding the bound hands of two hooded prisoners.

"Ah, shit." Ryder dialed his FBI contact. "Get me an exact location, quick."

"There's a property listed under a company name that might be it," Teagan said. "Ivy, can you verify? Here's the address."

Ivy plugged it into the satellite feed. "Yep, it's a match."

Ryder waited for the call to connect, his heart beating fast. Then a third man stepped out of the aircraft and walked at a leisurely pace behind the others. "Can you enhance the image so we can see his face?" he said to Ivy.

"Trying." She typed more commands.

"Palmero," the man Ryder had called answered.

"Darren, it's Ryder Locke. We've got a situation—"

"Oh, holy shit," Ivy breathed.

The others all leaned in closer, staring at the screen.

"Hang on," Ryder said to Palmero, moving in next to Callum. The image on screen was clear, the night-vision capability allowing them to see the man's face. The angle wasn't great, but holy shit was right, because… "Max de Vries doesn't happen to have an identical twin, does he?" he asked Palmero.

"What? No, why?"

"Then we've got a really serious damned problem." He quickly explained what had happened, then got put on hold while Palmero sounded the alarm on his end.

"Bella's probably safe," Ivy said as she studied the screen, saying what he'd been thinking. "But Creed's on borrowed time. They're going to kill him. It's only a matter of when."

Ryder nodded, hating it but knowing she was right. "We have to get them out."

"I'll go with you," Decker said.

"Me too," echoed Walker.

Ivy looked up at him. "Call Matt—"

"Yeah," Walker said, already dialing someone on his own phone.

"Who?" Ryder asked.

"Matt DeLuca, married to my sister Briar," Ivy answered.

"He commands one of the FBI's HRTs. I just talked to Briar yesterday, and she said the team's on a training exercise in Idaho, so they're close."

"Okay, good." He felt the first spark of hope since he'd received the initial alert from Creed. "Grab what you need, and we'll head out," he said to Walker and Decker, then hurried for the door.

What Ivy said was dead on. Creed was on borrowed time, and even if the FBI authorized deploying the HRT, it would still be hours before the team could mobilize and get down to the target.

And Ryder's gut said Creed didn't have that long.

SEVENTEEN

Creed bit back another groan and struggled to shift his position to relieve the unrelenting ache in his shoulders and the strain in his legs. It was dark and cold as a morgue in here, every shiver sending more pain through his tired, battered body.

There was no give in the ropes at all. The angle they had his arms wrenched at behind him had long since made everything numb from the shoulders down. Everything else *hurt*.

They had strung his arms up just high enough that he had to balance his weight on his tiptoes or risk tearing his shoulder joints apart. Every time his legs gave out he had to bite back a scream as his shoulders threatened to dislocate from holding up his body weight.

But he was still alive.

He had no idea how long he'd been in here, or how much time had passed since he'd alerted the CPS crew. Had to be at least an hour. They would have alerted the Feds immediately, and a tactical response would be in the works. He figured it would be at least six to eight hours to get a team here. And he also knew he would probably be dead by then.

Blood dripped down his face from the wound in his scalp where they'd pistol-whipped him, sealing his swollen eye shut. A shudder rolled through him. He bit back a guttural moan as the vibration of muscle and bone made every single nerve ending scream in protest.

They'd left him alone for hours in between beatings after using fists, boots, and a rod on his back and ribs. He didn't know exactly how long it had been since they'd first strung him up in here, and it made no sense. Why bother doing this? If they wanted him dead, why not just kill him and get it over with?

It was almost like they were waiting for something.

Or someone.

He lifted his head at the sound of footsteps outside the door, dread rolling through him in an overpowering wave. His exhausted leg muscles quivered as he braced his weight on both sets of toes, stomach clenching tight as he dug down deep for the strength to endure whatever they were about to do to him this time.

Every time, he wondered if it was the last. Wondered if they were going to beat him to death or slit his throat the way Bella had described her father doing to one of his own. So why hadn't they? What were they playing at?

The door opened and the lights switched on in a blinding rush. He turned his head away, closing his good eye until it had partly adjusted to the light coming through the lid, then opened it slightly to squint at whatever horror was coming his way.

Bella appeared at the threshold. Someone gave her a rough shove forward. She stumbled into the room, fell to her hands and knees before she caught herself.

His heart constricted. *Bella*.

He wanted to scream her name. To order her to turn around and run. Get the hell out of here so she wouldn't have to see what they did to him.

But then she looked up at him, and the naked agony on her face nearly broke him. She shoved to her feet, both hands flying to her mouth to cover a tortured sound of distress.

He knew how bad he must look. Hated that she had to see him like this, that he couldn't protect her from any of this.

He licked his dry lips. "Bella," he croaked out, trying to warn her off while trying to think of a way to delay his tormentors.

There were only two reasons they would have allowed her back in here. Either to force her to agree to whatever other terms her father had demanded. Or, she'd already done that and all that was left was to kill him in front of her as punishment.

His guts twisted, fear coiling deep. God, he should have told her he loved her when he'd had the chance. Had been a fucking coward to hold it back from her when she'd poured her heart out to him and told him everything she'd been through.

Bella bolted toward him, crying openly as she grabbed hold of his bound wrists behind him and frantically started trying to undo the rope to free him. "Let him go," she screamed at whoever had come in with her, her distress and fear hurting far worse than anything he'd endured so far. "You're already getting what you want!"

"No." His throat and mouth were bone dry, his pulse thudding in his ears.

The way she was talking, it sounded like she'd made a deal with them for his freedom. Or tried to. What had she promised them?

"You fucking cowards, beating him when he's tied up and helpless. If you kill him, I swear to God I'll kill you, even if I have to wait the rest of my life to make it happen. You'll never be safe." She gave another tug on the ropes but nothing budged.

He winced, sucked in a breath and regretted it as a sharp blade seared through his ribs.

She took his face in her hands, her beautiful blue eyes filled with tears that rolled down her face. "Oh, my God. Creed, no. No, no, no." She pressed her cheek to his, wrapped her arms around him. Holding him as best she was able, trying to take his weight off his shoulders. "I'm so sorry. So sorry, I—"

"Step back, Lara," a hard voice said behind her. Max.

She shook her head and kept holding him, still crying. Great, gulping sobs that shook her whole frame. "You fucking animals! How could you do this? He hasn't done anything to you."

"But you have. Step back *now*."

One of the men standing next to Max stalked forward. Creed tensed and gritted his teeth, preparing to fight as best he could, struggling to keep his balance on his toes, the muscles and ligaments in his shoulders pulling ominously. But Bella whipped around to confront him, her arm still solidly around his waist to help hold him upright.

The man stopped in front of them. Half-smirked before landing a punch right in the sorest spot on Creed's ribs. He let out a throttled growl, eyes squeezed shut against the white-hot pain splintering through his side. And he was suddenly afraid that the moment would come when he would welcome death rather than endure the full extent of the torture they had planned for him.

"Enough!" Bella tried to place herself between them in a futile effort to shield him.

The man simply shoved her aside, wound up and delivered a blow to Creed's other side.

Creed inhaled sharply against the sharp jolt of pain, fought to hold back the scream trying to climb its way out of his throat as his footing slipped. He scrambled upright, her pleas and attempts at comfort barely registering in his brain. Trying to take it without scarring Bella more or giving them the satisfaction of seeing him break.

He would rather die than give them that. And he would protect her with his last breath. *Hold on. Just hold on a little longer.* And then a little longer after that. Help was coming. He had to somehow stay alive until it got here.

"Don't do it, Bell," he rasped out, shaking from the cold and pain. Desperately searching for the strength to endure whatever they did to him. "Whatever they want, don't give it to them. Please. Not for me."

They both knew she couldn't save him. Just as he knew he'd failed her by not keeping her safe.

Unless a miracle happened and a rescue happened in time, Max would kill him as soon as whatever he was waiting for happened. He had to withstand this for as long as he could. Had to at least spare Bella the trauma of seeing him break.

Bella shook her head at him, her expression tortured.

It was so damn hard to talk. To think. But there was one more thing he had to tell her. "I love you. Always have, always will. Until…day I die." And hopefully beyond.

"That's today," Max said with smug satisfaction. "As soon as Andreas arrives."

STILL TRYING TO hold Creed upright as he dangled from the cruel ropes holding him hostage, Bella shoved the lackey back with the heel of her hand on his chest and turned her head to confront her father.

Andreas was on his way, or might already be here. And he was going to kill Creed.

Hatred suffused her. Deeper and more volatile than anything she had felt before, venom putting steel in her spine.

Max had brought her back in here to drive the point of the

knife deeper into her heart. To make her witness Creed's suffering and death. Underscore her helplessness and show that she had no power to stop this.

The hair on her nape stood on end, rage pumping hot and fast through her veins. "I'll kill you. I'll kill you for this, I swear to God, if it's the last thing I do on this earth."

For Creed. For her mother. For her*self*.

Max stood watching them dispassionately near Stanton and his other lackeys just inside the door. She wanted to attack him. Claw his eyes out with her fingers. Tear him apart with her bare hands.

She lunged at him. Barely made it a step before Stanton intervened, grabbing her and stopping her cold. "Fucking cowards, taking your orders from a soulless monster who would turn on you just as fast if it served his purpose. All for money and power." Disgust coated every word even as she again thought of the CPS crew. *Where are you guys? Hurry!*

She drew in a deep breath, battling to shove the fury back down into a hard, scalding ball in the pit of her stomach. *Think, Bella. You have to calm down and think.*

It was useless. She'd run out of distractions. Max had refused to negotiate with her. She knew that, and attempting it again would not only be laughable, the show of weakness might make him more furious. But Stanton… If she could get him alone, maybe she could make him feel guilty enough to delay Creed's death a little longer.

Maybe. She had to try.

"Well?" Her father lifted an eyebrow. "Say your goodbye to him, Lara. Your fiancé is almost here."

"Fuck you."

Max turned and walked out without another word.

She stood there shaking, sick to her soul. This was her darkest nightmare come to life. It killed her to see Creed hurting this way, to know what was going to happen to him. All because of her.

Stanton walked up and gripped her upper arms. "Let him go," he said quietly.

"Never." Not in this lifetime.

"Lara. Let him go now," he warned.

She glared up at him, refusing to back down. "My name's not Lara."

He looked away quickly, guilt filling his expression.

A tiny thread of hope twisted inside her. She seized on the guilt. Would use it. Twist it, force the weak bastard to step up and do the right thing for once. Stanton held a lot of sway with Max and was the only one who could keep Creed alive now.

With a sigh he finally wrenched her free of Creed, who stumbled slightly, scrambled to find his balance, half of his bruised, swollen face covered in blood. Her heart shattered at the sight of him. At not being able to stop this. This was her fault. All of it.

"Come on," Stanton said in that same low voice. That same fucking tone that said he thought he was being reasonable. "You'll only make it worse for him the harder you fight." He dragged her away, toward the door.

She threw a glance at Creed over her shoulder. Stifled a sob at the sight of him dangling there, bleeding and broken, his one open eye fixed on her. Couldn't bear to think that this was the last time she would ever see him.

Then his mouth moved. She had to strain to hear his voice, barely audible.

"I love you. Forever."

The lights went out before she could utter a single word, plunging them into sudden darkness.

Stanton grabbed her harder this time, his fingers digging into her flesh as he continued to drag her away. Moments later, she was forced outside and marched across the courtyard to the main building. Max was nowhere to be seen.

Stanton pushed her into a small, dark closet, and gave her a pitying look, hesitating with his hand on the outside of the door. "I wish it didn't have to be this way."

"Fuck your pity." It was empty and meaningless. "And fuck you for standing by and letting this happen."

His eyelids flinched slightly.

"You get him out." Her voice was rough with emotion. Stanton had always had a soft spot for her. He was her only hope now, her only possible ally. "You didn't help me or my mother before. Never lifted a finger to help or protect either of us back then. But you know what Max has cost me, and you know what he means to take from me still."

He looked away, jaw tight. A clear indication that he didn't like Max's plans for her at all. She could use that too.

She pushed. "He's not going to give me a choice, and neither will Andreas. But killing Creed is wrong, and you know it. I've never asked you for anything, but I'm asking now. Please find a way to keep him alive. That's all I want."

He met her gaze again for a long moment, his eyes tormented. She could feel the guilt writhing inside him. Had to capitalize on it. "I can't stop this, it's too late. Andreas is—"

"Not here. Yet." Was he? She didn't know. "There's still time." Her heart pounded her ribs with bruising force. "You couldn't save my mother, and you can't save me. But you can at least do this. It's the right thing. You know it is."

His jaw worked, more turbulent emotion churning in his eyes. "I can't promise you anything." Then he shut the door, engulfing her in darkness.

Bella laid her forehead against the cool metal and closed her eyes with a shuddering sigh, fighting a wave of weakness and a growing sense of claustrophobia. Had she gotten through to

Stanton? Convinced him to release Creed before Andreas arrived?

Hold on. You have to hold on and not give up. Someone would come for them. Was hopefully already on the way. She couldn't give in to the hysteria and defeat pulling at her. Had to snap out of this, stay sharp. But it was so damned hard to think clearly right now.

All she could think about was Creed. All she could see in her mind's eye was him strung up like that, beaten and bloody. A sick helplessness filled her at the knowledge that he would hurt a lot more before they inevitably killed him.

Her eyes flew open when she heard footsteps approaching. The door was wrenched open. She blinked against the light, a wave of revulsion hitting her when she came face to face with Andreas, Max standing a short distance behind him.

No.

Her stomach dropped. He couldn't be here already. It couldn't be too late. Stanton wasn't with them. Was he with Creed? Was he trying to release him in the other room right now?

Andreas's good looks made her situation that much worse, the twisted, violent monster concealed beneath a polished, attractive veneer and charm he used to manipulate everyone around him. Tall and fit with short black hair, his bone structure was the stuff of a renaissance sculptor's dream. But his physical beauty was only skin deep. She'd always seen him for the predator he was.

He reminded her of a tiger. Coiled power waiting to spring on his prey. His deep brown eyes swept over her like she was a prized steak he couldn't wait to devour.

She wanted to drive her fist into his handsome face. Break his nose and keep on hitting him until she pulverized every bone and he was as ugly on the outside as what lay within. But it wouldn't stop any of this. Wouldn't save Creed. They had her trapped and backed into a corner she had no prayer of escaping, and they all knew it.

I'll never give in to you, she vowed, looking him dead in the eye. Refusing to cower or show fear or any hint of her suffering. *Even if it looks like it on the surface, I will never give you what you want.*

He didn't know her. Didn't *want* to know her, only wanted to see the fantasy he'd created in his mind years ago when the betrothal was first drawn up. The object he could use and control to satisfy his ego and whims, and get heirs from.

That would be his downfall. Because she would rather die than be the prize trophy wife selected to breed with him to give him children.

I will never stop trying to escape. And if I get the chance, I will kill you for what you've done.

She would appear to give in now to protect Creed and buy him time to escape. If Stanton got him out, then she would go through the motions to survive and find a way out again one day.

She'd done it before and could do it again. Whatever it took to get back to Creed. They would both go into WITSEC, start over together. And their love would be that much stronger because of all they'd endured.

She bit the words of hatred back, reached down deep for the last ounce of calm she possessed, and raised her chin. Andreas was too arrogant to recognize the defiance in her eyes and understand her mettle. But he would find out soon enough. They all would.

"Good to see you again, Lara." He eyed her in that proprietary, predatory way that made her skin crawl. "You've lost a lot of weight." He tutted. "I liked you better curvy. We'll have to delay the actual wedding until we fatten you up a bit."

"Kill him and you lose me too."

Andreas laughed in surprise. "You think you can make demands?"

"Yes. And he knows why." She forced herself to look at Max, standing a dozen or so feet behind Andreas. He might not care about her or her life, but he very much cared about her welfare in one sense.

He wanted children from her. Children fathered by Andreas, to carry on his bloodline and eventually take over his place within the organization. But neither man would get them if she killed herself. And she needed them to see that she was prepared to take that step if they killed Creed. "I would never allow a child of mine to go through what I did. *Never*."

As for Max... Looking at him was like having a dagger plunged into her heart, then twisting sharp and cruel.

Before the night she'd seen him kill that man long ago, he'd been different to her. She'd experienced kindness from him in those early years, and it hadn't been fake. It had been real. And back then, way back when she'd been a small child, she'd had no doubt of his love for her.

Was there any of it left now? There didn't seem to be any shred of humanity left in him at all. She had to be imagining the flash of emotion that moved through his eyes. It was tiny and fleeting, extinguished as quickly as it had formed.

She was desperate enough now to plead and beg with either him or Andreas, but that was pointless. Her only card was still delay. Delay, delay, delay. Keep them all here for as long as possible and pray that either a rescue would happen in time, or Stanton would grow both a conscience and a spine and was doing something to help Creed right now.

Looking amused, Andreas folded his arms and regarded her. "And if I don't?"

"If you don't…" She shrugged. "I'll make the same choice my mother did."

There was no way in hell she was going to live in a world without Creed while knowing his death was because of her fucked-up sperm donor and the criminal, poisonous organization that had consumed him.

Andreas scoffed. "You wouldn't have the guts."

"I promise you, I would. It might take some time before I get the chance to act on it, but you can't watch me every minute of every day and night, forever. Eventually you'll drop your guard, and when you do, I'll seize my shot. End my suffering and deprive you both of your prize brood mare and the fucked-up dynasty you want."

Max didn't answer. He stood unmoving, jaw bunched as he studied her like he'd never seen her before. As if she was a puzzling opponent he was trying to analyze. Trying to decide whether she would actually follow through with the threat.

"I'll do it," she told him. "You know I will."

He stared at her for another long moment. Then, without a word he turned his back on her and walked away.

His abrupt reaction filled her with unease. What did his dismissal mean? Did he believe her or not? Had she bought Creed enough time to get out of here?

Her heart thudded in her ears, the bubble of hope in her chest painful. She didn't know what Max's sudden departure meant. But she knew he didn't want her to die and cost him the blood dynasty he wanted so badly. That much she was certain of. And a rescue was coming. Hopefully sooner than later.

Please, God, just let Stanton get him out of here.

Cruel fingers seized her jaw and twisted her face up. Andreas's eyes blazed down at her with a blend of arousal and contempt that shriveled her insides. She could read his intent so clearly. Could tell that her defiance had aroused him.

Because he wanted to break her and could hardly wait to get her behind closed doors wherever they planned on taking her.

"You're mine, Lara. Always have been and always will be. Better get used to it." He let his gaze travel over her again, visually stripping her until she felt naked. "Get ready, because you're going to be my wife as soon as we touch down in the Bahamas."

A shiver of dread rolled through her at the thought of having to endure his cruelty over and over again until she found a way to escape. She narrowed her eyes. "Not happening. You disgust me."

A slow smirk spread across his face. "But I gotta admit, I like seeing this fire in you. It'll make breaking you a lot more enjoyable. There's just one last thing I need to take care of before we go."

She gritted her teeth and held his gaze, refusing to back down. She fantasized about kneeing him in the balls, watching him crumple to the ground and whimper like a child. But she couldn't push him too far right now. Couldn't afford to slip until she had proof that Creed was safe.

Something in her face must have shown her defiance, because he released her with a snarl and proceeded to rip off his jacket. "Time for me to finally meet your lover, sweetheart. He's waiting for us."

A bolt of fear threatened to choke her, all her desperate hopes suddenly crumbling to dust in front of her. Was it true? Had Stanton not helped Creed?

It took everything she had not to show fear and hold his gaze as she responded. "Kill him, and I'll kill myself the first chance I get. It's that simple. There's nothing more you can take from me."

A cruel sneer twisted his face. "We'll just see about that."

He spun on his heel and stalked off, signaling to one of his men to follow. "Bring her."

She tried to fight off the man who grabbed her, but he was too strong. She was dragged along in his wake, a rising tide of panic about to drown her.

She'd done all she could to save Creed. There was nothing more to say, no other tactic she could use to buy more time. If by some miracle Creed wasn't there when they entered that room, she would appease Andreas and Max long enough to ensure Creed's escape and lull them into a false sense of security. And if he was still there…

Max and Andreas would find out just how determined she was to decide her own fate.

EIGHTEEN

Walker had been on the phone constantly during the two-hour flight up here into southeast Washington State. Now that they were finally on scene, he was screening his calls more carefully.

But when he saw Ivy's number, he answered immediately. "Hey, anything new I need to know about?"

She and Teagan were still back at CPS with Walker, monitoring things on their end and forwarding bits of intel as they happened. "No, I was just checking in with you. Feds there yet?"

"Yeah, got here about forty minutes ago."

"Did you see Matt?"

"No, just spoke to him over the phone. CIRG and HRT are both set up in a mobile command center a few hundred yards from us. I gave him everything we have so far. They've got a drone up now trying to get more intel."

"The satellite I was using is in a blind spot right now. We're waiting for it to come back online."

"Were you able to verify the number of heat signatures on site before you lost the feed?"

"Unfortunately not. Did you get a visual at all when you flew in?"

He stepped farther away from where Ryder and Decker were talking next to the vehicle they'd parked in a small clearing between the trees. "No. Helo landed a couple miles from here. We had to drive in to this point."

It was two in the morning. Creed and Bella had been captured a few hours ago already, and at the very least Creed was in a life-or-death situation. Walker and the others were here to lend whatever assistance they could to get him out and bring him home safely. "I don't know anything more yet, and won't until this is over."

Unless Ivy could get the satellite feed back again.

"I'm sorry."

"Not your fault." She'd taken a huge personal risk in hacking the satellite for them in the first place. "Without you, we wouldn't even have known where they were taken or been able to call in the Feds. At least now Creed and Bella have a chance."

A small one, he admitted, but still a chance.

"I hope Matt's boys get in there in time and get them both out."

"Yeah, I do too." No one here had to be told that time was running out. Hostage situations were always intense, but the backstory on this one made the likelihood of both Creed and Bella surviving slim.

"You all right?" Ivy asked him.

"I'm good. Just wish I could do more to help."

"I know how you operate, and I love your cool, calm, and collected thing. But you're also my husband, and I know this is hard on you. Especially since you're sidelined."

"I'm fine," he repeated, glad to hear her voice. He, Ryder and Decker had arrived on scene a couple hours ago after the flight from Crimson Point and had been forced to sit back and wait ever since. Meanwhile they had zero intel on Creed or Bella.

"Too bad the Feds brought their own hostage negotiator. You'd be better."

He smiled a little at her faith in him. "Can't be impartial, since I'm not arm's length from this one."

"Doesn't matter. You'd still be better."

His expertise was in interrogation and intelligence, not negotiating. "How's Callum? He say anything about Nadia?" Walker had only talked to him about Bella and Creed and logistics, no time for anything personal.

"He's fine. She's tired, but the baby's nursed a couple times already. That PJ Grady is apparently on shift on the L&D ward, so they're in good hands."

Ryder called Walker's name from near the SUV. "I gotta go. Keep me posted if you get eyes on again."

"I will. Love you."

His heart squeezed. It had taken her so long to be able to say the words. Not a surprise given her solitary and violent past. "Love you too." He ended the call and strode quickly over to where Ryder and Decker were waiting. "Any update?"

"HRT's getting ready to go in," Ryder said, just as two big SUVs rolled out of the makeshift parking lot up ahead in the middle of a campground half a mile from the target.

That was fast. Though not fast enough in Creed or Bella's opinion had they known, Walker was sure. Given the density of the surrounding forest, the team would have to cover the final hundred yards or so to the target on foot.

He glanced at his watch. It would be the better part of ten minutes before they arrived at the drop-off point, and then a while longer before they were set up at whatever entry point they'd chosen. Likely somewhere along the fence line, close to the building where the hostages were being held.

After that, it was just a matter of waiting for the signal to commence the op. DeLuca had final say and would give the command from inside the command post. "Ivy's still trying to get us eyes on."

"All right." Ryder expelled a breath, set his hands on his hips and stared after the departing vehicles, their red taillights glowing in the darkness. "Man, I hate sitting here on the outside of this when it's two of our own in there."

"Tell me about it," Decker muttered darkly.

Walker hated it too. And Decker was strung tighter than anyone, had barely said a word the entire trip up here, and kept pacing around the clearing.

Walker got it. Creed was Decker's friend and teammate. This was more personal for him than anyone else here.

"We've been reviewing the footage Ivy sent earlier," Decker said, showing him some images on his phone. "There wasn't much movement visible in the compound in the past few hours. The last we saw, three people moved from this building to this one just over twenty minutes ago. Hopefully the Feds' drone is getting some good images."

"Ivy's working on it on her end."

"Hope she can get us something soon," Ryder said. "I wanna see what's happening."

Walker's phone rang. Ivy. "Hey," he answered, tension humming through him.

"I've got a feed. It's not awesome, and I can't stop to share the images right now so I'll talk you through it."

He put her on speaker. "Go."

"There's been more movement. Two people leaving the larger building and entering the smaller one. I'm working on accessing infrared capability on the satellite and will get you a live feed as soon as I can."

Walker held out his phone for them to see. "Perfect."

Decker and Ryder moved to flank him to get a better look.

Moments later, a video feed appeared on screen. Grainy and indistinct at first until the focus sharpened. "Can you see?" Ivy asked.

The camera moved around a bit, then zeroed in on the helicopter sitting on the ground inside the compound's perimeter fence. "Yeah. Shit, the rotors are turning."

"Looks like de Vries is getting ready to do a runner," Ryder muttered darkly.

Walker clenched his jaw, his instincts demanding that he *do* something. He knew DeLuca and his people would be seeing all this too and reacting accordingly, but shit, Walker felt useless standing there.

His heart rate picked up, all his muscles tensing.

He took a breath, consciously relaxed his body. The HRT was the FBI's most elite unit, most of them with backgrounds in tier-one SOF units. Every single guy on the team was a pro, and as good an operator as they came. And right now, they were Creed and Bella's only hope of making it out of this alive.

He, Walker, and Decker waited tensely, all of them riveted to the live feed. They could clearly see the heat signatures moving around the fenced compound. And a solitary one in another building. Unmoving.

"Think that's Creed?" Decker asked.

"Must be." Walker's heart sank.

That he was isolated and unmoving weren't good signs.

"So where's Bella?" Ryder said. "You think de Vries would…"

"He won't kill her," Walker murmured.

Not a chance after all the risk and effort he'd put into

finding her. But he would kill Creed. Might have already, and they all knew it.

A line of heat signatures appeared in the lower left of the screen. The HRT formed up and ready. "There they are." *Go get 'em, boys.*

They watched the team move into a stack along the western fence line, close to the building where Walker thought Creed was being held.

He watched in silence, counting down the seconds. The rotors turning on the helo worried him. Because if de Vries was about to leave, it meant he'd finished his business here.

Everything was riding on the coming assault. If it failed, there was zero chance of getting Creed out alive.

∾

COMMANDER MATT DELUCA stood in the mobile command unit watching the split-screen monitor in front of him, giving him simultaneous views of the drone feed and the team leader's helmet cam. "Good visual of the target building. Can confirm one suspected hostage inside. Over."

"We're in position," Tuck said in his low Alabama drawl.

"Roger. Stand by." He could see the boys all stacked up next to the entry point they'd chosen, a section of chain-link fence next to the small building where a single heat signature registered on the drone's camera.

They were ninety-nine percent certain it was Creed Morgan. And given that he hadn't moved the entire time DeLuca had been watching the feed, there was a high likelihood that he was already dead—or dying.

The second hostage was currently being confined in a tiny room in the other building, but was moving around slightly. Almost certainly Bella.

DeLuca shifted his focus to his team. The boys were ready to rock, waiting for the command to begin the assault.

Tuck's helmet cam showed Bauer standing second in line holding the tactical shield, his huge frame almost obscuring Evers at the front of the stack. The remaining four members brought up the middle and rear of the formation.

More activity appeared on screen. Someone running toward the helo. He keyed his mic. "Be advised, someone is approaching the helo. Single suspect." He waited a moment. "Suspect has entered the helo." Had to be the pilot. As far as they knew, de Vries didn't know how to fly. "The rotors are starting to turn."

"Copy that. Any visual on tango alpha?"

De Vries. "Negative." But their window of opportunity was closing fast, because this meant he was planning on leaving shortly. They had to take de Vries down before he boarded that aircraft, but the hostages were first priority. "I don't see anyone else outside the buildings yet. Can you confirm?"

"Confirm."

As soon as Tuck answered, the drone picked up two new heat signatures exiting the small room where hostage B was located.

"Be advised, two suspects just exited the larger building on the south side. They're heading toward the smaller building, not the aircraft. Should be visible for you in three, two, one."

"I see them," Tuck answered.

DeLuca stayed focused on the drone feed. "They're about to enter the building where hostage A is being held."

The good news was, it meant they still had time to get de Vries. The bad news was they were going after Morgan—if he was still alive.

If they were going to save him, they had to act *now*.

"Stand by." He stared at the monitor. Waited for the two

men to enter the building where they wouldn't be able to see the team coming for them. Neither of them had any clue that Blue Team was less than fifty yards away and about to go tactical on their asses.

He quickly checked both feeds one last time, then made the call. "Execute."

NINETEEN

Creed carefully shifted his weight from his right foot to his left, balancing on his toes. His exhausted leg muscles quivered with the effort, made worse by the deep, penetrating cold.

At first the effort of balancing his weight had been manageable, shifting from one foot to the other to rest one leg at a time. But now his legs were so tired he had to switch feet every few minutes.

At this point he didn't know how much longer he could keep it up before his muscles quit altogether. If that happened it would mean dislocating both his shoulders, because no way in hell could they sustain the strain of holding up his body weight at this awkward angle. He had to have been in here a few hours by now. A rescue attempt would take a few hours more at least.

The latch on the door turned. His stomach dropped.

He was out of time.

He lifted his head as it opened, clenched his jaw to keep it from chattering. He'd be damned if he would let them mistake his shivers for fear.

A tall, fit man around thirty or so walked in with one of the others from before. Clean cut, dark hair, wearing tailored pants and a dress shirt. He paused inside to study Creed, and though they'd never laid eyes on each other before, there was no mistaking the hatred in the other man's gaze.

"So, you're him," the asshole said, his tone laced with disgust. "The one who thought he could save Lara from her destiny."

Andreas. Had to be. Creed hated him with an intensity that stole his breath and filled his ears with a high-pitched ringing.

Andreas stalked forward. "You know who I am?"

Creed didn't answer, mentally gearing up for what was coming. Because there was no doubt as to why Andreas was here.

He was going to die in the next few minutes. The look on this asshole's face guaranteed it.

A flash of fear shot through him, and then an agonizing spasm of grief. This was it. Bella had only just come back to him. They had started to rebuild what they'd had, and now…

He'd held out this long hoping and praying the CPS crew might somehow have been able to track or locate them. They would have alerted law enforcement as soon as they hadn't been able to establish contact with him or Bella. The FBI would be involved by now.

But none of that mattered at this point. The moment Andreas had entered this room, it was obvious that any help would come too late to save him.

He just hoped rescue came in time to save Bella. He couldn't bear to think of her being enslaved and controlled by these animals for the rest of her life.

"I'm the one who's going to have Lara," Andreas continued, a malicious gleam in his eyes. "Because I own her. She's *mine*."

Creed almost lunged for him. Barely caught himself before he struck out with his legs, deciding that dislocating both shoulders was worth it just for the chance to plant his foot in the bastard's face.

Andreas slid a hand into his pocket and pulled out a switchblade. He hit the button to deploy the blade and held it upright so Creed could see it, the light catching on the wickedly sharp edge.

Creed drew in a painful breath, braced himself for what was coming. Fuck. This was gonna hurt bad. And it wasn't how he'd hoped to go out.

But Andreas stayed several feet away, watching him, his enjoyment of Creed's torment evident in the half-smirk. Then he sobered. "You dared touch what was mine," he said in a low, taut voice that vibrated with barely suppressed rage. "You dared to defile the woman who was always going to be my wife. Now you'll pay. And with every slice of this blade, I want you to think about what I'm going to do to her when I get her under me."

Creed's whole body tightened, a roar of fury building deep in his chest. He choked it back and hung there, poised to fight with every bit of strength he had left. His body was like a cable pulled to its breaking point. Stretched until it was about to snap as he awaited the first hot swipe of the blade across his flesh.

"Bring her," Andres snapped to the man standing behind him.

He went instantly cold all over as the man hurried to the door. *Oh, Christ, no.*

He didn't want Bella to watch him die. And never like this, sliced and stabbed while he struggled on the end of this rope like a pig being slaughtered.

For a fleeting moment, he almost goaded Andreas. Contemplated trying to push him into a towering rage so he would end him here and now before Bella arrived.

But survival instinct was a funny thing.

Even now, trussed up and unable to fight back with death staring him in the face, he wanted to live. Wanted it so bad it was all he could focus on. Bella was still alive. He couldn't give up. He would fight until the end, in the hope that somehow they could both still survive this. Somehow.

"She's gonna learn the hard way what happens when she turns on us." Andreas shifted his grip on the knife. Holding the blade outward in his fist, telling Creed he knew what he was doing. And how to inflict maximum damage with the weapon. "By watching what I do to you."

Creed glared back at him, refusing to look away, his jaw so tight his molars were about to crack.

They waited in a taut, deadly silence as Bella was brought in. She tried to wrench free of the man holding her, gave him a disgusted scowl before looking at Creed. Pain filled her face, then she turned a lethal glare on Andreas. "If you kill him, I will bide my time until I can do the same to you, you son of a bitch."

"I thought you said you'd kill yourself," Andreas said, but then his amused smirk vanished. "You were mine as of sixteen years ago, and nothing's changed."

"Try me," she fired back, and Christ she was magnificent. Even held captive and facing unimaginable horror with her future and his life on the line, she refused to be cowed, the molten fury in her eyes threatening to incinerate Andreas where he stood.

The fucking idiot had no idea who he was dealing with. He thought he could force Bella into becoming some meek, submissive slave willing to give into his every demand?

Andreas's expression darkened. He faced Creed once again. Took a menacing step forward and lowered the blade, angling it pointedly at Creed's groin, his intention all too clear.

Creed bit back a snarl and shifted his weight onto both sets of toes, preparing for the fight of his life.

"*Stop!*" Bella commanded, trying to wrest free of her captor.

Andreas ignored her. "I'm gonna cut your balls and dick off and shove them down your fucking throat, so you choke on them while I gut you," he snarled, fury burning in his eyes as he took another menacing step forward.

Creed gauged the distance between them, coiled and ready to attack. *Yeah, come closer, motherfucker.* Just another step, and he would be within range…

Andreas suddenly bared his teeth and lunged forward with the blade. Bella's scream shattered the air as Creed drew one foot back and rammed his knee into the bastard's face with all the strength he could muster.

The top of his knee connected with the bottom of Andreas's chin with a loud *thunk*. Andreas's head snapped back. He stumbled, lost his balance, and toppled over, falling on his ass as he cradled his jaw. The blade clattered to the concrete.

Creed's heart lurched as he fought to catch his balance. Barely steadied himself before the bastard scrambled to his knees, looking dazed. Then his gaze locked on Creed, and a look of pure rage contorted his face.

He bent to snatch up the fallen knife and shoved to his feet. He lunged at Creed again, his enraged bellow echoing off the walls.

This was it. Do or die.

Bracing for the pain, Creed distributed his weight on the tips of both boots, gritted his teeth and levered upward to drive both feet at the fucker's chest.

He caught him dead center, sent him flying backward, arms pin-wheeling and his breath leaving in an audible whoosh.

But the move came at a great cost. Creed's momentary

triumph was cut off by his own scream of agony as his shoulders were jerked in their sockets. Something tore with a hot pop.

He frantically tried to regain his footing on the floor. Through the haze of pain blurring his vision, he saw Andreas rising to come at him again, and knew this was the end. He had maybe one more kick in him, and it wouldn't be as good as the first.

Finding his balance once more, he looked at Bella. Wanting her to be the last thing he saw on this earth. She was screaming his name, fighting like hell to break free of the man holding her.

She was everything. The love of his life. His guiding star and his reason for living.

"Sorry, Bell," he rasped out. "I love you. I'll never stop loving y—"

The lights went out, plunging the entire room into complete darkness.

Creed stilled for an instant, his heart careening in his chest as everything seemed to freeze for a split second. Before he could even begin to guess what was happening, the door burst open.

Three deafening explosions rent the air one after the other, the brilliant flashes of light momentarily searing his retinas.

Even through the confusion, he understood what was happening.

Flashbangs. The cavalry was here.

"Bella, get down!" he roared, just before another voice rang out from near the door.

"FBI! Drop your weapons and get down on the ground!" A team of men barreled into the room, a backlit line of silhouettes with rifles up.

"Down, down!" one of them yelled as the team split into two and veered in opposite directions. One toward where Bella and her captor had been standing. The other toward him and Andreas.

Creed frantically tried to make out what was happening through the smoke and darkness, the only illumination the thin stream of moonlight coming through the open door. He lost sight of Bella and the man restraining her. Thought he saw Andreas trying to scramble to the side of the room in his peripheral vision.

The asshole was quickly swarmed, then someone was standing in front of Creed. Whoever he was, he was huge, his massive silhouette almost blotting out the light as he towered over him. "You Creed Morgan?" he asked, grasping the ropes holding Creed's arms behind him.

"Yeah," he managed, the dual shock of pain and relief making him lightheaded.

"I'm getting you outta here." The man sliced through the ropes with a few quick cuts of a blade.

Creed bit back a howl of pain as his injured arms flopped down behind him. He would have crumpled to the ground, but the big guy caught him, quickly cut through the bindings on Creed's wrists to free his hands, and then bent to lever him around his shoulder.

"Bella," Creed croaked, struggling to move his arms. The pain made his stomach roll as the guy carried him toward the door. He could hear rotors turning somewhere nearby.

FBI? Or de Vries trying to get away?

"She's okay, we got her." His rescuer hurried him out into the cold night air.

Creed grimaced, managed to brace his forearm weakly on the guy's shoulder and lifted his head to look around. Andreas and the other men were facedown on the ground nearby with their hands secured behind them, two men standing over them with pistols drawn.

He didn't see Bella.

"FBI! Stop and get on the ground!" someone yelled.

The man carrying him stopped instantly, rolled Creed to the ground and knelt over him in a protective stance, rifle raised. Creed swung his head around in time to see someone racing toward the distant helicopter.

De Vries, trying to make his escape.

MAX BROKE FROM cover and sprinted for the helicopter as if his life depended on it. Because it did.

The motherfucking FBI was here? They had already taken Andreas and the others down. How the fuck had that happened without any warning?

He didn't have time to think about that now. Didn't even have time to find Lara and take her with him. He needed to cut his losses and get his ass onboard that chopper, get the hell out of here before they caught him.

Lara was a lost cause. His sole priority now was to save himself.

His thighs burned as his legs pumped up and down, his breath sawing in and out of his lungs as he tore across the open space. Stanton had the engine powered up, increased the speed of the rotors when he saw him coming. The chopper was only a hundred feet away or so. All he had to do was get inside, and they would be—

"FBI! Stop and get on the ground!"

A bolt of terror streaked up his spine, the rush of adrenaline giving him an added burst of speed.

"Stop, or we'll open fire!"

No fucking way.

He was so goddamned close to escaping again. He wouldn't let them take him, not after all he'd suffered to win his freedom

GUARDING BELLA

back. And there was no fucking way he was going back to prison.

Panicked, he drew his pistol and whirled to fire at whoever was behind him.

The crack of rifle shots ripped through the air at the same moment the bullets slammed into his chest.

Hot, burning agony suffused him. Stealing his breath.

The impact knocked him over, sent him crashing to his knees. He stared in shock at the bleeding holes in his chest. He hadn't worn a vest. Hadn't seen a reason to.

"Down!"

He stared at the darkened outlines of the men closing in on him. Bared his teeth as blood rushed into his mouth, dripped down his chin. "Fuck you," he wheezed, dragging his weakened arm up to aim the pistol at them.

Fuck all *of you.*

Another round punched into him dead center.

He toppled backward. Arched and bucked as he choked on his own blood.

His lungs were shattered, the pain so hideous his vision sheeted to white. His open mouth gasped for air and found none. His legs kicked, a terrifying weakness invading. Spreading throughout his body. Turning his limbs to lead.

The kicking slowed. His eyes bulged. The haze cleared momentarily. Long enough for him to see the men racing up to kneel next to him.

He could hear them talking. Above that, he could hear the noise of the helicopter's engine throttling up. Stanton was about to lift off and abandon him here to die.

His gaze slid right. Found Lara crouched off to the side in the shadows with an FBI agent protecting her.

For a moment he swore their gazes locked. Then her hand

came up. He clearly saw the outline of her extended middle finger.

His own daughter had betrayed him for a second time. Now she'd cost him his life.

His eyes rolled back to stare up at the sky. He saw the stars glittering in the inky blackness above him as his vision began to dim.

He drew his last breath gazing up at a heaven he would never reach.

TWENTY

Creed tensed as the shots cracked through the air. Watched de Vries topple backward and the agents converged on him. Then, maybe fifty yards behind them, the helicopter started to move.

The agents with de Vries fired at the cockpit window. The rounds punched through it and the sound of the engine changed instantly. The pilot must have collapsed onto the controls because the helo suddenly veered hard left and tipped in Creed's direction.

"Oh, shit, look out!"

The guy with him picked him up and ran like hell behind the corner of the closest building for cover. From his view draped across the agent's shoulder, Creed watched in stunned awe as the tip of a rotor caught the ground.

The sudden shift in momentum flipped the whole thing over onto its roof. The engine continued to run at full power, tearing the spinning fuselage apart.

The mortally wounded helo went airborne for a second before colliding with the perimeter fence with a bone-rattling impact that shook the ground. Within a heartbeat it went up in a deafening explosion that knocked the air from Creed's lungs, the flash of heat whipping across his exposed face and arms even at this distance.

"You good?" the guy carrying him asked.

"Yeah," he managed. De Vries and the pilot were both dead. "Where's Bella?" he demanded. He needed to see her. Needed to be sure she was okay. Was dying to hold her in his arms—even if it was just with the right one.

"With one of our guys. She's safe."

Oh, thank God. He groaned in relief, closed his eyes, and let his head drop. Struggled to process everything through the pain throbbing in his shoulders and ribs.

The agent carried him to a spot near a gap that had been cut into the chain-link fence and carefully set him down with his back against it. "Doc," he called, waving someone over.

Another agent hurried over and crouched beside Creed, setting down a medical kit. "Where's the pain the worst?"

Honestly? Everywhere. "Shoulders. Ribs." It was a tie.

"Okay. I'm Schroder, by the way. Team medic."

Creed nodded and kept looking around for Bella. He trusted that she was safe, but he had to see her with his own eyes—

"Creed!"

His head snapped left. Bella was racing toward him across the open space between the two main buildings. His whole chest tightened. His brave, sweet baby.

She ran straight at him. He tried to raise his arms, ready to catch her. Winced at the searing jolt that shot through his left shoulder.

"Yeah, maybe wait on moving the left one for a bit." Schroder moved aside for them as Bella pounded up and dropped to her knees beside him.

She threw her arms around his neck and buried her face there, holding on tight. Creed managed to get his right arm around her, suppressing a howl as every ligament and tendon screamed in protest. But holding her again was worth any amount of pain.

"Bell," he whispered hoarsely, squeezing his eyes shut against the burn of tears. She was real and warm and solid. More precious to him than anything, even his own life. "I'm okay."

She shook her head, her tears wetting his neck. "No, you're not."

No, he wasn't. But he would be. As long as she was okay, as long as they were together, then his injuries didn't matter. "Did they hurt you?"

She shook her head again, her small frame wracked as she choked back a sob. "Max is dead."

"I know." He didn't say he was sorry, because he wasn't. He hoped the evil bastard was already burning in the hell he so richly deserved. So he pressed his cheek to Bella's hair and just held on to her. "The pilot too. They've arrested everyone else here, including Andreas, and his fucking evil father will be taken down too. So it's all over. They'll never hurt you again."

She expelled a shuddering breath. "No," she agreed, and clung harder. "I'm so sorry."

"No," he said firmly. "None of this is your fault. *None* of it. The Feds didn't even know Max was still alive until tonight. There was nothing you could've done differently to prevent this."

Schroder came back over and crouched down beside them. "Mind if I take a quick look at you, Bella, just to make sure you're okay?"

"I'm fine," she answered, holding Creed tighter.

"Let me make sure of that."

"He's the team medic," Creed told her, kissing the top of her head. "Let him check you over."

"Former PJ," Schroder said.

"There you go," Creed said. "He's a pro." He wondered if Schroder knew any of the Air National Guard PJs back in Crimson Point, but now wasn't the time to ask. "Here, sit up a bit," he said to Bella, easing her away gently and masking another wince.

A few minutes ago, dislocating both shoulders had been the least of his worries, but now he was starting to worry that he might have long-term or even permanent damage.

"Are his arms broken?" Bella asked Schroder as he began doing an assessment on her, checking her eyes and head first.

"Not a hundred percent certain, but I'd say from my initial exam that it's unlikely, though his ribs might be cracked. Won't know until he gets X-rays taken at the hospital. Right now his biggest issue is that his left shoulder's dislocated."

Fucking A. "Thought so." And it sure as hell felt like it. "Any chance you can reduce it?" Waiting until later risked all sorts of complications he would rather not deal with.

"Yep. Won't be any fun for you, but I'm down if you are—as long as you're sure you don't want to wait for X-rays."

"Nah, I'm good to go." God knew how long it would be until X-rays could be taken. His left hand was already almost completely numb. Not a good sign. The nerves and maybe the blood supply were being pinched. "Rather do it now and stave off any permanent damage if I can help it."

"I got you." Schroder finished checking Bella over, eased back on his haunches and gave her a reassuring smile. "You're fine, gold star for you. You up to helping me with his shoulder?"

She quickly wiped at her face, her shoulders hitching with a residual sob. "Sure."

Creed allowed her and Schroder to lay him down on his

back. The big guy from before came over and pulled off his ski mask. "What've we got goin' on here?"

"Anterior glenohumeral dislocation," Schroder said. "Gonna reduce it with the old external rotation technique."

"Oh, yeah, that's the best," the big guy said, kneeling beside Creed and looking at his teammate. "You need a hand?"

"Sure. Plant one of your paws on the middle of his chest and hold him down. This is Bauer, by the way."

"Hey," Bauer said to them, and set a big hand in the middle of Creed's chest.

"Hi." Creed felt a twinge of misgiving as Schroder sat down facing him and stuck the sole of his boot in Creed's armpit while taking hold of his left hand. "Okay, I'm gonna apply traction and turn your arm outward. Try not to fight me. It'll go easier if you don't tense up."

Okay, he was starting to break out in a cold sweat now. "Just—"

"Deep breath in, and hold it a sec." Schroder firmed his grip on Creed's wrist.

Creed sucked in a big gulp of air. Held it. Bella was here. She was okay, and their nightmare was over. He could handle the pain. This was nothing compared to what they'd already been through.

"Nice. Now let it out, nice and slow."

He closed his eyes, tried to relax and focused on Bella. She was holding his head, her gentle fingers stroking his temples. He exhaled.

Schroder applied force to Creed's armpit with his boot and pulled on his wrist, upping the traction more and more, subtly turning Creed's arm as he did.

Fuck! Creed gritted his teeth as his muscles started to grab again, was just about to yell for Schroder to stop when suddenly, he felt a *clunk* in the shoulder joint and the pain stopped.

"There we go." Schroder released his wrist, removed his boot from Creed's armpit and knelt to palpate the joint. "Humeral head's back in the socket. You feel anything in your hand yet?"

"Pins and needles," he said weakly, feeling dizzy. But his arm bone was back where it should be.

"Awesome. You can let him go now," he said to Bauer, and the mini anvil on his chest lifted away. "Let's sit you up and get this in a splint, and then we'll get you guys to the command post."

"What's their status, Doc?" Another agent Creed hadn't seen until now walked over. He had a Southern accent.

"They're good to go. Air ambulance on the way?"

"I'll check with the boss." He strode away through the gap in the fence.

Schroder and Bauer sat Creed up. He felt woozy as hell, a little nauseated. Bella hovered over him anxiously, while Schroder wrapped his arm up in a sling and they lifted him to his feet. The agents escorted them through the fence to where a cluster of vehicles waited near the tree line.

Spotlights had been set up around the area. Andreas and the other surviving prisoners were all kneeling in a circle off to the side, wearing hoods and hands secured behind them. Three FBI agents in windbreakers stood guard over them.

The HRT members took him and Bella toward the largest vehicle that had to be a mobile command post of some sort, where a man stood talking to some of the team. He was dressed in cargo pants and a dark T-shirt and wore a Chargers ball cap. He nodded at them. "Creed, Bella, good to see you both. I'm Commander Matt DeLuca."

"Good to see you too," Bella said. "Thank you so much."

"It's what we do. Just glad we could get down here in time." He checked his watch. "An air ambulance is en route to transport you to a hospital in Spokane, but there are a few things we need from you before it arrives."

"Whatever you need," Creed said, his right arm wrapped as securely around Bella as he could manage. His left arm felt way better now. The shoulder joint was sore and throbbing, but nothing like before. Actually, his ribs were bothering him the most now.

"Right this way," DeLuca gestured to the trailer behind him, then nodded at his men. "Good job, boys."

"Thanks, boss."

Creed led Bella past him and inside the trailer. "Almost over, baby," he murmured to her, anxious to get through the rest of this so they could finally draw a line through the entire nightmare and start to put it behind them. And they *would* get past this.

As long as they had each other, they could get through anything.

TWENTY-ONE

Walker waited just outside the secure perimeter with Ryder and Decker, resisting the urge to pace. They'd all heard the gunshots. No one involved realized he and the others had all watched the op live via satellite feed while it was happening, and then they'd heard the helo crash and seen the fireball erupt into the sky beyond the screen of trees blocking their view.

Only thing was, they didn't know who was dead or alive.

The pilot was obviously dead, whoever he was. Best Walker could tell, the guy who'd run toward it was also dead, but they didn't know who it was. Ivy was scrambling on her end trying to get a clear enough picture of the victims' faces to run them through the FBI database she'd just hacked into. Three others had been arrested, but again Walker had no clue who any of them were.

Man, he hoped de Vries was one of the dead guys, for Bella and Creed's sake. No, for the world's sake.

His phone buzzed with a text from DeLuca. *We have Creed and Bella safe in the command trailer.*

He expelled a relieved breath, grinning like an idiot as he

relayed the message to Ryder and Decker, standing nearby. "They're both safe. They're with the HRT commander right now."

"Yeah, baby!" Ryder shouted and high-fived Decker, who looked like a completely different person. an ear-to-ear smile transforming his hard face.

Excellent news, he typed back. *Thank you for the update.*

Of course. Agents are interviewing them now. I'll let you know when you can see them.

Appreciate it. He grinned at Decker and Ryder. "I'll tell the others." He texted the team back at CPS, then sent a quick message to Ivy thanking her for her help and put his phone back in his pocket. "What a hell of a night."

"No shit. Any word on de Vries?" Decker asked.

"Nope. But we'll find out soon enough."

It was more like an hour later when they finally got the okay to come and see Creed and Bella. Creed's left arm was wrapped up in a sling, and he looked like he'd taken a beating. Otherwise, he appeared okay as he grinned and accepted careful hugs from them.

Decker was last. He surprised everyone by grabbing hold of Creed and holding on.

Creed chuckled. "Hey, man. Ease up a little, will ya? My ribs are killing me."

"Sorry." Decker instantly released him and stepped back, running a critical eye over him. "You good?"

"Yeah." He smiled at Bella, reached out his good arm with a slight wince and grasped her hand. "Real good now. Thought for sure it was gonna be lights out for me there."

The unmistakable sound of an approaching helo penetrated the quiet. They all looked up, and through the spotty cloud cover above the towering evergreens, the outline of the helicopter appeared. An air ambulance.

"There's your ride outta here," Walker said.

"One question first," Decker said. "Is de Vries…" He shot a guilty look at Bella and left the sentence unfinished.

"He's dead," she said flatly. "They shot him as he was trying to escape. Him and the pilot. I'm guessing you guys saw the explosion." Her tone made it clear how much she hated the both of them and wasn't the least bit sad they were gone.

"Good, they both deserved what they got," Decker said. Then quickly added, "What I mean is—"

"No, it *is* good," Bella agreed. "Best news I've had in a long damn time, and I hope there really is a hell, because if there is, both of them will be burning down there right now. As for the others…" She looked over her shoulder in the direction of the compound, the hatred on her face unmistakable. "At least they'll all be locked up for the rest of their lives."

"Damned right, they will," Walker said, then went silent as the helo grew louder during its final approach. It circled the area once before landing in a clearing on the north side of the fence line. "Y'all ready to get outta here?"

"Fuck, yes," Creed said, looking exhausted.

"I'll walk you guys over." Decker stayed close to Creed as if he was afraid his buddy might topple over without him.

"We'll meet you guys at the hospital in Spokane," Ryder called out.

Creed raised his right hand slightly, gave them a thumbs up and kept going, flanked by Decker and Bella.

"I honestly didn't think he'd make it," Ryder said to Walker when the others were out of earshot.

"Yeah," he answered. "I thought maybe five, ten percent chance tops. Never been so happy to be wrong."

"Same. Damned glad they're both okay."

He nodded. "They beat the odds." He'd seen enough hostage rescue missions go down to know that they rarely ended with such positive results. Creed and Bella had been damned lucky.

His phone buzzed with another message. This one with a response from Ivy. *Thank God for that!!!*

They're being flown to a local hospital, he typed back. *Go home and get some sleep.*

Okay. Love you.

Love you too. See you soon, he answered.

He and Ryder waited there while the helicopter took off, then Walker spotted someone near the fence waving them over. He and Ryder approached the edge of the perimeter where all the FBI taskforce vehicles and some local cops were gathered. The prisoners were nowhere to be seen, but the HRT guys were all still there.

One of them broke from the group to walk over to them. Dark blond hair, brown eyes. He nodded. "You Walker?" he said in a Southern drawl similar to Walker's.

"That's right."

"I'm Brad Tucker. Team leader." He held out a hand.

Walker shook it. "Damned nice to meet you."

"Same." Tucker looked at Ryder. "You're Locke?"

"Yes." They shook. "That was good work tonight."

Tucker smiled. "We love our job." He looked at Walker. "So, I hear you're DeLuca's brother-in-law."

"Not officially yet. And we actually haven't met."

Tucker waved a hand for them to follow him. "Come on then. I'll introduce you to the boss."

"Perfect," Walker said, a lightness spreading through him as he fell in step with the others. This had been one hell of a night, and it had ended with the best outcome possible.

A group of agents stood talking outside the mobile command center. "Hey, boss man," Tucker called.

The one wearing a ball cap and cargo pants looked over.

"Found someone you oughtta meet."

DeLuca came toward them, backlit by the lights setup. "You Walker?"

He nodded. "That's right. Good to meet you finally." He held out his hand, grinning. It felt weird to meet the guy like this.

"Pleasure's all mine." He smiled and clapped him on the side of the shoulder. "And hey, congratulations on you and Ivy. Welcome to the family."

They grinned at each other, the unspoken secret hanging between them. They were two of only a small, select group who knew the truth about their significant others and their siblings. Every single one of them was a deadly assassin, trained by the government in a top-secret project that had only recently been shut down for good. "Pretty colorful family. I heard something about a possible reunion in the works?"

"I heard that same rumor." DeLuca chuckled. "God help us."

∼

BELLA FIDGETED RESTLESSLY on her makeshift bed, one of those pullout chairs hospitals claimed could be used as a bed but were more like torture contraptions. She'd been trying to find a comfortable position for the past hour or more since Ryder, Walker and Decker had come in to see Creed. Decker was staying at a local motel and flying back to Crimson Point with them once Creed was discharged.

In spite of the abrupt crash in energy level that had hit her once Creed had been brought up to this private room for observation overnight, sleep continued to elude her.

Maybe it was a good thing. After what had happened tonight, she would have nightmares for sure, and there was no way she was crawling in beside Creed on that narrow bed and waking him up after all he'd been through.

They'd overridden his protests and given him a sedative to make him sleep. Waiting for all the test results had taken hours after arrival and he'd been exhausted. The good news was the X-rays showed no fractures in his arms, wrists or shoulders—which was kind of a miracle—though there were possible hairline cracks in two of his ribs on the left side.

Thankfully, there was no internal damage from the kicks he'd suffered and no concussion. His left shoulder had remained in the correct position, and they'd secured it to his chest to keep it that way until the soft tissue could heal. So apart from being bruised and battered, he was doing really well.

God knew it had almost been far worse.

"Bell."

She rolled over and sat up at the sound of his groggy voice, straining to see him in the dimness. "You okay?"

"Drugged as hell, but otherwise, yeah."

She got up and went to perch beside him on the edge of the bed, smoothing his hair back from his forehead. "You look bad."

He huffed out a laugh, grimaced. "Thanks a lot."

"Still gorgeous though," she reassured him. "You still make my heart skip a beat."

He reached up to capture her hand and brought it to rest on the center of his chest, right above where his other arm was secured. She could feel his heart beating calm and steady beneath her palm. It soothed her on a deep level.

"Can't sleep?" he asked.

"No." She would eventually. There was just too much clutter going on in her head at the moment. Too many things for her to process.

She'd thought Max was dead once before. This time there

was no doubt about it, however. She'd seen him get shot down, and the FBI commander on scene had told her he was deceased.

Creed rubbed a thumb over the back of her hand. "Do you feel any closure now?"

"Some. I'm glad he's gone. But finding out about my mom that way, and then seeing what they did to you…" She didn't know how she was supposed to move past all that.

"I'm okay." He squeezed her hand. "We both are now. And I'm just so damn sorry for everything you've gone through."

"For what *I've* been through? What about you?"

"I'm sorry for that too. But mostly I'm sorry for all the time we lost."

"Me too. And I can't believe I didn't realize they'd planted something on my watch. I led them right to us without having a clue."

"It wasn't your fault."

"Seems pretty obvious now that they'd put a tracker on me somewhere."

Creed was quiet a moment. "You told them you'd go with them and marry that asshole to save me, didn't you?"

"If they let you go, yes."

"They wouldn't have let me go, Bell."

"I had to try. And I'd do it again."

He studied her for a long moment. "Why do I get the feeling there was something else you're not telling me?"

"No, there's nothing. Anyway, that's all behind us now, and every last one of them got what was coming to them." She'd meant what she'd said to them about suicide, though. She would never have subjected herself to the life her father and Andreas had wanted to force on her.

But enough. That whole nightmare was over. There was no point in torturing herself by second-guessing her actions now. She leaned down and gently kissed him, so damn grateful that he was still here with her. "I really love you, you know."

He cupped the back of her head, his fingers knotting in her hair to hold her there. "Just don't leave me ever again. I can take anything but that. Anything but losing you."

"You won't lose me. Not ever again," she vowed, her throat tightening.

"You're worth everything to me. Worth any amount of risk or any sacrifice. You're the most important thing in my world, the center of my universe. So promise me, Bell. Swear that no matter what happens from now on, we'll handle it together."

"I swear," she whispered, his impassioned speech choking her up. They'd been through a horrific experience. Surely things had to get easier from here on out. But even if they didn't…

She was sticking with Creed until the end.

TWENTY-TWO

Two days later

Creed winced as he pulled his shirt over his head, getting his first good look at his chest and ribs in the mirror just before the hem covered the deep purple and blue bruises along his ribs. The doctor had told him he might have a hairline fracture or two. He was just glad it wasn't worse than that, because they hurt enough as it was.

"Creed? You almost ready? They're here," Bella called up the stairs.

All his local friends had been calling and texting. Bella had taken it upon herself to invite them over for breakfast. He'd been surprised, but if keeping busy and being around friends helped her right now, then he was all for it.

"Yeah, coming." The hot shower had helped ease some of the stiffness in his muscles and woken him up more. Mostly, he was just tired and sore. The past two days had been a blur of meetings and interviews with various agencies, medical experts, and travel. He and Bella were both glad to have that part behind them and to be home.

Home, he thought, as he headed down the upstairs hallway.

It felt strange to think of this place like that. Before Bella had reappeared on his doorstep, this house had merely been a roof over his head. He hadn't spent much time here, using it mostly as a crash pad in between work assignments. She had changed all that. Because *she* was his home.

He could hear voices coming from the kitchen as he descended the stairs and walked in to find everyone gathered around the island while Bella served up fresh waffles hot off the iron. Walker and Ivy, and Marley and Warwick.

"Hey, there he is." Ivy eyed him with a frown. "You look like shit."

"Good to see you too, Ivy."

"I already thanked her for the criminal hacking of the satellite," Bella said.

"Yeah, *thank* you," he added. Without Ivy, no one would have known where the hell they were. Bella would have been taken away by force, and he would have been dead long before anyone found him. "We both owe you."

Ivy frowned again and waved the thanks away. "You don't owe me anything. It was my pleasure."

"How much trouble are you in?"

Ivy looked down her nose at him with a highly insulted expression. "None."

"She's, ah, good at covering her tracks," Walker said with a wry grin, sliding an arm around her shoulders. "How're the ribs?"

"Not bad."

"He's black and blue from his chest and halfway around his side." Bella lifted another waffle off the iron with a fork. He loved that she had made herself at home here and seemed comfortable in her new surroundings. "But I gotta say, he's been a better patient so far than I thought he'd be. He's actually complying with the doctors' orders."

"What about the shoulder?" Marley gestured to the sling binding his left arm to his chest. "Decker and Teagan said they'd be over with the twins later, by the way."

"Great." His small circle here in Crimson Point and the CPS crew had rallied around him and Bella the past forty-eight hours, but Decker and Teagan had really gone above and beyond. "Yeah, the shoulders are the bigger issue. I managed to get an emergency appointment with an orthopedic surgeon in Portland yesterday on the way back from Spokane. All the bones are intact, but the soft-tissue damage confirmed by the physical testing and CT isn't so great. I've got torn ligaments and inflamed joint capsules. Obviously, the left one's worse than the right."

"Will you need surgery?"

"Maybe, we're not sure yet. Surgery can tighten and stabilize everything on the left side, but for now it's wait and see. Once the swelling goes down and I start physical therapy, we'll have a better idea of the prognosis."

"Did you call Everleigh? I texted her yesterday about your situation, and she said she'd get you in this week even if it's after her last patient of the day."

"I did, thanks. Booked in with her two days from now, so fingers crossed for a good outcome. In the meantime, thankfully I'm right-hand dominant." He stepped up behind Bella to settle his hand on the curve of her hip and placed a kiss on the back of her neck. "Hi."

"Hi. Hungry?"

"Starving."

"Good. Here." She passed him a plate loaded with two waffles.

"Thank you. But I'd rather eat you," he whispered against her ear, low enough that no one else could overhear.

Her cheeks flushed. "You're in no condition to follow through with that."

"Wanna bet?"

She turned and planted her lips on his. "Go eat." She shooed him toward the table.

Warwick moved over to make a spot next to Bella's plate. "Smells amazin'," he told her in his northern English accent. "I'm clammin'."

"You're what?" she asked, sitting down beside Creed.

"It's Newcastle slang for 'starving to death.'" Marley cut a square of waffle. "You'll get used to it."

"It's Geordie," he clarified, digging into his breakfast.

It all felt so normal. Sitting around eating together with the late-winter sunshine pouring through the windows.

"Any word on the investigation yet this morning?" Walker asked.

"Got a call this morning from the FBI," Bella said. "Apparently, Andreas's father was arrested last night by the DEA on a major op, acting on intel they'd gathered on Andreas and Max."

"Glad to hear it."

"Us too," Creed said.

Now that criminal bastard and his son would both die behind bars. It was a far better fate than either of them deserved, but at least there was some level of justice in it. They had lost their freedom, their wealth, and their empire.

The others stayed for about an hour after finishing breakfast, helping clean up and then visiting for a bit longer. "Well," Ivy said, laying a hand on Walker's shoulder, "we'd better let you guys rest up."

"Yeah, especially since the twins are comin'," Warwick added.

Marley poked him in the shoulder. "They're not that bad."

"No, they're good lads. Interviewin' next week, are they?" he asked Walker, who nodded.

"That's right."

"I'm just excited to have all of us in the same city again," Marley said. "Been way too long."

Bella smiled at her. "I'm happy for you. I never had any siblings, but I always wanted some."

"Well, if you still want some you can borrow mine anytime, and then you might change your mind," Marley said with a laugh. "Call us if you need anything."

"Will do," Creed said. "Thanks for coming."

"Happy to. We're all glad to see you guys safe and sound."

He and Bella saw them out. He shut the door and wrapped his right arm around her waist from behind, setting his chin in the curve of her shoulder to nuzzle her cheek. "You doing okay, baby?"

It was going to take a long time for her to deal with all of this.

She shrugged. "Doing the best I can. Just glad you're okay and we have each other." She turned to face him, gently ran a hand up and down his back, her eyes sad. "I hate what they did to you. Every time I close my eyes, I see you strung up like that, and it's straight out of my nightmares. It's why I agreed to leave Tucson in the first place, when the news broke that he had escaped. I knew what they were capable of."

"I don't want you to remember me that way." He wished he held the power to wipe it from her mind permanently.

"Well, it's gonna take a long time before that image stops being seared into my brain."

"I'm gonna put so many good memories in your head, you won't have time to think about it," he half-teased, and kissed her softly. "Have you decided what you want to do now?"

"What do you mean?"

"Where you want to live."

She frowned up at him. "I thought you liked it here."

"I do. But I want you to love it too."

"I haven't had a chance to spend much time here, but what I've seen I like, and I already love the people. You have good friends."

"They're your friends now too. What about the house? We could look for something else together if you want."

She glanced around them for a moment. "No, I really like this place. It has a cozy, homey feel and it's not too big. Maybe we could paint the—"

"*Mrreow.*"

She stopped talking, looked down as Nick Furry emerged from the staircase and came over to stand in the doorway. He seemed to stare right at Creed for a long moment with his one eye, his tail twitching in agitation. Then he took a cautious step forward, and another. And another, until he was close enough to sniff at the leg of Creed's jeans.

Creed stood absolutely still, not wanting to spook him.

Nick sniffed around some more, then bowed his head and rubbed his cheek across Creed's pant leg.

Bella gasped. "Oh, my God, you hear that?"

"What?"

"Listen." She was smiling as she watched her pet.

It took Creed a moment to pick up on the low, rhythmic purr. "The purring?"

"Yeah, he's totally purring," she said in excitement, bending to scoop up the cat. She kissed the top of Nick's head, earned an annoyed look and a paw pressed to the middle of her chest. "I'm so proud of you, buddy." Then to Creed. "He likes you. Wanna pet him now?"

Creed lifted his hand to scratch the top of the cat's head, but

Nick had other ideas and flattened his ears, a warning growl coming from him. Creed stopped. "Whoa, okay."

"Yeah, too soon." Bella laughed. "Okay, buddy. Baby steps." She set Nick down and the cat paused to give Creed a warning look before trotting away and disappearing back up the stairs. "They have any animal rescue groups around here?"

"I'm sure they do. Ryder's wife works at the vet clinic in town. She'll know. Why, you thinking of adopting another cat?"

"Maybe, but I really just want to start working with animals again. A shelter is okay, but I'd prefer to work with a sanctuary. Or open up one of my own. By the way, there's something else I need to tell you that I didn't get the chance to before."

That sounded ominous. "Do I need to brace myself first?"

"No," she said on a laugh.

"Okay, what?"

"I'm rich."

His eyebrows shot up. "Rich?"

She nodded. "I received a large amount of money from the courts back when Max was first put in prison. I hired a personal investment firm to manage it and my portfolio has performed well. I've been really careful with it, didn't touch it much while I was in WITSEC."

"Like, how much?"

"A lot." She shrugged. "Enough that neither of us would ever need to work again if we didn't want to."

He stared at her in shock. Holy shit.

"Anyway, it doesn't really matter," she said with a flap of her hand. "I don't need money to be happy. I just need you."

"You've got me forever. But…the money doesn't hurt."

She grinned and looped her arms around his waist, gazing up at him adoringly. "No, it doesn't, does it?"

He raised a hand to cup the side of her face, gazed into her eyes. "I'm so glad you came back to me."

"Me too."

"I'll forever be grateful for that. No matter what we went through to get here, it was worth it, and I'd go through all of it again to have you here with me."

"Me too," she whispered, and lifted onto her toes to kiss him.

The doorbell went off.

He laughed. "Perfect timing. Must be Decker."

Sure enough, Decker stood there with Teagan and his younger twin brothers behind them. "Y'all sure about this?" he asked. "We can come back another time."

Teagan nudged him with her hip. "Stop with that. Hey, handsome," she said, reaching out to gently hug Creed. "How you feeling today?"

"Bit better. Glad to be home."

"I'll bet." She stepped past him to hug Bella, gave her a megawatt smile. "Hey, girl."

"So, these are them," Decker gestured behind him to his brothers.

The twins were identical, with Decker's build and Marley's coloring, though their hair was a lighter shade of auburn compared to hers and their eyes were green. "I'm Creed," he said to them. "Which one's which?"

"I'm Gavin," the first one said, stepping up to shake Creed's hand. "And it's actually not that hard to tell us apart when we're together. I'm the better-looking one. Obviously."

His twin rolled his eyes. "I'm Tristan, the better one in general."

Creed shook with him, grinning. He could already tell they were both polar opposites of their older, remote brother. "Good to know. Come on in."

"So we missed out on all the excitement around here *again*, huh? It's like a hotbed of criminal activity in these parts, never a dull moment." Gavin said as they joined Bella and Teagan in the living room.

Decker smacked him on the back of the head.

"Ow! What the hell, Deck?"

"That's for being an insensitive shit."

Gavin blinked at him in astonishment. "*I'm* insensitive?"

"You're an idiot," Tristan said as he walked past them.

Decker shot Gavin a warning look and took the chair at the end of the coffee table. "Sorry about him. His mouth flaps before his brain catches up."

Gavin sank down next to his twin on the love seat, looking contrite. "Didn't mean anything by it," he said to Creed. "Sorry, man."

Creed waved it away. "No worries, and you're not wrong. So, you're both interviewing next week?"

"Wednesday morning," Tristan answered, then looked at his twin. "Separately, thank God."

Gavin didn't answer, just narrowed his eyes at him.

"They keep things interesting," Teagan said, fighting a grin. "Constant banter. But they're both good people, great teammates, and they've got solid backgrounds for the industry. They'll be great assets to the company. Right, Deck?"

Decker inclined his head. "They can both handle themselves."

Gavin grinned at him. "It was physically painful for you to say that just now, wasn't it?"

"Don't poke the bear, Gav," Tristan said in that long-suffering way that only a close relative could.

"I'm sure they'll both be great," Creed said. "Who's doing the interviews?"

The twins looked at each other and Tristan answered. "Ryder Locke, Callum Falconer, and Walker. I don't know what Walker's first name is."

"I do, but I'm sworn to secrecy," Bella said. "Ivy told me," she said to Teagan, who looked scandalized.

"What? She didn't tell *me*. What the heck?"

"Apparently he's really touchy about it."

"Is it bad?" Teagan asked with interest. "Something hideous like…Gaylord or Elmer or something?"

Bella laughed. "No, I actually really like it. But he doesn't, and that's why he goes by Walker."

"Well, now I have to get it out of her."

"Good luck with that." Ivy probably wouldn't give up anything she didn't want to even while being tortured.

Teagan laughed. "Oh, but you know I love a challenge."

"All three of 'em, huh?" Creed asked, bringing the conversation back to center. He didn't know Walker's first name either, and now he wanted to. "They're all good guys. Walker's pretty quiet. Ryder and Callum will be taking the lead."

"They're a good team, and they're fair," Decker said. "You'd both be lucky to get hired on there."

"In other words, don't mess it up if you do," Tristan said to his twin.

"Yeah, got it," Gavin answered with a good-natured grin at Decker. "Like I would ever do anything to embarrass you."

Decker grunted, his usual stony expression back in place. But everyone in this room knew him now, and he wasn't fooling any of them with the forbidding, impregnable fortress routine. He'd moved here to be close to his sister and wanted the twins to get the job so they could all be together again. He just didn't want *them* to know he wanted it.

"You want a beer?" Creed asked the others.

"I'll take one," Decker jumped up and hurried to the kitchen ahead of him.

Creed chuckled at his buddy's concern. "I think I can handle opening a couple beers."

Decker ignored him, pulled two chilled bottles from the fridge without answering, twisted them open, and handed one to Creed. "Cheers, brother."

They tapped bottle necks and each took a pull.

"Anything from the Feds yet? About how in hell de Vries escaped prison?" Decker asked quietly so the others wouldn't overhear.

"They're still investigating, but the working theory is that the riot and fire were planned. Someone in the morgue was paid off to have a body pulled aside and faked the dental records to match de Vries."

"Daaamn. It's right out of a movie."

Creed nodded. "His boss was arrested last night."

"Really?"

"Big DEA op that had been in the works for a few months, and they moved up the timeline once they got word about de Vries."

"Awesome. Love to see it. How's Bella handling everything?"

"Okay." He was worried about her though. "She's just been through so fucking much, and I don't know how to make any of it better."

"You be there for her," Decker said, in that matter-of-fact way of his that saw things so clearly and cut through all the clutter and bullshit. "That's all you can do—and all she really needs right now. You just be her anchor, and let her be yours."

Creed blinked at him. Well, holy fuck.

"What?" he said when Creed kept staring at him.

"Nothing, it's… For a guy who makes a point of letting the world think he's a closed-off island, you're amazingly astute and thoughtful, that's all."

Decker made a face. "Thoughtful," he muttered as if the word tasted bad in his mouth.

"Yeah, and compassionate."

Decker grimaced. "Christ," he said, and took another pull of beer. "Don't fuckin' tell anyone else that."

"I won't. But I think the secret's already out, brother. At least to everyone here." He nodded at the others, who were all still talking amongst each other on the other side of the great room. "Also… Did we become best friends?"

Decker paused, bottle partway to his lips. "I dunno. Did we?"

"You tell me."

Decker had insisted on staying behind in Spokane the night of the incident, then spent the following morning running around town getting Creed's prescriptions and driving them to various meetings and appointments before making the trip back here to the coast. No way he'd done all that just because they were work partners.

He sighed. "Jesus, fine. You scared the shit outta me the other night. You know that?"

"It scared the shit outta me too."

"Yeah, well, don't ever do it again."

Aww, hardass Decker had a squishy marshmallow center. "I won't." Creed set his bottle down and extended his right arm. Lifted his eyebrows.

"What."

He knew what. "Come on. Bring it in here, brother."

Decker eyed him for a moment, considering it. Darted a look over to where the twins sat to make sure they weren't looking, then moved in, and gave him a quick hug. A careful one, mindful of him being bruised and battered, with a slight tap on the middle of his back.

Creed held on.

Decker stood there, stiff as a board. "What are you doing?"

"I just…I can't let go."

Decker grunted. Tapped him on the back once more.

"*Whoa.*"

At the shocked voice, Creed looked over at the living room side of the great room. The twins were gaping at them from the love seat in utter astonishment. Teagan and Bella were smiling.

Decker immediately broke away and stepped back, scowling at Creed. "Now look what you did. Asshole."

Creed grinned and picked his beer back up, not the least bit apologetic. He and Decker were best buds for life. "Not sorry."

TWENTY-THREE

"I can't believe you said that. 'We missed out on all the excitement around here *again*'? Really?" Tristan said to Gavin under his breath as they strode down the walkway to Decker's SUV waiting at the curb out front of Creed's house. Deck and Teagan were still saying goodbye to him and Bella.

"Yeah, okay, I fucked up." Upon reflection, it *had* been a little insensitive, and probably not the finest first impression he'd ever made. He'd been going with what he now had to agree had been a pretty lame attempt at lightening the mood. "But I apologized, and he seemed cool about it."

"Honestly, it's like I need to follow you around and do damage control with people you meet."

He stopped walking and put a hand to his heart. "*Ouch*. That hurts, Tris. You know how charming I can be."

Tristan didn't respond, just strode to the vehicle and got in the backseat to wait.

Gavin slid in next to him, waited in silence for a full minute before speaking. "You think I should apologize to Deck, or…?"

Tristan twisted his head around to stare at him. "Are you insane? Just leave it."

"Yeah. Right." He tapped his fingers on the armrest, watching out the window. Decker and Teagan were walking toward them now. "So what now? You wanna go check out the town more?"

"Later. I could go for a hike, though."

"I'm down with that. Along the cliff up to the lighthouse maybe."

"Yeah, okay." That would give Decker time to cool off if he was still pissed at him.

Decker got in the driver's seat, and Teagan in the front. "You guys wanna head over to Marley and Warwick's place now?"

"Nah, think we'll go back to your place, change, and head out to do a little exploring."

"Okay, sure. Don't forget though, Marley wants us there at five for dinner."

"Got it," he said, looking forward to it. Marley was an awesome cook.

It was hard to tell if Decker was still pissed or not on the drive back to the condo. He didn't say much at the best of times. Gavin took the win and went straight to the room he and Tristan were sharing to change. He'd just pulled on a sweatshirt to protect him from the chilly weather when some new messages popped up on his phone.

Autumn had sent him pictures of Carly holding an honor roll certificate. "Carly made honor roll again last term."

"Awesome. Never doubted it," Tristan replied from the bathroom.

Way to go, kiddo! he responded, adding hearts and kisses. *Proud of you.* He made a point of telling her so whenever she accomplished something big. Because that was important for kids to hear, and God knew he'd never received it from his parents growing up. None of them had.

His phone rang a few seconds later. Autumn calling. "Hey, gorgeous," he answered. He'd called her that for forever. Now he really meant it. "Carly there?"

"No, she's at a friend's place. We've got draaaama going on here though. She's got a crush on this boy, and he's kind of the class bad boy. Word got out, and some of the other girls are spreading it around on this app they all use. Carly doesn't have a phone yet, of course, but she's really upset because the boy found out. Now she's saying she can't bear to go to school and face him because she's humiliated."

Well, he didn't like that shit at all. "You tell her from me, that kid's lucky she's interested in him in the first place. And that if this keeps escalating, I'll step in and take care of it."

Autumn laughed lightly. "I think I can handle it without backup, but thanks for the offer. Just hate what social media does to kids. They're way too young to have to deal with this shit." She yawned.

"Hundred percent. You sound tired. Late night?" Yeah, he was fishing. Didn't care.

"Sort of. Late dinner, is all."

His attention sharpened. "Like a date?"

"Kind of."

He frowned. "Whaddya mean, kind of?"

"Okay, it was."

"With who?" She usually told him about guys she was seeing, but hadn't mentioned this one. That could be good or bad.

"A guy I met through a dating site a while back. He travels for business a lot, so we never made plans to meet until now."

Uh huh. A lot of guys claimed they "traveled for business" on those sites, when in reality they were just using it as a cover for not having to be up front and accountable with the women they met. He knew plenty of guys who pulled that shit. Lying assholes. "What's he do?"

"IT contractor for the military."

Right. "What's his name?"

She laughed softly. "Why, you gonna run a background check on him?"

"Maybe I am." He'd always looked out for her when he could. And while he was well aware that she had dated over the past year or two, the thought of her with another guy now made him feel irrationally jealous and territorial.

"I'll pass on that offer, but thank you. How's your trip going so far?"

He still wanted to know this dick's name. "Good. Got some drama of our own happening here. Well, already happened a couple days ago. So how did the date go?"

"Why are you being so nosy?"

He wasn't touching that one. "Good? Meh?" he pressed.

"It wasn't bad."

"Wow. Ringing endorsement for the guy." He felt better already.

"He's perfectly nice."

"*Nice*?" He snorted, rolling his eyes. "Please tell me you're not going to settle for *nice*."

"Why not? Nice is refreshing after all the dating horror stories I've racked up. You think it's easy to find someone willing to date a single mom my age?"

He blinked. "That's such bullshit. And don't you dare settle for a guy just because he's *nice*." That was almost worse than the thought of her dating.

"Okay, you're really hammering on that word."

"I'm serious. Same as what I just told you to tell Carly. Any guy would be lucky to have you interested in him. And if he's too stupid to see it, then you need to kick him to the curb

ASAP." Because God, there was no one like Autumn. She deserved to be worshipped. He would worship her if she was his.

But she's not.

She sighed. "It's not that simple, Gav."

"Sure it is." Dead simple. And none of the dipshits she'd dated so far deserved her. That was for damn sure.

She deserved someone who saw her for all her incredible attributes, not just her looks. Someone who understood and respected the job she was doing as a single working mother. Everything she'd sacrificed along the way to love and nurture her daughter. She deserved someone…

What, like you?

Well…shit, yeah. Why not him? They had history together. He had known her for most of her life and seen what she'd gone through. He understood her in a way no one else ever would. He would take care of her, share the load and be there through thick and thin.

"Easy for you to say," she continued, jerking him out of his thoughts. "Anyway, let's drop that and talk about what's going on there."

"One more thing. Are you gonna see him again?" *No. Say no.*

She paused before answering. "We're supposed to go out this Saturday night."

Saturday night. Way different from a regular weekday date. Sex-date territory.

Jealousy streaked through him, swift and hot. The thought of her going to bed with another guy turned his insides to cement.

His mind flashed back to that night before he left for boot camp.

He thought of what had happened after he'd climbed

through her window. Cringed inside when he thought of how awkward and clueless he'd been back then.

He wished he could go back in time and do it over again.

No. He wished he could do it over again *now,* and show her how it should have been between them. Show her how good he could make it for her. He'd fantasized about that way too often lately.

"Okay, enough about me and my dating life—I've got some other news," she said.

"Yeah? What's that?" He was still stuck on this coming Saturday night. And that Mr. Nice Guy was probably going to put the moves on her and try and get her into bed. Fuck.

"My company just announced they're sending a team to a huge conference in Seattle in June, and they picked me to head it up."

"That's fantastic, good for you." He was happy for her. Proud of her. Still didn't want her going to bed with her date on Saturday.

"Thanks." He could hear the smile in her voice. Could picture it so clearly. It was one of his favorite things about her, so real and warm. There was nothing fake about her. "So if you get hired on there, maybe we could meet up when I come out."

"Hell, yeah, we will."

"Great. Listen, I gotta go, but…just wanted to wish you luck again on your interview."

Yeah, there was definitely a wistful edge to her tone. As if it was already a foregone conclusion in her mind that he would be moving out here permanently soon. And there went that twinge behind his sternum again. "Thanks. Nothing's set in stone yet though. We'll see what happens."

"You'll get it," she said. "Both of you will."

"If we do, it's not like we'll be living on Mars. We're on the other side of the country, not the other side of the world."

"I know. Just feels like it sometimes."

Yeah, that was definitely wistfulness he heard. Made him think she really missed him. Or was afraid of losing him or whatever. Which was insane. "You think I'm gonna up and disappear on you or something?"

"No." But she didn't sound convincing. "Just ignore me. It's been a long week."

"Week just started," he said to lighten the mood.

She laughed softly. "God, don't remind me. You'll let me know about the job?"

"Of course I will. You okay though? For real? You sound... down." He didn't like that either. Wished he was there to hug her and make her laugh.

"No, I'm good," she said with forced cheeriness. "Say hi to Tris. And try not to bug Decker. I know how much you love it."

He chuckled. "No promises. I'll call you after the interview. Give Carly a hug for me."

"Will do. Bye."

"Bye." He lowered the phone, that ache in his chest getting stronger instead of fading.

"How's Autumn?" Tristan said as he came out of the bathroom changed for their hike.

"She's all right." Sad though. Lonely. Now he was missing her like hell. And absolutely hating that she had that goddamn date coming up Saturday. "Said to say hi and told me not to bug Deck."

"I love her."

"Everyone does."

But Gavin was starting to think he might love her in a far different way than he had before.

∽

"HEY. YOU ALMOST READY?"

Standing over his dad's duffel laid open on his bed, Finn stopped rolling the last of his T-shirts and looked over at Ryder in his doorway. "Yeah, gimme five minutes."

"Kay. Meet you outside."

"Yep." He quickly finished packing the last of his stuff, zipped up his bag, and paused to look around his room one last time. It was weird to know he was leaving home, for a few years at least. These four walls had been his refuge from the day he and his mom had moved in. Now it felt like he'd outgrown them.

He hefted the duffel and walked down the hall, doing his best to shove aside the nostalgia and building nerves. He wanted this. The adjustment would be tough at first, but he'd get through it. It would be worth it, and he was excited for the challenges that lay ahead.

His mom and Ryder were both waiting in the vehicle when he locked the side door. He opened the tailgate to toss his gear in, then got in the back behind his mom. She reached back a hand, and he took it, squeezed in return. She was holding it together much better than he'd expected so far, thankfully. He didn't think it would last much past when they got to the airport.

"Are we picking up Shae on the way?" she asked him.

A concrete block formed in the pit of his stomach. "No, she was busy."

"Oh. Okay."

"And we're off," Ryder said, turning out of the driveway.

Finn released his mom's hand and looked out his window, resisting the urge to look back at the house before it disappeared from view, his mind stuck on Shae. He'd reached out to her every day over the past week since he'd told her the news, and every time she'd had some excuse why she couldn't meet up.

She hadn't answered his calls when he'd phoned, and hadn't been home when he'd stopped by her place last night. He was pretty sure that was deliberate on her part, because the only form of communication she allowed now was texting.

As if on cue, his phone buzzed. He grabbed it from his pocket, heart jumping when he saw a message from her. A short response to his text a few hours ago saying goodbye and telling her he'd contact her from base when he could.

Safe travels! And good luck. I know you'll do us proud. She'd added a smiley face and a heart.

"That her?" his mom asked, glancing back at him.

"Yeah. Just saying goodbye." But he was still stuck on the heart. Was it a friendly heart? Or did it mean more?

And that last bit. *I know you'll do us proud.*

Yeah. He *would* make her proud.

Just you wait and see.

TWENTY-FOUR

"Okay, little man, in you go." Bella coaxed the young lab mix back into the kennel and shut the door with only a small twinge of guilt.

While she hated seeing any animal locked up, she was exhausted, soaked, and bedraggled after that hour-long on-leash wrestling match in the rain, and she needed a break. Although she was happy to see him so energetic. He'd almost died after being hit by a car several weeks ago, winding up with two broken legs and a fractured pelvis, along with internal damage. Now he was as good as new.

The dog immediately whined and started clawing at the kennel door with one paw. "Aww, buddy, I know. I'm sorry, but I need a rest because you wore me out."

At not quite one year old, this one was a handful. All go, all the time, with a healthy side of canine ADHD to go with it and a spastic, bull-in-china-shop energy. Bella's arms ached from constantly pulling back on the leash for the past forty minutes on their "walk" through town.

The dog had absolutely no training or manners whatsoever, but thankfully didn't seem aggressive. He'd been found dragging himself along the shoulder of the coastal highway, skinny and broken. No tags, no collar or microchip.

It made her blood boil just thinking about it.

His piece-of-shit "owner" had abandoned him. They had probably gotten him as a cute little puppy and had quickly grown frustrated by the bad behavior. Rather than putting in the time and effort to correct it, they'd dumped him on the side of the road and left him, nearly getting him killed in the process. Asshole people like that didn't deserve to have an animal.

The good news was, this young pup was friendly and had lots of potential. She was hopeful she and the others here at the shelter would be able to rehabilitate him into a good canine citizen and get him adopted within the next few months.

"Thought I'd find you here."

She turned to find Ivy watching her, framed by the archway that opened into the hallway leading to the office. "Hey! What brings you down here?"

"Just checking up on you. Been a couple weeks since I've seen you." She nodded at the lab mix, who was now running around his kennel like a lunatic throwing his toy for himself. "He looks like a lively one."

"Oh, man, ten times worse than a toddler full of caffeine and sugar," she said with a laugh.

"Is he up for adoption?"

"*No*. Lord, no, he's nowhere near ready to go home with anyone. Well, unless that person's extremely experienced with high-energy dogs—and a saint. He needs major training and discipline first. And about a billion hard runs to burn off some of that frenetic energy." She paused, eyed Ivy. They'd definitely bonded since she had arrived in town. Well, bonded as much as Ivy would allow, anyway. "Why, you thinking of adopting a dog?"

"Noooo, are you *kidding*? Mr. Whiskers would disown me."

"Fair enough. Nick Furry wasn't too thrilled when I brought a puppy home last week for a sleepover." Sometimes she took dogs and cats home with her for sleepovers. Partly to assess them in a home environment to judge their suitability for adoption, and partly to give animals a break from the stress and monotony of the shelter. But she knew she wanted to do more.

"Yeah, I'd guess not. How'd it go?"

"There was a lot of hissing and spitting, and I've been getting the cold shoulder ever since. That pretty much sums it up."

"You're such a softie."

She shrugged. "Can't help it. I like animals better than most people I know, so getting hired on here was a godsend." This was a no-kill shelter, which was important to Bella. She would never, *could* never work at a facility where animals were at risk of being euthanized.

"You're preaching to the choir about the people-versus-animal thing."

"I know. That's partly why I like you so much."

"This kind of work suits you. Truly."

"I love it. It's the most rewarding work I've ever done." It gave her such a sense of purpose and satisfaction to help these innocent little souls that asked for nothing. Even if the animals didn't get adopted and wound up being long-term residents, at least they were safe here and got good food, clean water, shelter, and people to love and care for them for the rest of their lives.

"Too bad it doesn't pay very well."

"I don't care about the money." She had more than enough of that, though only Creed knew it. She knew exactly how privileged she was and how lucky she was to be able to follow her heart and dreams and do this instead of a job she didn't love just to pay the bills. Every day she was grateful for it.

"Hey, I heard something the other day I wanted to ask you about."

"Oh?"

"Something about a reunion involving all your sisters."

"Ah." Ivy gave an enigmatic smile. "Marley and Teagan told you."

"Yep. So? Is it true? And they're both mad that I know Walker's first name and they don't."

"Well, they'll just have to deal, and the reunion is in the works. My sisters are all so damned busy and hard to pin down at the same time. That's the problem. But it's happening. Why, you wanna meet them too?"

"*Hell,* yeah, I wanna meet them. Are you kidding?"

"I'll send you an invite when it happens then." She glanced to her left, down the hall. "Looks like you've got another visitor, so I'll make myself scarce. See you later."

"Yes, you will." Curious, Bella leaned out to peer down the hall and broke into a wide smile when she saw Creed coming toward her. Without the sling. "Well, hello, sir. Are you here to look at adopting a dog? Or maybe fostering to adopt? We have both kinds of contracts, and lots of amazing pets waiting for their furever homes."

"No," he said on a chuckle. "Just finished physio and thought I'd swing by and check on my best girl." He wrapped her up in a hug. With both arms.

"Ohhh, I've *missed* this." She buried her face in his chest and inhaled. It had been weeks since he'd been able to hold her like this. The scent of his soap combined with laundry detergent and something that was intrinsically Creed surrounded her. Yum. "So the rehab's going really well then?"

"I think so, yeah. The inflammation in the joint capsule is way down, and Everleigh thinks if I can keep strengthening the rotator cuff, I won't need surgery."

"That's incredible news."

"I was pretty happy, not gonna lie." He took her by the shoulders and gently eased her away from him to look at her. "You look like you've been through the wringer."

She laughed. "It's his fault." She jerked a thumb over her shoulder at the lab mix. "He's a project, that one. Dragged me along for two miles like a windsock hanging off the end of the leash, and he's still got a full tank."

She looked back to see the dog continually throwing his toy and pouncing on it in the confines of his kennel. "I hate seeing him in a cage. This one needs space to run. A farm, maybe."

There were plenty of those in the area. She would document his progress on video and post it on their social media. His perfect home was bound to be out there somewhere.

"Maybe he can be the inaugural dog at your rescue once you get all the permits."

"Maybe," she agreed with another smile. She had recently purchased a ten-acre parcel of land up in the hills above Crimson Point with the intention of creating a sanctuary for unwanted dogs and cats. Applications were pending for building permission from City Council.

Once they were approved, she planned to have several buildings put up on the property with big, spacious kennels, an enclosed catio for the kitties, and lots of different exercise and training areas for all the dogs. "By the way, Sierra was in to see me this morning." The town vet, and one of the project's biggest supporters, along with Ryder's wife Danae, who worked at the clinic with her.

"Oh? What about?"

"Her husband Becket has offered to build the structures and take care of the landscaping at a discount. Can you believe it?"

"Yeah, I can. This is a tight-knit community, and people like to step up and help each other out. Especially if it's for a worthwhile cause like this."

"I just love it here. You picked the most incredible place to move to." He'd taken her up to the lighthouse on the point last week, and they'd walked the forest trails together. The raw, rugged beauty of the place was something she would never get tired of.

"What can I say, I have good taste." He reached into his pocket. "Speaking of, I brought you this."

She gasped when he held out an exact replica of the watch he'd given her. "Oh my God!" She took it, flipped it over and got a little emotional when she saw the same engraving on the back as the original. "When did you get this?"

"Picked it up at the jeweler's on my way here. It arrived last week, and they just did the engraving this morning."

She pulled up the sleeves of her jacket and sweater and put it on. "I love it, thank you." She slid a hand around the back of his neck and lifted up to kiss him.

"Welcome. And I also brought this." He reached into his other pocket and pulled out a ring.

"Oh…" She covered her mouth with her hand, looked up at him through a veil of tears. "Oh, you kept it," she breathed. Her diamond engagement ring. She'd left it on the kitchen island that day with the note. And he'd kept it all this time.

"I couldn't give up hope that you'd come back to me someday."

She held out her left hand, fingers trembling slightly. "Put it on."

Creed slid it onto her finger. It was a bit loose now. "We can get it sized down, I already talked to the jeweler about it."

"No, it's perfect. I plan on gaining all that weight back and maybe then some. I like food."

He grinned, brought her knuckles to his lips to kiss where the ring rested. "Will you marry me, Bell?"

"Yes." She flung her arms around him.

She would marry him right here and now if she could. And this time, her promise was going to last forever.

EPILOGUE

Three months later

As far as wedding days went, this one had to go down in history as one of the best.

The Oregon Coast weather was notoriously fickle and changeable all year long, and today was no exception. A storm had rolled in overnight, dumping a drenching rain on the region and bringing high, gusty winds to batter the rugged coastline. Not exactly beach wedding weather.

Then, three hours ago, the storm had suddenly blown itself out ahead of schedule and a big pocket of blue sky had appeared on the horizon. It was almost directly overhead now, the warm May sunshine pulling moisture out of the sand in columns of misty vapor that were carried away on the light breeze.

Creed stood in front of the mirror in the hotel room overlooking the beach where he and Bella would spend their wedding night and removed his tie again. He'd tried twice already and couldn't get it tied right.

"What the hell, didn't anyone ever teach you to tie a tie in the Army?" Decker muttered, batting Creed's hands aside to tie the Windsor knot himself.

"Didn't think I'd be nervous, but I guess I am." His hands felt clumsy, and it had nothing to do with his left shoulder, which was now almost back to normal, no surgery required.

Decker scowled as he worked. "What the hell for? She's everything you've ever wanted, and you've both waited forever for this."

Leave it to Deck to lay it all out there in just a few words. "I'm not nervous about getting married." He was well aware that Bella was the best thing that had ever happened to him. "I guess…I dunno, I just don't wanna fuck it up."

"You're not gonna fuck it up," Decker said with tried patience, expertly finishing off the knot and tucking the tail of the tie through the loop in the back before putting the tie clip in place. "There. Now don't touch it."

Creed glanced down, saw it was perfect now. "You've had some practice with that, huh."

"I helped raise those two ding-a-lings out there when they were young, so, yeah." He jerked his chin toward where Gavin and Tristan were visible, currently racing up and down the damp sand throwing a Nerf football. They were barefoot and had their pants rolled up to their thighs in a useless attempt to keep them dry.

Creed clapped a hand on the side of Decker's meaty shoulder. "In case I forget later, thanks for everything you've done, man. I appreciate it."

Decker was his best man for a reason. They were tight, and Decker had been awesome, helping get everything ready for today. There was no one else Creed would have wanted to stand up with him.

"Yeah, no problem. But don't hug me."

"Too late." Creed hugged him. Received a half-assed pat on

the back in return. "I'll do the same for you when you and Teagan tie the knot." Decker hadn't said anything, but Creed figured his pal would be popping the question soon.

Decker grunted and grabbed the flower thingy to go on Creed's lapel from the dresser. A pink rose to match the ones in Bella's bouquet. Whatever made Bella happy.

He checked himself in the mirror, reached up to fiddle with his hair a bit. Was one side sticking up a bit more than the other? He'd just had it cut, but...

"Hold still unless you want me to impale you in the heart with this thing," Decker muttered, securing the flower in place. "There." He stepped back, eyed Creed critically and gave an approving nod. "You're good to go."

"Thanks. You got the rings?"

"Yeah, of course I got 'em. What did you think—I'd leave 'em at home or something?"

"No. Just checking."

Deck clapped him on the shoulders twice. "You're ready."

Creed nodded. "Yep." He was. More than ready to do this and make Bella his officially for all the world to see.

A crisp knock came at the door. Marley poked her head in. "Y'all ready? Minister's here, and everyone's already seated."

"Everyone except our errant brothers," Decker said.

"Right. On it. You look hot by the way, Creed," she said with a wink before hurrying away to corral the twins.

Creed led the way downstairs and out through the lobby where a lush green lawn stretched out toward the ocean. It was a simple setup, because both he and Bella wanted it that way. This was about saying their vows in front of the people most important to them—and having a hell of a good party afterward.

The salt-scented breeze rushed over him as he stepped outside. Several rows of white chairs were set up facing an arbor in the center where the minister waited, with the rolling ocean as a backdrop behind it. The CPS staff had turned out in force, along with the tight-knit circle of friends he and Bella had here in Crimson Point.

"Hey, there he is, the man of the hour." Ryder got up and shook Creed's hand, followed by Callum and Walker.

"Thanks for coming." They'd wanted a small wedding, but it meant a lot to have everyone here.

"Wouldn't have missed it," Callum said, sitting back down next to Nadia, who was holding their infant son. Donovan and Anaya were beside them with their little daughter.

"Hey, buddy," Creed said, reaching out to tickle the baby's cheek.

"Showtime," Decker said.

He shook a few more hands, waved and smiled to others on his way up the aisle, and spoke with the minister briefly. Decker took up position next to him, and they stood waiting with hands clasped in front of them. Harp music started up.

All eyes turned toward the end of the aisle.

Ivy came out first, dressed in a turquoise bridesmaid gown and carrying a bouquet of pink roses. Creed's heart started to pound. His gaze moved past Ivy, locked on the place she'd just emerged from, and then Bella stepped out in a formfitting white dress that hugged the curves she'd finally regained.

His throat tightened and a ridiculous, sappy smile took over his whole face. She smiled back, held his gaze, and strode purposefully toward him. Not a slow, sedate wedding march, but a brisk, confident pace that underlined how ready she was for this.

She joined him at the altar and he took her hand. "You look so beautiful, Bell," he murmured, his heart trying to pound its way out of his chest.

"Thanks. You look gorgeous." Then she bit her lip, tears flooding her eyes an instant before she threw her arms around his neck. "I'm sorry. I can't believe this is finally happening," she choked out.

His chest hitched, and he hugged her to him as chuckles and awwws from the guests filled the air, smiling even though his own eyes stung. "I know. Me either." He took her face in his hands and kissed her.

"You're supposed to wait until I tell you to do that, but I'll allow it," the minister said dryly behind them.

Creed ignored him and slowed the kiss, his fingers sliding into Bella's hair. Whistles and cheering broke out but Creed ignored it all, focused on his gorgeous bride and the long, winding road their love story had taken to bring them here.

They almost hadn't made it to this day. They'd been through so much, overcoming terrible odds to earn this chance. But all the pain, all the hardship they had endured along the way made this moment that much sweeter.

"You guys wanna get married, or just make out in front of us?" Decker said, drawing laughter.

"Seriously," Ivy said. "Let's get 'er done."

Creed lifted his head to smile down at Bella. "You and me, Bell. Forever."

"Forever," she echoed, then took his hand. Together they turned to face the minister, and the future they'd both fought so hard for.

And won.

—**The End**—

*read Gavin and Autumn's story next in *Guarding Autumn*!*

Dear readaer,

Thank you for reading ***Guarding Bella***. If you'd like to stay in touch with me and be the first to learn about new releases you can:

• Join my newsletter at: http://kayleacross.com/v2/newsletter/
    • Find me on Facebook: https://www.facebook.com/KayleaCrossAuthor/
    • Follow me on Instagram: https://www.instagram.com/kaylea_cross_author/

Also, please consider leaving a review at your favorite online book retailer. It helps other readers discover new books.

Happy reading,
Kaylea

Excerpt from

Guarding Autumn
Crimson Point Security Series
By Kaylea Cross
Copyright © 2024 Kaylea Cross

Prologue

Twelve years ago

Maybe it was the alcohol. Or maybe it was because this was his last night in his hometown. But standing here beneath the thick branches of the old sycamore and looking up at the two-story white colonial bathed in moonlight, Gavin was overcome by a wave of nostalgia. Almost homesickness.

Which made sense. In a lot of ways this house had been more of a home to him than his own.

Autumn's window on the second floor was dark. He knew she had to be in there. She hadn't shown up to the party, and it just wasn't the same without her. And there was no way he would leave without saying goodbye.

Her family had given him a key when he was nine, but he never used it this late at night. Instead, he jumped up and caught the lowest limb of the sycamore growing beside the house and swung himself up on top of it. From there it was a short climb to the sturdy branch that ran close to her window. He'd done it so many times over the years that the bark was worn away in places.

Crouched on the gnarled branch, he wobbled once before steadying himself, then peered through the window. A shaft of moonlight revealed Autumn lying curled up on her side on her bed, hugging a pillow to her chest.

He tapped on the window quietly. Her head came up.

She pushed up into a sitting position when she saw him, pushed her long sandy blond hair back and switched on the bedside lamp to its lowest setting. Gavin lifted the sash and climbed over the windowsill into her room as she pulled the folds of her silken robe around her more securely, covering her bare legs he refused to let himself stare at.

His mischievous smile faded when she watched him with a sad expression that twisted his insides. "Hey." He paused there just inside the window. "You didn't come to the party, so I thought I'd stop by and check on you." Pretty much their entire class had gone down to the river to celebrate grad, and as a sendoff for him and his twin Tristan.

"I wasn't in a party mood." Her voice was dull. Flat.

He came over to sit on the edge of her bed. Only a few feet separated them, but it felt like a mile, and he felt a flicker of worry. The antique grandfather clock on the upstairs landing struck one. The house was still and quiet, her parents sound asleep in their room down at the opposite end of the hall.

Gavin reached for her hand, held it gently, unsure what to say. "Bad night, huh."

She nodded, swallowed and blinked a couple of times.

"Wanna talk about it?" Her dad had cancer. She was upset and scared about that. But he knew it was more than that. And that it was partly his fault, because he was leaving town tomorrow.

"Not really." She pulled her hand free, lay back down and curled up on her side facing him.

He studied her for a long moment, willing the lingering haze of alcohol to clear from his brain so he could figure out what to do, then leaned over to switch off the lamp. "Scootch over."

She shifted over to make room so he could lie down next to her. He stretched out on his back, hands resting on his stomach, their shoulders touching. "Did your dad hear back about his treatments yet?"

"He has his first chemo appointment Tuesday."

"That's good. I mean, that he gets started so soon," he added quickly. "But I'm sorry you guys are going through this. It sucks."

She closed her eyes, drew in a breath and let it out in a sad sigh that made him wince inside. "I'm just…worried."

"Yeah." He reached for her hand again, needing the connection. It was hitting him hard now that he was down to his last few hours. How their lives were about to change forever, and that after tonight he wouldn't be climbing through her window again for a long time. Maybe ever. "That's rough."

"How was the party?" she asked in that same dull tone.

"It was all right." He turned his head to look at her. "Not the same without you there." Not even close. He'd left early to come here, bothered that she hadn't at least wanted to see him before he left.

She frowned at him. "Are you drunk?"

"A little, yeah."

"You didn't drive here, right?"

"Course not," he said, insulted. "I walked."

"You walked all the way here from the river to see me? That's…miles."

A little over five and a half. "Yeah." Why wouldn't he? Had she really thought he'd just leave without seeing her? They'd been friends for thirteen years. Close friends, and he was going to miss her. A few times he'd wondered if they could be more, but she'd never given any sign that she was interested so he'd shoved all that down.

"What time is your bus tomorrow?"

"Eight. I gotta be home by seven to spend a bit of time with Marley before we go, but I can stay until then." His house was only two blocks away down a well-worn path through the woods.

The moonlight washed across her face, lighting up the depths of her pale green eyes as they stared at each other in silence. An overwhelming rush of sadness hit him, along with a surge of protectiveness he'd been feeling a lot lately for her.

Who was going to look out for her when he left? Who would be here for her if things didn't go well for her dad? She and her parents were such a big part of his life, had treated him as one of the family since kindergarten. They were family to him as much as his brothers and Marley were.

Autumn hitched in a breath and reached for him.

He rolled to face her, drew her to him and wrapped his arms around her, not knowing how else to make it better. He remained uncharacteristically silent as he held her there in the moonlight, giving her the only comfort he could.

The heartbroken sound she made hurt his heart. He kissed the top of her head, already missing her. He'd wanted out of this town for years, and he and Tris had always dreamed of becoming Marines. Now that the moment was at hand, it was harder than he'd imagined. Because it meant leaving her behind too. He knew they would stay in touch, but everything was going to change now.

Autumn wriggled closer, and he tried to ignore the sudden rush of arousal at the way they were pressed flush together. The way his pulse kicked. He'd held her like this before a few times, the most recent when her dad was first diagnosed a few weeks back. But tonight…was different.

Because this was goodbye. They both knew it. And right now with only that thin, silky robe covering her, he was struggling like hell to repress every non-brotherly thought and feeling he'd ever had for her.

She felt so small up against him like this, and the way she burrowed into him stirred all sorts of confusing feelings. Along with certain parts of his anatomy that he had no control over.

Thankfully she didn't seem to notice. She pressed her face into the crook of his neck, enveloping him in the fresh scent of her shampoo. He went rigid when she moved closer still, because there was no way she could miss what was happening in his jeans.

But she didn't pull away. And just as he went to ease his hips away from her, she nuzzled the spot at the side of his neck.

He froze, all his muscles tensing, even as tingles spread out from where her lips caressed his skin. Was she…?

He eased his head back to peer down into her eyes, convinced that either he or the alcohol was misreading the situation. But Autumn stared back at him and cupped the side of his face in her hand while his pulse tripped and went into double time.

Because the look on her face told him he definitely wasn't imagining this, or the intent in her pale green eyes. More arousal shot through him, leaving him hard and aching.

He hadn't planned this. Hadn't dreamed this would happen when he'd climbed into her room minutes ago, or that she would ever want him this way. He'd only meant to comfort her. But if she really wanted him, there was no way he was stopping this.

They both leaned in at the same time. Their lips touched. A tender grazing that shot sparks right through him before he settled his mouth over hers and brought one hand up to cup the back of her head.

Autumn slid her hand into his hair and pulled him closer to deepen the kiss. He moved slow at first, his brain still trying to process that they were kissing. Then her hands started moving over him and he stopped thinking entirely as they slid up under his T-shirt to glide over bare skin. Tracing every ridge and dip of muscle she found before trailing down to cup the aching bulge between his legs.

Shit. He sucked in a breath, broke the kiss to stare at her. The feel of her hand blocked by only a layer of denim was the sweetest torture. His breathing turned unsteady.

Say something. He felt like he had whiplash. Had to be sure she truly wanted this and exactly *what* she wanted before they did anything else. "What—"

Her lips cut off whatever he was about to ask, her tongue delving in to play with his. The question he'd been about to ask withered and died under another rush of heat, the feel of her hand stroking him through his jeans taking over everything else.

Autumn sat up suddenly, got to her knees and undid the sash of her robe. He stared up at her in shock, barely able to breathe as it fell from her shoulders to puddle around her legs. The moonlight made her pale skin glow, the shape of her round, firm breasts and tight pink nipples making it impossible to speak, let alone think.

Before he could move or find his voice, she was undoing his jeans. The moment he was naked she straddled his thighs and bent over to look for something. He grasped her waist in his hands, still unable to believe this was happening, and was about to take her breasts in his hands when she sat back up and ripped open the condom he'd been carrying in his wallet since last summer.

Like everyone else in their class she probably assumed he'd

had sex before, but he hadn't. Not full on. Had she? He didn't think so. If she had she'd never told him, and he hadn't heard any rumors around town.

By the time she got it rolled onto him he was struggling to breathe, every tiny touch and caress of her hands sending pleasure shooting up his spine. He shifted his hands to her hips as she straddled him, steadying her. Stopping her, using his last few functioning brain cells to give her a chance to stop this before they crossed the point of no return.

Even though he was dying for her to continue. The thought of her being his first was every one of his deepest fantasies come to life.

They stared at each other wordlessly for a long moment, the sound of his uneven breathing harsh in his ears, then she eased him into place and slowly sank down on him.

Warm, wet heat enveloped him, unlike anything he'd ever known. His eyes slid closed and his head moved back on the pillow, his whole body arching. Ecstasy rocketed up his spine, the intense pleasure knocking the air from his lungs.

"Autumn," he managed to choke out, his fingers flexing deep into her hips. He wasn't sure if he was trying to give her one last chance to stop, or beg her not to. Chances were high this was her first time too. Was she okay? Was he hurting her?

She placed her palms flat on his chest and began to ride him. Slow at first, a little hesitant and unsure, and his heart practically exploded with tenderness. But the friction was incredible.

He sucked in a sharp breath, groaned low in his throat and fought to hold back as she picked up her pace. Tried to tell his brain that he needed to hold on, make sure she was enjoying it too. But he couldn't even force his eyes open. The pleasure was too much, rendering him helpless, and suddenly he couldn't take it anymore. He thrust up into her, his breathing coming faster, face contorting and jaw locked an instant before he started to come.

Autumn muffled his strangled groans with another kiss. It felt like his whole body was melting into hers. He sank into the kiss and moaned into her mouth, the intense pulses gradually fading into soft ripples until they left him boneless against the bedding. His head spun. The whole room did, a deep lethargy stealing through him.

Autumn eased off him and lay down on his chest, tucking her face into the crook of his neck. He wrapped his arms around her, struggling to get his bearings and find his voice. He'd been so caught up in the moment he hadn't even made an effort to try and make it good for her.

He stroked his fingers through her hair, unsure why she'd done it. Why him? Why now? Because he was leaving? "Are you okay?" he whispered, worried it had hurt and that she hadn't enjoyed it at all.

She nodded and made a soft affirmative sound, her soft hair caressing his cheek.

He was still stunned. "Autumn, what—"

She put her fingers over his mouth to stop him. "Don't." Then she cuddled closer, telling him without words how much she craved the comfort of being held. "Don't leave yet."

His heart turned over.

"I won't." He drew the covers over her, savoring her warm weight, the silken softness of her skin as he held her to him. He didn't know why this had happened, but he was grateful it had and wasn't going to spoil this memory by asking for explanations she obviously wasn't ready to give.

They only had a few hours left together before he had to climb back out her window and follow the path through the woods back to his house. Before he left her and this town behind to begin the next chapter of his life.

He would get answers from her later. For right now he was going to hold onto her and this moment for as long as he could.

End Excerpt

ABOUT THE AUTHOR

NY Times and USA Today Bestselling author Kaylea Cross writes edge-of-your-seat military romantic suspense. Her work has won many awards, including the Daphne du Maurier Award of Excellence, and has been nominated multiple times for the National Readers' Choice Awards. A Registered Massage Therapist by trade, Kaylea is also an avid gardener, artist, Civil War buff, Special Ops aficionado, belly dance enthusiast and former nationally-carded softball pitcher. She lives in Vancouver, BC, with her husband and family.

You can visit Kaylea at www.kayleacross.com. If you would like to be notified of future releases, please join her newsletter:

http://kayleacross.com/v2/newsletter/

COVERT SEDUCTION

Printed in Great Britain
by Amazon